Honeymooners

Delver Maddingley

Honeymooners
BOULEVARD *editions*
London 2007

BOULEVARD *editions*
is an imprint of
Erotic Review Books
formerly The *Erotic* Print Society
ER Books, 17 Harwood Road
LONDON SW6 4QP

Tel: +44 (0)20 77365800
Fax: +44 (0)20 7366330
Email: enquiries@eroticprints.org
Web: www.eroticprints.org

Erotic Review Books is a publisher of fine art, photography and fiction books and
limited editions. To find out more please visit us on the web at
www.eroticprints.org or call us for a catalogue on 08000262524 (UK only).
Overseas +44 1905727476

ISBN 978-1-904989-42-4

Delver Maddingley

Honeymooners

with illustrations by
Mazzza

boulevard
editions

Foreplay

She could still feel a kind of tingling in her sexual parts from the thorough seeing-to her husband had given her the night before as she bent over the kitchen table. Far from subsiding, the tingling was gathering strength with anticipation as she hurried from the Fulham Road into the straight street lined with parked cars, their tops sprinkled with almond and cherry blossom. Sophie, who had come over from Barnes on the bus to avoid the hassle of parking, was also surprised at the force with which her heart was thumping inside her ribcage. Yes, she had to admit it to herself: she was dying for her first proper orgasm with a woman. Or even just to have the delicate, sensitive fingertips of a woman sliding over her smooth body, and to feel the teats of that woman's proud breasts swelling up hard between her lips.

Until the previous night's intimate dinner that she and her barrister husband Peter had given for his old school chum Mark and Mark's wife Cathy, Sophie had had little inkling of this sapphic tendency. If, deep down, she had always harboured such urges, as she now began to suspect, she had certainly not been aware of them. Her job as a junior in Peter's chambers had kept her far too busy during the day and, all too often, in the evenings and at weekends. And when the couple did find time to forget work, Peter's unremitting sexual energy had kept her alternately eager for his maleness and happily sated. But across the dinner-table on that warm spring evening she had become conscious of the elegant, dark-haired Cathy's flirtatious glances.

For some reason she had been more fascinated by these glances than by the more obvious ones shot sidelong at her by Mark, who had taken advantage of being seated next to her by missing no opportunity to touch her. (Had he realised that, at her husband's request, she was sitting there knickerless?) After a few glasses of wine Sophie had been slightly shocked to find herself giggling as she responded to Cathy's glances even as Mark's hand squeezed her upper thigh, his fingers feeling for a tell-tale but nonexistent panty-line, and then she had picked up, or thought she picked up, more and more little hints and signals in Cathy's outwardly innocent conversation. Well, *innocent* was hardly the word, but on the surface her discourse was hotly heterosexual in its orientation.

This heterosexuality had spiced the discussion following the proposal sprung on the guests by Peter. He had already obtained Sophie's agreement, and indeed it was hard to see any obvious objections to the plan, which was the offshoot of a successful piece of litigation he had brought off on behalf of a wealthy if somewhat shady client. The case had involved fraud, money-laundering and control of prostitutes, and was overshadowed by hints of blackmail. Enough reasonable doubt had been thrown on all these charges by Peter's brilliant defence to secure the acquittal of Giles Rosper, although the judge's glare as he dismissed him had left no doubt, reasonable or otherwise, in the minds of those present that he was sure the jury had been bamboozled. Since Rosper spent most of his time nursing his financial and other interests in Greece, he was untouched by the indignation of the tabloid press, which would hardly have bothered him in any case. But before leaving the country, he had made Peter the offer that was conveyed to the others at dinner.

'How would you two fancy a second honeymoon?' he had asked them over the brandy. 'A really sexy one? And how would you feel about the two of us doing the same and coming with you?'

Relaxed by the evening's liberal hospitality, Mark grinned. 'Not sure about us all *coming* together,' he replied. 'At least, not all in the same bed. But I'm ready for a break and think I can vouch for my lovely wife too.'

Peter had explained that one of his grateful client's interests was the running of a hotel on a tiny Aegean island, dedicated to satisfying the needs of honeymooners. Sophie couldn't help wondering how this would be achieved when it came to those needs that distinguished honeymooning couples from regular holidaymakers. She could only think of endless supplies of condoms, clean sheets, and maybe those little blue pills, but the look her husband had given her when she raised the matter in bed with him suggested that there were other things she would find out about soon enough.

Although the proposed plan appealed to her for its holiday aspect—who would not jump at the chance of a free week of luxury in spring on a Greek island?—to begin with she had had certain private reservations. Peter, Mark and Cathy all went back a long way, to their schooldays in fact. And they were all two or three years older than the twenty-three year-old Sophie, who was not sure how well she would fit in with them as a group. The dinner party was the first time she had met the other couple, and she had awaited it nervously.

When they had arrived, casually dressed, attractive and skilled at putting her at ease in their company, she immediately felt better about the prospect. And when Cathy began surreptitiously flirting with her, she had realised that the possibilities of fun on this shared second honeymoon were quite considerable. How far would the sharing go? Was Mark's rather tasteless objection altogether out of the question? She had an inkling at the time, which grew stronger now as she approached the house, that something about Mark appealed to her almost as much as his wife's flirtation. Yes, it suddenly dawned on her: Mark was doubly appealing because of his access to Cathy's beautiful body.

Cathy had expressed some doubts about the honeymoon scheme. 'Suppose all the other guests are middle-aged and fat? Doesn't sound like the kind of place young ravers could afford or would care to go to. Do you really want ugly stockbrokers and their gross second wives gawping at your gorgeous young bride, Peter?' She had fluttered her eyelids at Sophie as she raised this point.

'No, no, no,' rejoined Peter. 'This is something special. This is one week at the start of the season reserved for hand-picked guests only. Rosper told me he subsidises most of them in return for favours—I suppose the favour I did him was quite a big one. No one's going to be much older than us, and they'll all be good-looking, at least in his eyes. And another thing: for us it'll be second honeymoons, but all the others will be bona fide first-timers. Rosper says it's fun watching them settle into their stride. The place sounds like fucking paradise.'

Cathy seemed to be really excited by now, and kept making remarks about guessing what randy young husbands were getting up to with their new brides.

'And not only guessing,' added Peter. 'The old reprobate says they pretty quickly get quite uninhibited. Even the shy ones start showing off.'

At this observation, Mark's excitement had registered itself through a fluttering of his fingers between Sophie's thighs. She felt, or imagined she felt, a tickling of her fine, blond hairs. 'Sounds like Mark's thing,' laughed Cathy. 'You'll find he really loves *watching*, Sophie dear.'

At last the evening had come to an end. As the visitors took their leave on the doorstep, Cathy had held Sophie for a few prolonged moments in a surprisingly close embrace, letting one hand rest on her lightly-clad bottom. Kissing her on the side of her mouth, she had whispered the early morning invitation Sophie was now hurrying to accept. It certainly seemed that the older woman might have something more in the way of surprises for her. And, as a result of a plan hit upon by Sophie and Peter as they fucked among the unwashed dishes after their guests' departure, she too had a surprise for Cathy.

Her breath quickened as she fumbled with the latch of the front gate and recalled that scene in the kitchen. Her husband had swept the plates aside and pushed her forward. She had rested her cheek on her forearm, her bottom twitching and quivering as he turned up her loose skirt and paused a moment, no doubt admiring the bare buttocks and thightops framed by her black stockings and suspender belt. Then the sound of his zip, followed by the sudden thrust up her cunt.

Soon Peter's right hand had squeezed between her belly and the tabletop. The hand curled like a claw in a velvet glove, and a finger pressed into the creases on each side of her distended vulva while the thumbnail scrabbled through the light fuzz and gently scratched the clitoris.

They agreed on their plan just as Peter filled his now sated and mewling wife with a flood of cream that leaked out over the edge of the table, dripping slowly to the floor and spreading between the remains of the meal, fresher and more tempting to her tongue than the smears of leftover cream on their guests' plates.

She snapped out of her reverie. Cathy opened the door in a flimsy and completely transparent gown of smoky gauze, offset by black ribbons securing it above and below her breasts and threaded round the hem, which floated at mid-thigh level. A matching but broader black ribbon tied back her dark hair. Below her bosom, the front of the flimsy garment kept opening and closing, but even when it was closed Sophie could clearly make out a pair of tiny black knickers. She felt awkward and over-dressed in the jeans and baggy sweater she had worn in the interests of relaxed informality.

'So good to see you, darling,' purred Cathy in the hallway as she kissed her visitor's cheek. 'I wasn't sure if you'd come.'

Maybe, it occurred to Sophie, I shouldn't make myself seem too much of an easy lay. Her response veered away from what was most on the minds of both women. 'I had to pop over to tell you about another suggestion we've come up with.'

'You could have phoned or texted me.'

'Well, yes, but . . .'

'But you thought it would be more polite to tell me in person. I expect you decided the honeymoon idea went too far—with all of us going on it, I mean. You've come to suggest something a bit more staid.'

The pouting look of disappointment Cathy flashed at her brought the colour to Sophie's cheeks. Unable to stop herself, she blurted out: 'Oh, no. Not at all. I can't wait for us all to be there together. I've been looking forward to it so much. Going there with just Peter wouldn't be the same. It'll be great to have a girl-friend with us—as well as Peter's best friend, of course.'

Cathy took her hand and led her into a cosy sitting-room. The heating was turned up high, and Sophie now felt her clothes were even more unsuitable, especially when she contemplated Cathy's composure in her wispy attire.

'Drink, darling?'

'Something to cool me down.'

Left alone for a moment, Sophie tried to take in her surroundings. The decor was comforting and far from minimalist. Most surfaces supported ornaments and knick-knacks of various kinds. On the Victorian mantelpiece stood an array of framed photos. To her amazement, she recognised one of herself. Peter had taken it on holiday a couple of years ago, when they were newly married. In it, she leaned against a rock, wearing a diminutive purple bikini. Her right hand was raised to shield her eyes from the sun. A tuft of yellow hair, matching that on her head, was clearly visible under the lifted arm. Her feet were planted apart on the sand, and the bikini bottom bulged with sexy promise between her parted thighs. How the fuck . . .

Cathy returned with two glasses of wine, and immediately took in the situation. 'You look shocked,' she said. 'So would I, I suppose. He's quite harmless, though, my Mark. Just a bit of a voyeur. Well, an incorrigible one, to tell the truth. And when he's not in a place where he can watch things actually happening, he's always drooling over pictures and DVDs. I must say, it hots up his performance when he *does* me, which he can't wait to do when he's in that sort of mood.'

Sophie was by no means reassured. Upset as she was, she scarcely took in the fact that while out of the room Cathy had discarded her knickers; instead of the little black triangle of lace, an even smaller black triangle of curly hair was now revealed as the front of her short gown fell open. 'How on earth did he get his hands on a photo of me?' demanded Sophie.

'I think he persuaded your Peter to have a copy done for him. He's always asking his friends for favours like that.'

'But what about you? How can you bear to have it up there on your mantelpiece, along with those pictures of yourself?'

In the mirror above the fireplace, Sophie saw her new friend approach her from behind to peer over her shoulder, and felt her smooth left cheek nestle against her own right one. 'I put it there myself,' came the murmured reply. 'Those legs are so slim and lovely, I just have to come over and admire them every five minutes. I've been dying to see them for real.' She fixed Sophie's eyes in the mirror. 'To stroke and lick and kiss them.'

Partly to hide her embarrassment, and partly in the hope of finding release for the sexual tension that had been building up in her all the morning, the blonde girl looked down at her own trembling fingers as they fumbled with the button of her jeans and slid the zip down. Immediately, Cathy's hands took the waistband and eased it down over her slender hips and the swell of her bottom. The garment slid down her legs; she kicked off her shoes and stepped clear.

Cathy took a couple of paces back to look at her from behind. In the mirror, Sophie saw her raise her eyebrows and bite her lower lip. She imagined the picture she now presented to Cathy's longing gaze. Her baggy black sweater, she knew, hung to about halfway down her buttocks. These were divided by the narrow strap of a scarlet silk thong, probably hidden between the firm cheeks, which tensed at the thought of how she must look. Between her bottom and the little white socks she wore, her admirer would be feasting her eyes on the backs of her long legs, flawless in their athletic slimness.

Cathy's head dropped down out of the reflection. She was kneeling behind Sophie, who parted her feet very slightly and waited for contact to be made. When it came, it was not quite what she had expected. The cheek-to- cheek nestling of a few moments earlier was repeated, but with the right cheek of the girl's bottom now cushioning Cathy's face.

A moist, pointed tongue ran round the crease demarcating the curve of the buttock from the firmness of the thigh. It probed between the very tops of both legs, thrusting in far enough to find the silk that half divided and half covered Sophie's trembling sex. As the tongue continued to prod, tickle and spread saliva over those parts it had access to, cool fingers played in a delicate dance on the fronts of her thighs, moving more and more to their insides, and gradually, teasingly higher.

Suddenly an open palm was spread across the triangle of red silk covering the pubic region. The heel of the palm rubbed against the mound, and Sophie responded by opening her legs wider until they were splayed at the angle she could see right in front of her, in the photo on the mantelpiece. She hadn't quite realised just how prominently the mound bulged and stretched out its purple packaging in the picture, but she was sure Cathy would not have missed that detail.

Cathy spoke. 'My God, darling. It's lovely to stroke this smooth silk and feel how it's sort of tangling your hairs inside it and scouring your skin. Can you feel that too?'

'It's driving me crazy. You wouldn't believe how I needed this. I can hardly believe it myself.'

'Turn round.'

Sophie did as she was bidden, resting her hands on her lover's shoulders to support herself. Cathy now contemplated the shiny triangle for a moment. 'You're getting a damp patch down there at the bottom of your slit,' she observed, and buried her face in the sexbulge as her hands ran up the backs of Sophie's legs and seized her buttocks.

'You've been licking there.'

'No, I was licking further back, round your arsehole. This wet stain must be fresh cuntjuice. Yes, it's spreading and getting bigger all the time.'

'I can't take much more of this treatment,' gasped Sophie, as the nerves of her overstimulated sex began to ripple.

'Let's go upstairs,' came the hoarse reply.

Sophie followed, her face centimetres behind her friend's athletic thighs and well-rounded bottom.

A bedside lamp cast a warm glow to fill the sphere of its potency, beyond which the room was dim, the curtains closed against the morning sunshine. Apprehensive but eager, Sophie stretched full length on the black satin sheet, but Cathy pulled her into a sitting position and roughly dragged the sweater over her head. A mass of blonde hair, released from the band containing it, tumbled over the girl's shoulders. She dropped back on the pillow, with her hands behind her head so that the provocatively fragrant yellow tufts under her arms were exposed to view.

These adornments evidently attracted the older woman, who placed a palm flat over each of them and curled her fingers into the white shoulders while she dipped her mouth to a pink nipple. As soon as the nipple hardened she moved to the other one, sucking it, too, into the form of a tight, pink peg. Her hands then followed her mouth down to the firm young breasts and her tongue tickled its way down to the dimpled belly-button and beyond. She caught the waistband of the skimpy red undergarment in her teeth and pulled it down to reveal the upper half of a plump mound so sparsely adorned with short, light fluff that the details of the slit were fully visible. Further removal of the thong was prevented by the weight of its wearer's buttocks, so Cathy released the elastic, allowing the waistband to snap back into place.

She rolled Sophie over on to her belly and kissed each soft cheek of her bottom in turn. Then she placed her hands on the waistband just in front of the hipbones to pull it clear of the girl's sexmound as she used her teeth at the back in the same way that she had done at the front. This time the thong moved fairly easily downwards, Every few centimetres the elastic bit into the yielding flesh, only to be tugged down to its next temporary stopping-point, until at last Cathy let it come snugly to rest round the tops of the thighs. The narrow central strap was pulled away from the crevice in which it had been buried, and the moist fruit of Sophie's sex pouted back. Only the thong binding her thighs together seemed to be stopping those succulent lips from falling yearningly apart. Sophie mewed and clenched the cheeks of her bottom, and Cathy, taking this as a sign, slipped the thong right down her legs and over her feet. The blonde girl now lay completely naked. Cathy ran a hand lightly up the inside of her left thigh until the edge of it rested against the labia.

Shocked by this touch, Sophie lifted her head from the pillow and supported herself on her elbows, her back arched up and her buttocks tense. Her friend was kneeling on her left; embarrassed to meet her eye, Sophie stared at the wall a couple of feet from the right-hand edge of the king-sized bed. At the level of her face a shelf contained an assortment of bedside reading, a small clock and a number of framed and unframed photos. One of the latter immediately caught her eye.

In spite of the dimness of the light cast by the reading lamp behind her, she could not possibly be mistaken. This was another of her husband's private holiday snapshots, taken one warm morning in Normandy during a spring bargain break a year or so ago, a break just long enough to take in the invasion beaches and Bayeux tapestry and to laze about a bit in the sun.

Strangely, it showed her in pretty much the same attitude she was in now, lying on her front with her shoulders raised up on her elbows as she looked sideways at the camera, or at Peter. It was an outdoor scene, taken on the rough lawn behind the little house they had rented for that short break. She lay on a rumpled blanket, and was not completely naked as she was now; a miniskirt of soft, red cotton material was bunched up round her waist, leaving her pale bottom bare to the sun. A small breast could be seen jutting invitingly forward above the blanket, its teat elongated. Her hair was tousled, her face flushed, her eyes narrowed and her lips rather swollen.

Cathy pre-empted her question. 'Hope you don't mind, dear. Another one he managed to wheedle out of his best mate. After all, what are best mates for? He'd never put it on display downstairs, or if he did I'd put my foot down. He shags me on the bed here with his eyes glued to it.'

Sophie was genuinely shocked. 'When was the last time he did that?' she demanded.

'Just before you arrived. Look, there are still some damp patches on the sheet next to you. I went to the window to watch him drive off on his way to the college, and you rang the bell just as he disappeared. Anyway, what were you thinking of to let your old man take a picture of you in that condition?'

Sophie blushed. 'What condition?'

'You look as if you'd just been doing sex.'

'To tell the truth,' replied Sophie after a brief pause in which she reflected that all the barriers now seemed to have come down, 'he'd just, well, masturbated me. I was enjoying a bit of sun when he got down beside me and stuck his hand up under my skirt. I tried to keep my legs together, but he put a knee between them and stuck his thumb in me. It didn't go in far at first because I was dry, so he shoved his fingers and the palm of his hand up under me and started stroking and scratching my hairs.'

'Like this,' said Cathy, suiting her action to Sophie's words.

'Yes. I soon got wet then, and the thumb went right in. He wriggled it about and tickled me with his finger and I came, just as he was leaning right over me and sticking his tongue in my mouth.'

Once more Cathy imitated the action described to her, and felt the pressure of the girl's teeth on her tongue as Sophie writhed in orgasm. It was a few moments before she was calm enough to continue her story.

'I was too far gone to care when I heard what sounded like an upstairs window slamming a couple of houses away. What a show that must have been for whoever it was!'

'I tell you, darling, if my Mark had been watching he wouldn't have slammed the window. He would have lurked there behind the curtains, jerking off—or more likely getting himself primed to fuck me. Was that the end of the performance?'

'No. Peter pulled my skirt up and fired off half a dozen

photos. Then he put both his knees between my legs, grabbed my hips, pulled me up on all fours and screwed me like a bitch. And I came again.'

On her left, Cathy was moving about, opening a bedside drawer and taking something from it. 'Keep your eyes shut, Sophie dear,' she ordered.

Sure enough, Sophie felt one knee, then a second, take its place between her own legs. Cool hands seized her hips and raised them while her face remained resting on the pillow. With no warning, a cold, hard knob was shoved against her gaping vulva and rammed up into her cunt. The huge implement was forced in and out while clever fingers spidered over her lower belly and teased her clit. She quivered and came. She felt the intruder being drawn out. Rolling over on to her back, she saw Cathy lift it from its slippery sheath and hold it out between them. Carved from pale green jade, it was a lifelike replica of an enormous phallus, the swollen veins faithfully represented and the surface now glistening with the juices of her vagina.

Cathy lay down beside her, and she guessed she was expected to reciprocate the favour. However, the older woman seemed to be taking things at a relaxed pace, perhaps not wanting to press a novice too hard (for Sophie felt sure her innocence and virginity as a lesbian were apparent). They gazed into each other's eyes, and Cathy was the first to speak.

'I bet you're not too happy about the thought of Mark ogling your picture while he's fucking me.'

'Of course the idea's disturbing. Kind of weird, pervy even. But I'm glad he finds me attractive.'

This, she thought, was probably the right time to spring her surprise suggestion on Cathy. Well, the suggestion had come from Peter in the first place, but she had eagerly gone along with it as he slid his stiff prick up her on the kitchen table—another fuck for which she had been sufficiently lubricated without foreplay.

'Cathy,' she began, 'Peter and I have had an idea. You'll have to discuss it with Mark, of course. It's about our Greek holiday, the second honeymoon.'

'I bet it's going to be a lovely idea. What is it?'

'Well, instead of a second honeymoon, what about a first one?'

'How do you mean?'

'You've guessed already, haven't you? We go there as two couples, like we agreed, but swap partners for the week. So we each get a new husband. It looks as if mine already has the hots for me, and I know Peter can't wait to get it together with you.'

Cathy grinned. 'I hadn't only guessed—I'd thought of suggesting it myself.'

'So you don't mind the idea of Peter having you?'

'Pete and I go back a long way—right back to school. It won't be the first time. Hasn't he told you?'

Sophie was dumbfounded. As far as she knew, her husband had never encountered Cathy except socially until last night. She pressed her to tell her story.

'I can't remember how young we were when we started getting close,' she began. 'But he never fucked me till we were in the sixth form, not all the way. Once we'd done it the first time we were at it two or three times a week. Of course, we had to find safe places to do it, and you know how difficult that is for teenagers. We used stock cupboards, changing rooms, the sports pavilion, the space behind the bike sheds, the woods at the back of the playing field, abandoned cars, occasionally our homes when our parents weren't there, and even empty classrooms, though that was taking a big risk. We never got completely undressed except on one occasion—that'll be something new for us to look forward to this time round.

'I was besotted with your Peter. At first, at least, he really seemed to care for me, and always pulled his dick out of me just before he came. All the surreptitious washing I had to do to get the stuff out of my clothes! The only problem with the relationship was that I got more and more jealous of his best friend, Mark. Pete seemed to spend much more time with Mark than with me—it was as if he only went with me when he wanted sex. Some time in the summer term I told him how pissed off I was getting.

'I felt a bit better when he said he was just as obsessed with me as I was with him, and that all he talked about when he was with Mark was me. And about the things he did with me. I wasn't the only one to be jealous—Mark had been too. "I've always been close to him," he said. "Sharing our experiences is like keeping it in the family."

'Well, this gave me an idea, and I asked if Mark would like to hang around sometimes and watch while we were doing it. "That's his big thing," said Pete. "He's really into watching."

'And so it began. At first, Mark would just hover in the background, his face contorted and a hand between his legs. Peter carried on as if he wasn't there, but I often gave the poor boy a smile or a wink and tried to encourage him to go further. Eventually he was kneeling quite close to us and wanking into his handkerchief. His wankerchief, he called it.

'By this time he and I would be gazing into each other's eyes as Peter was pumping away. I could tell from the way he looked that he was falling in love, and I felt the same about him. Peter, I reckoned, was just using me—but so what? I liked being used for sex, and still do. That's my way of using my partners.

'One day the three of us were down on a mat in the sports pavilion. Peter slipped out of me and spurted his come all over my tummy. Luckily I'd taken my skirt and knickers off and pulled my blouse right up, so none of it went on my clothes. I don't know what came into me, but seeing that Mark hadn't shot his load yet, I asked him to wipe me clean with his "wanky".

'He eased forward on his knees, his stiff cock sticking out of his flies, purple-headed and ready to explode. Instead of doing what I'd asked, he wrapped the handkerchief round that purple head and buried his face in the slippery puddle on my belly. I heard slurping noises, and realised that he was sucking it up and swallowing it down, licking me clean like a cat with spilt cream. When he'd finished, he dipped his mouth lower till his lips just found my pubic hair. At that moment he came, and sort of rolled over sideways on the mat.

'That was only the beginning of our activities as a threesome, which went on for the rest of that term. Sometimes, while he was screwing me, Pete let Mark suck my tits. I had a kind of urge to take that cock in my mouth, but Pete and I had never done that ourselves and the idea seemed too over the top to suggest, especially as Mark seemed to be impossibly big. It would have been like trying to swallow an orange. But I got a taste of my new admirer's spunk when he was allowed to jerk off over my face. Some of it hit my lips, and I sucked it in. This time it was Pete who licked me clean, churning his tongue about all round my tongue in the stuff that hadn't gone down yet. But he never let Mark fuck me.

'Then things changed because Peter, who had done very well at school, was leaving to study law while Mark and I were staying on for another term in the Upper Sixth. After the official leaving party we had our own celebration in one of the changing rooms. The two boys had me completely naked for the first and only time, and we repeated the business with Mark coming in my face. He managed it at the very moment when Pete fired off in my cunt. Then, after he'd kissed me clean, my boyfriend said he really loved me (he'd never actually said that before, and maybe it wasn't entirely true), but we had to get real as he was going away. He had been looking for a present for me, and the very best thing he could think of was to let me have Mark as my full-time lover.

'Well, I was delighted. Mark and I enjoyed each other for our final term, and then on and off all through the time we were studying and getting qualified. Sometimes I found Mark's voyeuristic activities a bit hard to stomach, but I adapted to his tastes and when he asked me to marry him I had no hesitation. There, now you know.'

Sophie was finding it hard to take all this in. Although he had often mentioned Mark, and occasionally Cathy, Peter had never given any indication of this part of their shared past, or even of the fact that he had known Cathy in person. At least she could now be fairly sure that the holiday would have its attractions for all four of them. Mark was a dishy bloke, and she would surely get used to his voyeuristic peculiarities. Not just peculiarities, or tendencies—Cathy had used the word *activities*. And what was it she had said about the size of his cock?

She clasped Cathy to her and ran her hand down the back of her gown until it rested on and caressed her soft bottom.

'Would you like me to do you?' she asked, rather shyly.

'I'm all yours, darling,' the more experienced woman replied. 'It's entirely up to you. I'll go with whatever you fancy.'

Sophie had already decided that she definitely did fancy Cathy. She rolled their entwined bodies until she had Cathy on her back. Lifting herself from her, she untied the black bows securing the transparent robe just above and just below the bust. When she opened it wide, the puckered areolas and engorged nipples she had glimpsed through the smoky gauze seemed to tighten and thrust up even more. Sophie knelt there for a moment admiring the beautiful breasts, firm even in this recumbent position. They were a creamy white, quite distinct from the light tan with which the rest of her body glowed.

Or most of her body. Hardly larger than the area of black curls, a white triangle showed that it had not been her practice to sunbathe in the nude. Perhaps it would be different on this forthcoming holiday, different for both of them.

Gingerly she used both hands to part the warm thighs, and then laid her right cheek on the nearer of them, Cathy's right, as she examined the outward appearance of the dark-fleeced sex. She directed a thin stream of breath into the hairs, which stirred like long grass in a breeze. Cathy moaned, lifted her left knee and began to fondle her own nipples.

Sophie's eye was caught by what she at first took to be a small patch of dead skin on the inside of the left thigh. When she scratched it lightly with a fingernail, it crumbled into powder. Something similar was visible tangled in the bush of pubic hair. Scrabbling into the thicket, Sophie found flakes and large crumbs of what could only be dried sperm caught up in it. Some of the flakes looked delicate and lacy; others were like tough rice paper. Lovingly she used her fingertips to comb through the bush and tease out this evidence of conjugal gratification. Cathy purred and let her left knee drop once more to the bed, spreading her legs more widely, a movement that caused her outer labia to part slightly and reveal a fragrant, pink gash.

With the palm of her hand resting gently on the triangle of hair, Sophie stroked along the gash with the tip of her middle finger. Now the inner lips parted. The finger probed up the unresisting vagina. It immediately ran into warm juice, signalling her partner's readiness for action. She rocked the heel of her hand on the pubis and probed deeper. There she found so much fluid that she guessed it was not all the product of Cathy's own lust. On withdrawing the finger, her eyes and nose confirmed that the viscous mass it sucked out could only be the residue of Mark's last fuck, shortly before her arrival.

'Take it easy, darling,' gasped Cathy. 'Just slip that finger in there again and stroke with it ever so gently while you tell me about your first time with Pete.'

'It was only a couple of years ago, of course. I'd just joined the chambers as his pupil. As you know, he's a bit of a workaholic. Always staying on late when the others went home. Well, he'd saddled me with a really complicated brief to master, and I found myself working late as well, to have all the law reports and stuff handy when I needed to look something up. Peter hardly seemed to notice me. He'd just give me what you might call a curt nod on the way through to his office.

'One evening, though, he called me in over the intercom. He was sitting at his desk with a stack of papers on it, and told me to sit on a couch facing the desk while he finished off what he was doing. Something seemed a bit odd, and I realised that the coffee table that usually stood in front of the couch had been moved out of the way. Oh well, I thought, why not? No one was going to serve coffee at this hour.

'Peter took off his reading glasses and sat staring at me as if he'd never seen me before. Then he started to smile, just a little, without opening his mouth. I felt uneasy. At last he spoke,

' "You want to stay with us, Miss Rogers?"

' "I think so, sir."

' "Well, you're not doing badly. But everyone has to fit in here, you know. Just unbutton your blouse and slip your skirt off, would you?"

'Of course, I was horrified and didn't know where to look or what to say. He just sat there drumming his fingers on the desk. And staring at me.

'There's something about the way he stares at you with those piercing blue eyes, isn't there?'

Cathy nodded. 'Isn't there just!'

'Usually they're sort of twinkly and friendly, right? But when he's in the sort of mood he was in that night they, well, I suppose they sort of hypnotise you. As I sat there being stared at I felt like I was sort of melting, especially, you know, down *there*.' Warming at the memory, Sophie stirred her finger with a deliberate firmness in Cathy's love channel before continuing.

'I was terribly self-conscious. My knees were trembling and I didn't know whether to cross my legs or just press them together. Whatever I did would seem to draw attention to what was happening to me. I felt so wet.

'To cut a long story short, I just gave way. Once I started unbuttoning my blouse I suddenly felt easier. After all, he hadn't told me to take my bra off. Then I stood up, unzipped my skirt and stepped out of it. Peter's smile got wider.

' "Now the knickers," he said.

'I peeled my little mauve briefs down and tossed them on the couch. I was now standing in my black business jacket, with my white blouse open to show the lacy mauve bra that went with the briefs, like the suspenders and stockings. No, they must have been navy, the stockings. He looked at my bush and actually whistled.

' "Sit down again," he ordered.

'I did so. For some time he still sat gazing at me. This time his eyes seemed to be focused on my pussy, and I felt a weird burning sensation in it. At last he got up and came round the desk. My God! He was naked from the waist down and his dick was sticking out like, well, like this thing you just stuck up me, but wagging up and down as he walked.

'He knelt in front of me, put his hands on my thighs and kissed my cunt. When I say kissed, I don't mean he was trying to do me with his tongue or anything. It was more of what you could call a *reverential* kiss. He was adoring me, and didn't need to tell me in words. Then he swung me round so I was stretched out full length on the couch. He put one of my feet up on the back of it and let the other one dangle on the floor. Of course, I was wide open.

'Then, without warning, he jumped me. I felt him stretching me right up to my womb. He bit one of my boobs through the bra and started to pump.

' "Wouldn't this be described as sexual harassment in the workplace?" I stammered out between his great thrusts.

' "Not really," he replied. "Not if you agree to marry me. Will you? And can I come inside you?"

' "Yes. And yes." '

Sophie finished her story and drew even more sexjuice out of her friend's vagina. Lubrication, then, was going to be no problem. She groped around on the satin sheet until she found that huge jade dildo. Using the fingers of one hand to hold Cathy's lovelips as wide open as she could stretch them, she introduced the lifelike head and worked it in with a twisting motion that became stronger as the penetration proceeded.

'Doesn't hurt, does it?' she asked.

'Not fucking likely, dear. That thing's exactly the same size as my husband's cock. In fact, it's an exact replica, hand crafted. It went into you, so you'll be able to take the real thing when he has you.'

'Where did you get it?'

'We had a great holiday in China last year. We went to Xi'an and saw the terracotta army—you know about it? Well, those old warriors are thousands of years old, but there are places everywhere making and selling imitations. Mark asked our guide quite brazenly if she could find someone who made terracotta sex-aids. Well, when she finally got the gist of what he wanted, she winked at him and said she could do better than that. She took us to a workshop where women sat at benches carving all kinds of objects out of this jade. The foreman gave us a packet of soft wax and made gestures. I knew at once what he meant.

'That night in our hotel, I sucked Mark up till he was just about as big as he was ever going to be. Then I wrapped the wax round his cock and squeezed it to get a clear impression of all the veins and things. I peeled the wax off just in time—he gushed all over the bed as I snatched it clear, ripping out some of his hairs, I'm afraid. The next morning we gave the mould to our guide to take back to the workshop, and that same evening she brought us the finished dildo, beautifully gift-wrapped. She explained that the women had made a plaster cast and used that to give them the exact shape and dimensions. It cost us quite a few *yuan*, but you might say it's worth its weight in jade. Oh yes, work it in and out faster!'

As she did so, Sophie used her free hand to press the fat outer lips tightly round the pistoning shaft. She gave a harder pinch at the top of the slit, and was surprised to see her friend's pink clitoral bud peep out of its hood like a pip being squeezed out of some succulent fruit. Could she bring herself to do what her nature prompted, she who had never (or hardly ever) dreamed of administering cunnilingus?

Nature kicked in and overrode her scruples. She dropped her head and tickled the pip with the tip of her tongue. Cathy erupted in orgasm, mounted Sophie and ravished her with fingers, lips, tongue and jade dildo.

Saturday

Light flicks of salt spray cooled Sophie's face as the motor launch frisked over the dancing waves. After a slightly scary landing on the short runway at Skiathos, a minibus had taken the party of good-looking couples down to the harbour. They were met by Giles Rosper in person, a gaunt, rangy man with a little white beard and a peaked yachting cap. Rosper welcomed them aboard and explained that the trip to Pothos, or 'Honeymoon Island' as he called it in his brochure, would take about forty minutes on this vessel. Late afternoon tea and *dolmades* would be available a bit later from an ad hoc buffet up in front of the wheelhouse; to start things off, though, as soon as everyone had found a suitably sunny or shady seat, drinks were served, a choice of ouzo or retsina. When someone commented on the generous supplies of these commodities stowed on the deck, Rosper said that the present party made up only about a sixth of the week's guests. He was running a shuttle service to the island, bringing over arrivals from a number of flights throughout the day.

Mark and Sophie had found a place on the starboard side near the stern, as the rather pedantic Mark insisted on explaining, while Peter and Cathy were somewhere nearer the buffet. Mark panned around the lively scene with his state-of-the-art camcorder, finishing the sequence with a close-up of his 'bride's' face. So far, things felt fairly normal, Sophie reflected. On the plane her new partner had gone no further than resting a tentative hand on her knee as they exchanged the small talk of near-strangers, mostly filling each other in on the details of their respective jobs. (It had occurred to Sophie that she probably earned a good deal more than this senior lecturer at one of the new universities with which London was so liberally endowed, and she hoped this would not somehow skew the balance of their relationship. Cathy, of course, would be getting a decent salary from her PR job, so he was not exactly on the breadline.) When they touched down with a bump at Skiathos, she rather forgot herself and hid her face in Mark's chest until the plane came to a standstill, while he reassured her by stroking her back and thighs. And now, on the boat, she didn't yet have any real sense that the man beside her was to be her 'husband' for the week.

Sitting opposite them was a couple they had noticed at the airport. They seemed to be in their early twenties, or more likely only eighteen or so, and were obviously deeply in love. Mark drew Sophie's attention to the way the girl kept glancing at her shiny wedding ring and twisting it on her finger. It was apparent that these newlyweds, who communicated with each other in whispers and giggles, were shy—at least in company. The girl's beautiful auburn hair had recently been professionally done, no doubt for her wedding. It hung down below her shoulders in a profusion of tight ringlets, which she allowed to cover half of her freckled face to afford her a kind of privacy. Her boyfriend's hair—no, that would be her husband's—was fair, and cropped quite short.

The auburn-haired girl made some complaint about the wine, to which the young man's reply seemed to be that she would have to wait till tea was being served. Mark nudged Sophie, who got the point immediately.

'Would you like some of this?' she asked, taking a plastic bottle of spring water from her holdall.

The girl leaned forward gratefully to take the bottle. As she did so, the top of her white sun-top, cut straight across and supported by broad shoulder-straps, gaped outwards. Sophie saw Mark dart a practised and appreciative glance down into the valley between two breasts the size of small grapefruits. Were his voyeuristic activities beginning already?

When her thirst had been quenched, or at any rate when she had taken a modest sip from the bottle, Mark extended his hand and introduced himself and Sophie. 'I expect we'll all be seeing quite a bit of each other in the next week,' he remarked.

Blushing, the girl handed the bottle back to Sophie. 'Yes,' she said, without much expression, and then went on in a slightly affected voice, 'Oh, I'm Tracy and this is Jason.' She let her hair fall back across half her face and seemed to consider this the end of the conversation. But for Mark, and to Sophie's embarrassment, it was no more than the beginning.

'Just married, are you?'

Tracy perked up slightly, crossing her slim legs. The operation seemed to be accompanied by some discomfort, due to the tightness of her little white shorts. 'First thing this morning. Got a cab straight from the town hall to the airport.'

'Congratulations. And to you, Jason. You're in the same boat as us, then. Well, in a way everyone in this boat's got to be in the same boat of course, but I dare say some are more newly wed than others, eh?'

Encouraged by Tracy's half-strangled, nervous laugh, he

continued. 'Of course, if you're anything like us I expect you'll have been living together for a while. Might be a bit jittery otherwise. Oh—hope I'm not speaking out of turn.'

Tracy was blushing deeply. 'Don't matter. I never been ashamed of saying no. That's how things are these days, know what I mean? Girls like to keep themselves for their husbands, like, till they get wed.'

The unintentional ambiguity of this blurted declaration escaped neither Sophie nor Mark: it was as if marriage was perceived as the green light for infidelity.

'Save themselves for their wedding night, eh?' said Mark. 'Well, I certainly envy your Jason. Hear that, Jason? I envy you. You've got a really beautiful bride here. See that you show her a great time.'

'That's it, mate,' replied the young bridegroom, speaking for the first time. 'Cheers. Let's go and get you some tea, Trace.'

The couple moved to the front of the boat and Mark winked at Sophie. While part of her disapproved of his behaviour, which she saw as taking advantage of the awkward and inexperienced, another part of her was quite excited at the half-formulated imaginings he had stimulated. This was to be her own supposed wedding night, and it certainly felt as if she had been saving herself up for more than the couple of days since the honeymoon plan had been agreed. She felt as nervous as a genuine, virgin bride.

They got up themselves, but instead of going to the buffet they decided to see how Cathy and Peter were getting on; not to sit with them, Mark suggested, but just to take a quick peep from a safe distance. They found them occupying a bench at the front of the vessel, obviously getting on like old friends, which of course they were, and more besides. Sophie concentrated on her rising but apprehensive lust for Mark, trying to suppress the twinge in the pit of her stomach that could have been a touch of jealousy at the thought of Peter and Cathy doing it. Like themselves, their spouses had struck up a conversation with a younger couple—a considerably younger couple, who, as Mark observed, hardly looked old enough to pass as married. These two, a lively blonde whose beribboned plaits made her look even younger, and a dark, pale-faced youth with a hairdo that would not have been out of place in a boyband, seemed to be the antithesis to—what were their names?—Jason and Tracy: really outgoing and full of fun. The girl was sitting with her feet up on the bench and knees slightly apart, and had let her short denim skirt fall right back to show off the bulging triangle of white cotton between her shamelessly exposed thighs. Sophie remembered the things Cathy had done to her that morning a few days ago back in Fulham. She tried to focus on the spotless trainers on this young lady's feet, but they were too close to the tempting crotch to be an effective distraction. She could not decide whether the girl had adopted this posture deliberately for the benefit of the new friends sitting opposite her, or was just careless and uninhibited, but Mark suggested that it was probably the former.

'And I don't think it's just for Peter,' he ventured. 'Partly for him, sure, and partly for Cathy if I know anything about it. But it's mainly for her bloke. To make him a bit jealous and give him a thrill. We lads like to get excited imagining other guys with our women.' He was standing behind Sophie with his hands around her just below her breasts. For the first time, she became aware of her 'husband's' penis stirring and nudging against her bottom through their light clothing. She thought of that massive jade dildo.

Giles Rosper had sidled up to them and was offering them paper cups of ouzo. 'Quite a view,' he commented. Sophie felt the blood rush to her cheeks, but soon realised he was referring to the fact that Honeymoon Island was now clearly visible on the horizon, a brown, craggy ridge descending to what looked like lush greenery on its lower slopes. Rosper explained that it was no more than a mile long and about half a mile wide, unpopulated apart from his hotel employees and a few peasants who looked after the goats and olive trees.

As the boat drew nearer, the hotel became more and more prominent as the main feature of the view. It appeared to be a large, modern, white, low-rise complex with windows of tinted glass, stretching up the slopes of a cove-like opening in hills that dropped steeply down to the beach. The twenty or so guests disembarked on the jetty just below this impressive building, and their host proceeded to give them a rapid guided tour while his staff took their cases to their rooms.

He led them into a cool atrium full of indoor plants. In the centre was a pool. A group of white statuary was displayed on a little islet in the middle of the pool; the three beautifully sculpted, nude figures seemed to represent a family. The man was like the deities Sophie had seen in museums and art books, except that instead of the usual fig leaf or apology for a dick he sported a ramping erection. (She couldn't help noticing young Tracy staring at her feet in embarrassment.) Rosper identified this god as Mars. The woman was your usual Venus de Milo or whatever, but with a full set of arms and with the slit of her sex shown gaping. And the little wings on the boy's back identified him as a pubescent Eros. As the party approached, a stream of water first trickled and then gushed from his little prick, the angle of which was such that it splashed on to Venus's rounded belly. As it found its mark, her nipples also turned out to be nozzles that fountained water. Because her tits were modelled to point outward and upward, these powerful twin jets squirted into the mouths of the man and boy. Finally (and Sophie saw that Tracy's eyes were now glued without pretence on the sculpted group), the Mars's cock began to emit its contribution. In his case, the water did not gush out in an unbroken stream, but spurted in orgasmic pulses to splash against the plump pubic mound of Venus (or, Sophie wondered, was it called *mount* of Venus?). In response, an arc of water burst forth from the shining twat. Mark made good use of his camcorder as they watched. Very good use.

Impressed, and in some cases visibly taken aback, the party moved on over marble flooring and shallow steps, following the upward course of a babbling stream that ran from pool to pool, from waterfall to waterfall, from fountain to fountain. It led them through reception rooms, shady courtyards, corridors, ballrooms, bars and restaurants, all these rising in tiers until a backward glance through tinted windows showed the sea sparkling far below. Rosper assured them that they would find lifts on every level, and escalators in the side wings of the complex.

In the corner of one small courtyard he pointed out a well. Instead of a bucket suspended from the rope coiled round the winding gear, Sophie was disturbed to see an uncomfortable-looking iron chair. The guests took turns to crowd round the stone parapet and peer down. Far below they saw the twinkle of water. Nearer the top of the wide, dank shaft, but still beyond the reach of anyone leaning over the parapet, was an iron grid. What looked like a viewing gallery ran around the wall at that level. They all looked to their guide for elucidation.

'We call this the Bridewell,' he announced gravely, 'sometimes pronounced bridle. *Bridle*, of course, is suitably ambiguous. Is it something to do with weddings, I hear you ask, or more to do with the medieval treatment of scolds?'

'Well,' interrupted the pedantic Mark, 'how do you spell it?'

'Me? I spell it B-R-I-D-E-W-E-L-L. Anyway, it's a short-stay cooling-off facility—for recalcitrant wives. You can't see them from up here, but we've got a good choice of chains, manacles and assorted, er, assorted implements ready for use. A quick word in my ear, lads, and we'll have your young lady down there in a jiffy. Yes, *have her down there* in all senses of the words.'

'What about a fair trial?' demanded the outraged Sophie, her legal instincts unleashed.

'Trial by ordeal. *Down there*. At the moment our regular dungeon-master's away doing a stretch back home for GBH. We're going to ask for volunteers if they're needed. Don't worry, ladies. No one's going to be put down there unless her husband gets her to sign a confession of disobedience and a form of assent.' This declaration evinced rumbles of protest, mainly from the women, but Rosper moved briskly on and they all followed him. Struck by what he had just told them, Sophie recalled a detail of the case in which Peter had successfully defended Rosper. One of the alleged minor characters in the scam had not been so lucky, having to rely on legal aid for his defence. And he had gone down for quite a lengthy spell, having been found guilty of grievous bodily harm. Hmm.

At one point the party skirted a heated outdoor swimming pool in which some of the earlier arrivals were already taking a dip. Rosper gathered the group around him and addressed them.

'Don't get the wrong impression of this place,' he cautioned them. 'Sure, things are pretty free and easy, but it ain't no bleeding Liberty Hall, know what I mean?' Rosper pulled a funny face and winked before going on: 'We do have a few simple rules, and you'll soon get used to them—they're posted in all the bedrooms. Drugs are an absolute no-no, except the blue ones. Hand over your gear at reception, guys. We get the *astinomía* over from Skiathos quite often—the law enforcement boys. We've got an arrangement with them about the sex, nudge nudge, but they'd close us down if they got a whiff of the other.'

Sophie whispered to Mark that it seemed odd that there should be any problem with the sex if everyone had valid marriage certificates, but he replied that she was probably being a bit naïve. Rosper was continuing:

'And take this pool. We don't mind what you get up to down on the beaches but up here, though topless is okay, we don't allow bottomless. Sorry about that, but we like a bit of variety, you might say. Oh, and we don't want any of you gents wearing those silly shorts down to your knees. They're ugly and unhygienic. The rule is, proper trunks or one of the posing pouches you'll find in your rooms and in these bins. Quite a colourful selection.' This was evident from the bright though minimal attire of the males in and around the pool. Mark surreptitiously took a scrap of red silk from the nearest container and slipped it into his pocket.

Sophie and Mark caught up with Cathy and Peter. At first Sophie was just a little disturbed to see that her real husband was idly caressing Cathy's bottom through her black hotpants. Mark laid a hand on Peter's shoulder. 'Those two kids looking at the statue over there,' he enquired, 'the ones we saw you chatting with on the boat. Pretty, um, well, let's say pretty lively, aren't they? Show off a bit, eh? Reckon they're, you know, up for it?'

'*Friendly*'s an understatement. Tim and Polly they said they were called.'

Cathy corrected him. 'No: *Poppy*. Said they were keen to get to know everyone.'

The statue Tim and Poppy were giggling over represented a crouching girl peeing clear water into a large scallop shell held for her by a kneeling boy, whose own piss mingled with hers in the receptacle. Tilted slightly, the shell allowed the water to overflow into the stream. Rosper saw the little group admiring it, or at any rate amused by it, and came over to them to explain.

'We had thought of putting a yellow dye in the water, but then we'd have had to use something like milk for the spurting nipples.'

'And for the spunk spouting out of the spurting pricks,' added the lad identified as Tim. Everyone laughed, though Sophie noticed that Tracy and Jason looked a bit uneasy.

'Quite right, young man. And maybe we'd have had to colour the statues, too, to be consistent. They're so lifelike it might have led to embarrassing incidents with the guests. As it is, you soon get used to it, like watching black and white films.'

Something seemed to be bothering Cathy. 'But wasn't it impossibly expensive, getting all this sculpture together?' she asked. 'It all looks new. You must have commissioned real experts to do the carving. And just the marble must have cost a small fortune.'

'They didn't come cheap. Nothing in this hotel came cheap, dear. But it's not real marble, and they weren't carved by real sculptors.' Rosper rapped the crouching girl's back with his knuckles. 'They've been moulded in a special hard plastic from casts taken from the bodies of beautiful young people who've all been our guests here. And to save electricity, which we have to generate ourselves, the fountains have hidden sensors and only kick in when someone comes in sight. Don't get me wrong though—we're not cheapskates. For instance, those of you who've been in these parts before will be relieved to hear that all the plumbing's well up to American or north European standards. And for that matter nearly all our staff are English-speaking. But you may not be so pleased that there's no reception for mobile phones.'

Although she refrained from commenting, Sophie wondered if children, definitely banned from the present holiday, were sometimes brought to the island. The urinating couple they were looking at were clearly not cast from moulds of honeymooners. At one or two points on their tour, hadn't she heard, or thought she heard, muffled childish voices in the distance? She had supposed these to belong to the offspring of Rosper's staff.

Soon they reached the highest point of this magnificent fun palace, and were directed to their rooms. The genial Rosper suggested that they should freshen up and relax for a couple of hours before dinner, to be served in the penthouse restaurant, after which they were all to present themselves on the next level down in swimwear. 'Don't worry about how much you eat,' he advised them. 'You're here to enjoy. No one needs to take a dip tonight.'

As soon as Mark had closed the door behind them, he threw himself on Sophie and covered her face and throat with kisses. The reality of this pseudo-conjugal arrangement hit her like a slap round the mouth with a wet fish, and she pulled back from him. Not wanting to seem a spoilsport, a killjoy, she explained that she wasn't quite ready after their arduous journey, and needed a bath or at least a shower. But first, as a distraction, she suggested they should have a look round their room.

This was spacious and airy. There were views on both sides: a picture window of tinted glass looked out to the south over the sparkling Aegean while, to the left of the bed, french windows opened on to a narrow first-floor balcony above a courtyard. Almost opposite their room, a stone staircase gave access to the ground from this first-floor level. Similar balconies ran round all four sides of the courtyard, and a rampant but continent Apollo Belvedere displayed himself on a plinth in the central pool.

The furniture was simple but spotless, and really comfortable, especially the large bed, as Mark reported when he threw himself on it. As well as a television set which might or might not have English channels but certainly, as a leaflet on it made clear, offered adult entertainment, there was a DVD player and a small collection of movies. A shelf over the bed contained a selection of appropriate reading in the form of paperbacks with sexy covers, novels by the likes of Maria Caprio, Delver Maddingley and Philip Mason, together with a boxed set bearing the imprint *Honeymooners Library* and a fat graphic novel, *Adventures of a Naked Girl*. Mark seemed to know the work of most of these authors, but doubted if they would have time to do much reading in the coming week.

Sophie cast an eye over some of the photos on the walls. She was struck by a sequence of wedding shots, displayed in a large frame at the top of which a pair of silver bells and a horseshoe added a nice touch. First, in front of a church door stood a lovely dark-haired bride with her groom, his best man and two bridesmaids. Then a couple of more informal outdoor shots, with the young people toasting each other and the camera in champagne as they hugged one another. Though the real action only started with the indoor pictures, Sophie found the contrast of these with the fairly decorous churchyard sequence highly arousing. The white bridal gown had now gone, but the laughing bride retained her gauzy veil, elbow-length mittens, little suspender belt and white stockings throughout. In the first few shots she also wore a tiny white thong, but this soon disappeared. Then came a sequence of frigging, fucking and sucking, concluding with the exhausted bride sprawled on her back, her clean-shaven cunt on full view and seeping sperm that was already puddling on the sheet. The other members of the bridal party stood around, half-naked and applauding. Sophie wished she had been there to palm the creamy breasts and taste that inviting slit. She looked timidly across the room at Mark.

The disappointed 'bridegroom' seemed to have too much sense to spoil things by being importunate. He opened one of the fitted cupboards and called Sophie over to look at the clothes hanging in it. Most conspicuous was a set of bridal garments. It seemed to include all the essentials except a wedding dress.

Mark laughed at Rosper's inventiveness. He patted Sophie's bottom, and let have her shower in peace. When she dried off and emerged with a towel wrapped round her, however, she had a shock and nearly lost her temper. Mark had switched on the TV, and on the screen she saw herself soaping her intimate places in the shower. Luckily her body was only seen from the back except for a brief glimpse when she turned to step out on to the bath mat. He had used his camcorder to take a sneaky sequence through the partly opened door of the bathroom, and was now playing it back to tease her and entertain himself. She stormed over to the set and switched it off indignantly, but Mark's sheepish grin won her over. After all, she knew perfectly well why she was here, even if it had been possible to forget this most of the time in the excitement of the last few hours. She switched the TV on again and sat down on the edge of the bed watching it with him as she pulled a brush through her damp hair.

He ran the film back to the beginning, and there she was, sipping ouzo on the boat, the engine drowning out any conversation on the sound track. The picture cut to a shot of Tim and Poppy chatting with Peter and Cathy, whose backs were to the camera. Suddenly the lens zoomed in on Poppy's crotch, her white knickers displayed between a pair of slim but shapely thighs almost as white.

Sophie stretched out on the bed and dozed off, the excitement of her day so far catching up on her. Drifting through a light slumber, she was still worrying and obsessing about her unusual circumstances. She had been so keen on the idea of the swap when she and Peter had first discussed it. The way Mark had eyed her at the dinner table that evening had turned her on almost as much as Cathy's flirtatious behaviour. But now that ideas were about to be transformed into carnal reality, she wasn't nearly so sure. Oh no, she couldn't deny that she felt stirrings of lust at his proximity, especially in this environment. That was part of the problem: she didn't trust herself not to lose control. The last thing she wanted to do was to fall for this darkly handsome guy, with all the shitty complications that would entail. And how secure did she really feel about Peter and Cathy? If she knew Peter (and surely she did), he would be screwing his new 'bride' even now—*using* Cathy, as she was starting to suspect he might have been in the habit of using her, his own wife. At least she and Cathy had established some sort of bond. Her new friend had promised to find a bit of time for her during the week, if that proved possible. If . . .

When she awoke, it was dark outside. Her 'husband' had dressed, casually but smartly, for dinner, and was picking a fleck of fluff from his shoulder. She pulled herself together and started to rummage through her open but still unpacked suitcase.

'Do what I did,' Mark advised. 'Remember what Rosper said about meeting after dinner? Well, I put one of his posing-pouch things on under my clothes to save having to come back to the room. A red one. If you do the same, we can take a bag to the restaurant with us, find a quiet corner to take our things off and stuff them in it to bring back afterwards.'

Sophie agreed this was a good idea, but was too modest to select anything from among the similarly scanty garments in her own luggage. She gathered up the things she deemed suitable for the occasion and shut herself in the bathroom, this time being sure to bolt the door.

She emerged in a high-necked black sleeveless dress and slipped her bare feet into a pair of open-toed black shoes with low heels. A black band gathered her hair in a golden ponytail. Mark complimented her on her appearance and they made their way to the restaurant, not forgetting the canvas holdall.

The excellent dinner passed fairly uneventfully. Each couple—many more had now arrived—was allotted a separate table, and Sophie was glad that they were nowhere near Peter and

Cathy. The meal was served by pretty, topless waitresses, who hardly flinched when some of the grosser husbands rubbed their mouths against their breasts *en passant*. Mark evidently enjoyed the sight of this larking, but thankfully kept his hands and lips to himself. At least he was housetrained. Music played in the background, not so loud as to drown out murmured endearments, and a pretty stripper moved languorously between the tables, responding with lewd gyrations to the signs of appreciation given by the diners, some of the women showing as much enthusiasm as their husbands.

Warmed by the wine provided plentifully by the house, as well as by the subtly lascivious atmosphere promoted in the restaurant, Mark and Sophie slipped out and found their way down to the next level. In a handy anteroom they removed their outer clothes, folded them and stowed them in the holdall. Then they stood in front of a full-length mirror and admired each other.

Sophie could tell from the state of her partner's crotch that his admiration was genuine, in spite of the relative modesty of her attire. She had selected her royal-blue, one-piece swimsuit, high at the hips and low at the back. A row of three buttons down the front extended a promise that was no more than a tease: they were purely ornamental. The effect of this outfit, which was well cut and had been fairly expensive, was to draw attention to the beauty of her slim figure, with her small but nicely formed breasts, firm hips, rounded thighs, pert bottom and inviting cuntmound.

Mark contrasted strikingly with her as he stood by her side, just behind her. He was considerably taller, and her slight body looked enticingly fragile alongside his. His pale-skinned chest, muscular but not particularly broad, was furred with dark scrub, and black hair lent something of an animal attraction to his powerful arms and legs. Sophie was used to Peter's smooth, tanned body, and found this unfamiliar hirsuteness arousing and slightly threatening. Mark's hips were narrow and his bottom tight, the centre strap of his scarlet thong lost between the cheeks as she saw when he turned slowly through three hundred and sixty degrees for her inspection. Beginning at his navel, a triangular strip of fur widened to disappear under the waistband of the indecent garment. In fact, *waistband* was hardly the word, as the elasticated band was slung really low around his loins. The lowest hair visible on his front was no longer belly hair but pubic hair. And dominating the whole of this impressive anatomical landscape, the outline of a fat prick was blatantly visible, held down over the magnificent bollocks by the containing pouch that was not quite able to prevent a limited degree of movement. Perhaps, Sophie thought, her reservations were beginning to break down under the growing pressure of her arousal. What a lark, after all!

Her eyes grew misty, and she smiled. Mark now pressed up behind her. He rested his face against her left cheek, brought his right hand round to squeeze her breast and lowered his left hand over the dimpled curve of her belly until it cupped her plump pubis and the fingertips pressed up between her legs. Then she felt a virile stirring against her bottom, and thought she was about to swoon. In spite of her relatively respectable attire, it was as if she was melting naked into the embrace of this powerful new lover.

Another couple entered the anteroom, and Mark backed off. His red thong could not conceal his excitement, but he behaved as if nothing had happened. The other couple were too engrossed with each other to be bothered, anyway. In one hand Mark carried the holdall, while with the other he led his 'wife' out to the main landing.

A loud, pulsing rhythm issued from a doorway opposite, above which they saw a banner proclaiming 'WELCOME TO THE HONEYMOONERS SWIMWEAR BALL'.

They entered, and Mark handed their bag to an attendant behind a counter. This person's main function seemed to be to collect and label the guests' shoes and stow them on an array of shelves. Mark and Sophie already had bare feet, and glided across the shiny ballroom floor to claim one of the empty tables round the periphery. As they ordered a bottle of complimentary champagne from a waiter, more and more of the couples were making their way in from the restaurant, or more likely from the rooms to which they had gone to change.

A lively and appealing multitude they made, in all possible varieties of bathing apparel, the colours of their costumes contrasting with the hues of their bare flesh and the aspect of the whole scene constantly changing under the flashing, multicoloured strobe lights.

At the far end of the ballroom, Giles Rosper could be seen spinning turntables and mouthing what was probably youth-speak into a microphone. He wore a black cowboy hat, dark glasses, and tight-fitting black leather trousers and boots. His scrawny torso was bare.

Some couples had already taken the floor and Mark pulled Sophie to her feet to join them. As they stamped and twirled to the thumping beat, Sophie worried that her partner's genitals might suddenly flop out of their flimsy pouch. Yet the security afforded by her own costume gave her confidence, and this was boosted by the knowledge that she looked really attractive in it. Mark's near-nudity made her feel slightly uncomfortable when he came close to her in his wild dancing, but as more and more couples took to the floor her concerns vanished; most people were showing off far more skin than she was, and were behaving with little restraint.

A slow number followed. Mark drew her into a close embrace and smooched about, hardly moving from the spot, like everyone else. Safety in numbers, she thought. And now his indecent exposure, far from alienating her, was turning her on. She let both her hands wander down to his buttocks, kneading them as she worked her tummy against his hardening member.

His height prevented her from looking over his shoulder, but because his arms were crossed behind her neck she was able to gaze out past his left side while inhaling the pheromonal fragrance of his armpit. Her impression, as far as the constantly shifting lights allowed her to judge, was that the way she and Mark were comporting themselves was indeed pretty restrained compared with some of the couples. Bikini tops had been pulled up to free breasts for the attention of sucking mouths. Couples were snogging belly to belly with their hands stuck down the fronts of their partners' trunks, G-strings or bikini bottoms. She was fairly sure she caught a glimpse of an erect penis as one woman pulled back from her bloke to adjust their mode of contact.

Faster music now blared out. As the dancers resumed their wild jigging about, some of them were caught out, with the parts they had bared during the slow number still on display and being shaken about in all directions.

One couple caught Sophie's eye, the ones Peter and Cathy had befriended on the boat. That was it, Poppy and Tim. The boy was wearing a pair of small, shiny yellow bathing trunks that he seemed to have outgrown, though that was unlikely, she thought. The appearance of this garment reminded her of many embarrassing moments on seaside holidays with her parents, when boys who had been kneeling and playing in the sand would stand up and dash into the sea to hide the way their trunks were sticking out so rudely in front.

But this Tim showed no inclination to hide his condition. He positively thrust his hips forward as he rocked and rolled in approximate time with the music. These movements were mirrored by Poppy, so that their pubic regions made contact every few beats. She was sporting a tiny thong in white lace that could hardly be strong enough to hold out against a really vigorous thrust. Nor could it be classified, conventionally, as swimwear, any more than could her upper garment, a narrow band of white lace tied at the back and supporting two artificial daisies, each about four centimetres in diameter, that just covered her nipples. The breasts themselves were small, but most of their shapely beauty could be seen bare, quivering and shining in the strobes as she danced.

Sophie decided she really must get to know this delightful young creature. Was she undergoing some crisis of sexual identity, she wondered, struck by the similarity between her response to Poppy and the feelings Cathy had aroused in her.

The music stopped and the dancers returned to their tables and drinks. As far as she could see, little conversation was being exchanged, and that was certainly the case between her and her new 'husband', who now struck her as a most desirable piece of masculinity, even compared with many of those so brashly on display, none of whom would have actually failed an acceptability test. She couldn't wait to get inside that posing pouch, and resolved to have a really good grope down there as soon as Rosper played another smoochie.

He did so almost at once. The treacly music had only just started when their table received a jog that nearly upset their drinks. Sophie looked up and saw the culprits were Jason and Tracy, the young couple who had been saving themselves up for each other to enjoy on their wedding night—tonight. They swayed together in a tight embrace, very close to the table. She noticed that Mark was leaning back in his chair, basking in their proximity.

By an odd coincidence, Tracy was dressed in an exact replica of Sophie's blue one-piece swimsuit. (Well, it was obviously a bit smaller, a perfect fit on the petite girl.) Where it dipped down in the front a constellation of freckles complemented those on her face, which looked slightly tense. Jason wore soft-looking, light green cotton trunks, and one of his thighs was thrust between his partner's. The girl's fingers were curled up into the trunks at the back, pulling them up on both sides so that the cheeks of Jason's white bottom were exposed. He gripped her hips, already bare below the high-cut swimsuit, and his knuckles were white as he dragged her against his loins. His head tossed from side to side while her tongue chased his open mouth; both of them flushed crimson.

'I don't think he can wait any longer,' said Mark. 'Saved himself up long enough.'

Mark was right. The young bridegroom's buttocks, concave with tension, began to heave with a rhythm that had nothing to do with Rosper's music but a lot to do with the urgings of Tracy's fingers. Suddenly he sagged against her. Their mouths met at last in a wet kiss, but almost immediately Jason pulled back, an expression of horror on his face. He pushed her away from him and looked down. Sure enough, the front of his trunks was stained with a huge and spreading wet patch of dark green, made even more obvious by the way his still swollen genitals filled the garment out. Holding one hand over this display, he laid the other on the nape of Tracy's neck and steered her ahead of him as a human shield. Her head was hanging in shame, but although her hair flopped forward it did not quite hide her deep blush. The couple hurried from the ballroom.

Even as Sophie, highly excited by what she had just witnessed, extended her hand to encourage the equally aroused Mark to take her out on the floor again, someone tapped her shoulder, and she turned to confront Cathy. Surprise, surprise: her elegant girlfriend had come over to ask her for a dance. Cathy's bikini was of shiny black silk, stretched tightly over her enticing curves. Mark grinned sheepishly and pushed Sophie out to join his real wife on the dance floor.

First the tempo was fast and they shimmied about in abandon. Sophie felt herself relaxing now. Only a couple of days ago the thought of dancing half naked with a woman would have seemed perverse to her; now it felt kind of normal compared with what awaited her in the bedroom on this first night of her 'honeymoon'.

The music changed to a slow dance and the two of them came together in a gentle clinch. Although the beat was now languid the volume was turned up high and Sophie was glad of this excuse for not engaging in conversation. She didn't want to know what her husband had been up to since their arrival—not yet. And she wanted to maintain her own privacy until the new arrangements were irrevocably entered into on both sides. She rested her chin on Cathy's shoulder and shouted in her ear: 'I hope we can get to do this more often.'

Cathy let her fingertips spider over her friend's thightops and the creases marking the outswell of her buttocks just below where the blue costume hugged into them. 'I'll try to get close to you every day, darling,' she laughed. 'No need to be shy.'

Back in their room, Mark stripped off his G-string immediately and slipped between the sheets. Sophie was in much less of a hurry, even though her sexuality had been wound up almost to its limits by the events of the evening. She disappeared into the bathroom and was in there for a considerable time. When she finally emerged she was wearing a short white baby-doll nightdress of thin cotton material. It was sleeveless and low cut, its edges trimmed with delicate lace. The neckline plunged to about halfway down her bosom, and a pink bow showed that the band that formed a high, empire-line 'waist' below her breasts could open to reveal even more. In front, the hem hung to the midpoint of her thighs, rising at the sides to a level about twenty centimetres higher. Her blonde hair hung loose around her shoulders. She switched off the bedside lamp. From outside, moonlight flooded through the open curtains and fell in a broad beam on the sheet.

Mark kicked this sheet off to disclose a magnificent upright erection as if offering it to the moon goddess in some lewd act of pagan worship. He extended his arms towards her, but Sophie ignored the invitation and moved across to the window looking down on the courtyard. Even as she looked out, a movement on the far side caught her eye. A pale figure tiptoed down the stone stairway and into the moonlight.

She recognised Poppy, slim and completely nude, and gestured to Mark to leave the bed and join her at the window. He did so, peering over her shoulder as his virility dug into her bottom through the flimsy cotton of her nightie. She made no objection, engrossed in the scene that unfolded below.

Poppy approached the rampant white Apollo in the middle of the central pool. The god reacted by spouting gushes of water from his penis; these rose to the level of his noble head before falling and splashing into the stone basin. At the first ejaculation young Poppy flinched back. She seemed on the point of moving round and stepping into the water behind the statue to avoid an overall wetting. Her toe entered the water. Changing her mind, she withdrew it, padded round to the front again, and mounted the low parapet. Then she made a quick dash for the plinth in the centre, squealing briefly as the cold splashes took her breath away. Sophie was distracted for a moment by strong hands squeezing her breasts as the phallus nudged against her bottom.

A second squeal drew her attention back to the scene in the courtyard. The athletic Poppy had flung herself up to clasp Apollo in a clinging embrace. Her arms were locked round his neck and her legs clutched his lean hips. And, yes, there could be no doubt that the girl was fucking herself on the spouting prick. Water still splashed into the stone basin in regular pulses, but these were flowing from Poppy's loins as her flushed cunt overflowed and became part of the fountain.

A second pale, naked form dashed down into the courtyard to join the girl delighting herself with this lifesize sex toy. It was her partner Tim, who mounted the plinth behind her. As he pressed himself against Poppy's back, Sophie felt one of Mark's hands releasing the breast it cupped and pushing his prick down. The hem of her nightie was lifted behind, and the slippery glans pushed between her thighs. She reached down and raised the front of the garment in dismay to see the purple monster peeping out obscenely just below her little bush of blonde fur. When she dropped the hem it remained caught up on the bulb. In spite of herself she quivered with excitement and writhed lustfully as 'her' man's thumb and finger teased the nipple of the tit he was still holding through her nightdress. Tentatively and with a sense of transgression she rubbed the tip of her thumb over that insolent knob and spread the clear fluid that seeped from the slit all over the sensitive surface. Mark spoke.

'Missed the target, I'm afraid. It was meant to slip straight in like it would have done with Ca—like it would have done if you'd been a bit taller. Or maybe you'd have preferred it the way that mad girl down there's getting it.'

A third, louder squeal caused Sophie to refocus on Tim, Poppy and the Apollo Belvedere. The first two were humping happily while the spouting god remained impassive. Dim faces could now be seen at the windows all round the courtyard.

'You mean from the front, with me clinging on to you like a monkey up a tree?'

'No. From the back. Can't you tell? He's got it up her arse, the cheeky bugger.'

Suddenly Sophie, whose moods had been swinging like Tim's balls ever since disembarking on the island, felt embarrassed and awkward with her unfamiliar partner. She tore herself away from him and threw herself on the bed, face down. The mattress bucked as he joined her, and she thought maybe this posture was not such a good idea after all. Her fear grew as the palm of a hand slid up the backs of her thighs and swept the hem of her nightie right up to the small of her back.

Now her bottom was being kissed, and the treatment was by no means disagreeable. Mark might be a gentle, considerate lover after all. Yes, her mood was swinging yet again. Remembering the scenes in the ballroom, she admitted to herself that she was, indeed, in a swinging mood. Time to let go.

She rolled on to her side, with her back to her 'husband', who took advantage of the movement to seize and massage a breast. His lips and tongue had now wandered to her flank and seemed to be licking their way down into the crease of her groin and over into her pubic fuzz. He sighed as he savoured the sexual fragrance released by his importuning mouth.

Ready at last to give herself—in fact unable to hold her lust in check—she now stretched out on her back and opened her thighs. Her only regret was that Peter and Cathy were not there to witness and perhaps share the excitement. Tantalisingly, Mark's tonguetip flicked over the bud of her clitoris before rasping up over her belly. She lifted her behind so that the tongue could drag the hem of her nightie up with it as far as that ridiculously high waistband. His fingers fumbled with the bow and he pulled the flimsy top wide open, easing the small, firm globes out to meet his wet mouth. The white skin gleamed with his saliva. Covering his teeth with his lips, he bit at the nipples in turn until they stood up red, hard and bigger than Sophie could recall them ever being when they responded to her Peter's attentions. Her arms were extended limply above her head on either side, and with the nearer one she reached out to switch on the bedside lamp once more. If he was going take her, let him see what he was taking. She knew, didn't she, that he liked to watch.

As he mouthed her teats, one of his hands cupped her sex, gently squeezed it and dipped a couple of fingers into her wetness. Then his mouth moved down and his hands moved up. Her breasts ached with lasciviousness as he toyed with them, but most of her sensations were now centred on her pussy as his skilled tongue lashed it and sliced the succulent lips apart. His nose played against her clit. She was about to come.

'Fuck me, you gorgeous man,' she whimpered. 'Fuck me now. Shoot your spunk up me. This is our wedding night, remember?'

Mark edged back. Instead of taking the immediate action she had demanded, he knelt there contemplating the juicing cunt exposed and open before him. 'You are beautiful, Sophie,' he breathed. 'I guess this is the moment I've been dying for. What a honeymoon this is going to be! Just feel how heavy my balls have gone with all the spunk in them.'

Sophie reached down and felt. She wanted them to release their load into her thirsty quim. But this maddening stud was not yet ready. He shifted on the bed until he was kneeling astride her chest, and she had no illusions about what was required. Putting one hand behind her head to support it, she leaned forward to take the oozing tip between her lips.

'Oh yes,' he murmured, giving a little shiver as she sucked. 'Oh yes, do it, baby. Let me see you do it. But not too much. Stop the minute I pinch your tits. I need to stick it up you and fuck you properly.'

She had not given more than half a dozen suctioning pulls on the bursting plum—just like that massive jade dildo, apart from the colour and temperature—when she realised his balls were tightening. A stab of pain in her right nipple gave her the signal and she expelled him from her mouth. With a catlike leap Mark planted his knees between her thighs and the head of his cock at the entrance to her vagina. One long thrust and he was right into her. Three more thrusts and he froze.

'Okay for me to come inside you—wife?'

'Go ahead. Give it all to me. Fill me up. Do it—now!'

Sunday

Sophie opened her eyes to brilliant sunshine. It was already hot in the bedroom at six o'clock. Mark was sleeping soundly, seemingly fucked out, and the smell of sex was heavy in the air. She slipped off the bed, stretched, and after a quick visit to the bathroom threw open the balcony window.

At first everything seemed quiet around the deserted courtyard. Then she noticed a movement on the balcony directly opposite, the balcony from which those two youngsters had descended for their encounter with Apollo and each other. She shrunk back into the shade of the room and watched intently.

Young Tim stood just outside the bedroom opposite, stark naked. The blackness of his abundant hair set off the pallor of his face and body. Unfortunately, he was standing behind a purple towel draped over the balcony railing, so that although the barrier was rather low Sophie could see no further down than his belly-button. This was far enough for her to register that he was masturbating as he stared across the courtyard. Could he see her as she trembled in the shadows?

A warm hand on her behind told her that Mark was now awake and had joined her at the window. He pushed her forward slightly. Now the sunlight caressed her as she stood on the threshold.

At this point Poppy appeared, naked, and stepped out to join the masturbating youth at the rail. Her plaits had been undone and her long yellow hair was piled up on top of her head. Like Tim, she too was partly concealed by the towel, but her pert little breasts winked proudly in the sun. Sophie undid the pink bow she had re-fastened below her bosom and let the nightgown hang wide open.

Poppy leaned forward. Her tits hung down, too small to be described as dangling, but she kept her head tilted back, staring wide-eyed at the astonished Sophie from below a golden fringe. Tim now moved behind her, grinned across to Sophie and appeared to be penetrating Poppy from behind. Whether he was using the same mode of entry as Mark had claimed to be the case last night was impossible to tell, though the girl's expression showed no sign of discomfort.

On the contrary, as her eyes widened still further, she blushed, grinned and stuck out her tongue.

Her partner drew back, turned and disappeared into the apartment, returning with a wooden chair. This he set down on the balcony, saying something to Poppy, who snatched the towel from the railing and draped it over the back of the chair. In full view of the spectators and sideways on, she now bent forward over it, her hands resting on the seat.

It struck Sophie that Tim, now fussing about behind the girl, had not the slightest visible trace of pubic hair around his sprouting prick and pink balls. Before she had time to reflect on this, he was thrusting into Poppy from behind, smiling across at the opposite balcony as he began to fuck.

The next thing Sophie knew was that Mark had backed away from her to fetch one of their own chairs. He placed it right at the front of the balcony and pushed his 'wife' face down across the back, a mirror image of young Poppy. And like Poppy, she too received the full length of an eager erection.

Mark was keeping time with Tim in his powerful shagging, having flipped the open nightie over to the side to give the younger couple an unimpeded view.

Which of the couples finished first Sophie couldn't tell. Just as Mark's sperm burst into her pulsating cunt, her own orgasm shook her so violently that she fell forwards and toppled the chair with her. With her bottom cocked up in the air, she felt her man pull back. He was still spurting, and some of the warm gobs landed low on her back. More of it bubbled out of her vagina, rolling down over her enlarged clit and dripping on to the tiled floor. 'What a lark!' she giggled.

After this bout, Sophie and Mark were hungry. They hopped on to their bed and Mark ordered a light breakfast from room service. They were still panting when the little brunette waitress from the night before slipped into the room with a tray, which she set down on a bedside table, introducing herself as Julie and hoping they had enjoyed their wedding night. She seemed unfazed by the way Mark's limp penis straightened out and stretched up under the gaze of her hazel eyes. In the restaurant she had been topless, wearing a black miniskirt and black stockings; now she was naked except for a tiny garment that just covered her sex with a diamond-shaped black pouch. Three little strings on each side secured this scrap of black lace to a band high on her waist. This held up a triangle at the back that gave no clue as to whether the item could best be described as a thong or regular knickers.

Observing Mark's interest in this piece of minimal lingerie, an interest emphasised by the way his purple knob grew even bigger and began to weep clear pre-come fluid, the girl bent back with her hands on her hips. 'Pretty, isn't it?' she laughed.

'My boyfriend encourages me to wear it on my rounds.' She then reached forward to straighten the sheet on the far side of the bed, and her left breast rubbed against Sophie's cheek. She adjusted her angle as if to facilitate her tidying task but in reality to place her dark red nipple against Sophie's mouth and press it into her lips. The lips opened and a wet tongue began to flick across the tip, bringing it up to rigidity.

'You're very naughty, madam,' she said. 'I like that so much, but I can only take a little of it. And what about you, sir? You can feel me up if you like—you know, down there—as long as you don't get inside my thongy-thingy. My boyfriend won't allow that, and he always knows. Here, let me get in a more convenient position.'

Julie jumped up on the bed and knelt between the honeymooners, who both sat upright and got to work on her. Mark's hand completely covered the diamond-shaped pouch, tugging at its black retaining strings; Sophie had one tit in her mouth while she caressed the other one manually. This messing about was really turning her on.

After just a few minutes, Julie, blushing prettily, pulled back. 'Got to go now,' she panted.

'Sure you wouldn't rather *come*?' asked Mark.

'Well, yes, but that's got to be with my boyfriend. Right now I'm so ready for him. He's usually too busy to get me going like this himself, so it's nice to find folks to give me a helping hand.' She blew them a kiss and skipped off, closing the door behind her.

Mark and Sophie decided to go for a walk and have a look at one of the beaches. They applied sun lotion, but being in hurry refrained from further hanky-panky. The young woman wore a minute black bikini with a transparent wrap-around skirt of white Indian cotton, and a broad-brimmed straw hat. Her 'husband' shrugged on a pair of jeans over the scarlet thong he had worn the night before.

Down at reception, Jason and Tracy, the couple they had spoken to on the boat, were conversing in low voices with the young man at the counter. Or rather, Jason was doing the talking while his auburn-haired bride stood beside him bashfully, staring at the floor. She was wearing the loose white top that had given Mark a glimpse of her tits when she bent forward, and the same white shorts. On her feet she had white trainers and ankle socks. The man produced what looked like a little map, marked something on it and handed it over. The couple left without noticing Sophie and Mark.

Advancing to the counter, Mark asked the guy if he knew a really private beach not too far off. A copy of the same map was brought out. The man indicated the location of the hotel and circled a cove on the opposite side of the island in red.

'Look,' he said, 'there's quite a few little coves over there, but steer clear of this one I've marked. I just recommended it to a pair of youngsters who wanted to have it all to themselves.'

Outside, it was a beautiful morning, sunny and fresh. They hurried up a track through a fragrant pine wood, holding hands. There was no need to articulate the destination they were heading for. When the young pines crowded close together, they stopped for a quick kiss and Mark asked Sophie to remove her bikini top. Her first reaction was one of shock, annoyance even. But his laughing eyes quickly changed her mood. Walking topless through the woods could be a bit of a lark . . . 'You like to watch, don't you?' she observed.

Mark had been hopping about and catching her from various

angles with his lightweight camcorder. He told her he was trying to get as many different effects of sunlight and shade dappling her pretty chest as he could. This explanation flattered Sophie, and she did her best to vary her posture and facial expression to add to the variety. For much of the filming Mark made sure that she was posing between him and the sun, so that her legs were visible through the flimsy cotton of her skirt. Every now and then she would pause to play with her breasts and offer them to the camera.

As they came to a bend where the track rounded a great boulder, they were so engrossed in this artistic endeavour that they almost gave their presence away to Jason and Tracy, who must have been loitering on their way and were now only ten metres or so ahead of them. Sophie pulled Mark back into the shadow of the boulder, from where they could watch fairly safely.

Sophie was shocked to see that Tracy had removed her shorts—bottomless seemed considerably more transgressive than topless. From the back the girl's bottom looked bare until Mark pointed out the white string of a thong just visible dipping down between the cheeks. Her legs were bare down to the little white socks and trainers. Her fair-haired husband, whose footwear, like Sophie and Mark's, consisted of sandals, had taken off his own T-shirt but retained his silly calf-length denim shorts. This was a fashion Mark said he had always despised. In one hand Jason clutched a hotel beach bag similar to Mark's. The other hand rested on his bride's hip. Sophie felt it was odd that this hand was not planted firmly on the white buttock just below it. Was the boy still shy? Even after the wedding night they had been saving themselves up for? Perhaps he had spent all his passion into those light green trunks on the dance floor last night.

Mark suggested a short pause to give the others a chance to get down to their secret beach unobserved. He stepped out of his jeans and stuffed them in the bag, paraded about a bit in his red pouch and gave his 'bride' a wide grin.

Taking her cue from him, Sophie stripped off her flimsy skirt and twirled about in her shiny black bikini bottom. Her breasts, small but firm, wiggled slightly in the dappled sunlight.

When she was about twelve, Sophie used to have these dreams or fantasies. She would be walking in the woods when she was surprised by a man—a fairy-tale prince in the colourful costume of a Pre-Raphaelite print on her classroom wall. ('Look at the *prints*,' her teacher used to say, and Sophie thought she meant this dashing guy, this *prince*.) Often his shirt was open, showing off a hairy chest in token of his mature maleness. The prince 'ravished' her, though at this age she didn't quite know what the word meant. Anyway, the experience was ecstatic and ravishing. With Mark she was reminded of this forgotten pleasure.

Assuming the active role of the prince she threw herself at her man and clasped her hands behind his neck. His right hand spread over her back and drew her to him so that she felt his hardness pressing into her lower belly. His other hand stroked her shoulder, then lingered in the damp yellow fuzz of her armpit before tickling down to her right breast—the left one was squashed against his chest, where his coarse hair scoured her nipple. She leaned back slightly to look up at him.

'Snog me, Mark,' she pleaded. 'I want to be snogged.'

He lowered his open mouth to hers. Their tongues flirted shamelessly with each other while his fingertips flirted with her right nipple. She pulled her mouth away for a moment and spoke again:

'Why don't you feel me up like you did with that little Julie in our room?'

Mark needed no encouragement. His kissing now moved down to her breast; his left hand slid down between their two bodies to cup the hot bulge in her bikini panties. Gently but firmly he began to knead the girlflesh, working his middle finger up into the outer reaches of her cunt and pushing the soft material into the wetness.

When she came with a great shudder, Mark released her. He adjusted his minimal garment to relieve the discomfort of his swollen cock.

'Saving myself up for you,' he laughed.

They came to the end of the track quite suddenly. Before them twinkled the unbelievably blue Aegean; on either side the undergrowth crowded to the edge of the small drop down to the beach. This beach was a tiny cove of golden sand, on which a couple might well think they could mess about unseen. Up here, on the right, the shrubs overarched a patch of moss. Mark signalled to Sophie and they both lowered themselves on to the cool bed.

Creeping right to the edge of the overhang, they were able to peer down through a fringe of long grass. Almost immediately below them, the attractive young couple lay side by side, face down, on an orange towel. Up at the top of the beach the sand was flat, though it sloped down quite steeply to the waves. The newlyweds had their heads towards the sea, which was ideal for the pleasure of their unseen audience. Jason was wearing those same pale green trunks from the night before. He or Tracy must have rinsed them out after he had disgraced himself. As for Tracy's outfit, she still had her white suntop on, but it was clear that she was now truly bottomless—the little white thong was there, discarded on the sand beside her.

Mark carefully placed his camcorder between two tufts of moss, tilted down so that it would take in the scene below them. Then he skinned off his G-string and Sophie's bikini bottom. He made her lie on her side with her head just over the edge so that, like the camera, she had a good view of the beach below while remaining more or less hidden. When she was comfortable he took a similar position right behind her. He lifted her upper leg and without further ado shoved his hot cock straight into her vagina. Instead of fucking her at once, he luxuriated inside her, gently stroking her bare breasts as the two of them stared down at the couple on the orange towel.

When Tracy spoke, Sophie was surprised that her voice could be heard so clearly. Perhaps the configuration of the bank above them focussed the sound and funnelled it upwards. 'Let's get you going,' she said. 'I'll play with your bum, like, to start with. Best not to go straight for that out-of-control dick of yours.'

'Just do it, doll,' came the reply.

Tracy's hand played over the green trunks, prodding and slapping. Inch by inch she eased them down with one hand while continuing her caresses with the other. At last the cheeks were fully exposed. The girl raised her own bottom, buried her face between her husband's buttocks and dragged the trunks right off over his feet. She now lifted her head from his backside, placed a knee between his thighs and concentrated on feeling his balls from behind. In spite of her position she was not entirely concealing the operation from the onlookers.

Without either of them taking their eyes off this developing scene, Mark started to slide in and out of Sophie in long, sensual sweeps. On each inward thrust he would squeeze one of her tits, giving the nipple a little twist.

Down below, there was a sudden movement. Jason rolled on to his back and pulled Tracy down on hers beside him. The spectators were astonished at the size of the young man's erection, as he was of no more than medium height, if that. His pubic bush was almost invisible, it was so fine and blond. In contrast, his bride's triangle of hair, though very small, was a fiery red, more intense than her auburn ringlets and clashing rather stridently with the orange of the towel. These colours were complemented by a splash of pink between the girl's thighs and the duskier pink of the boy's scrotum as well as the gleaming purple of his glans. Even more than from behind, Mark found the combination of white suntop with naked lower parts irresistible. He began to plough more urgently into his partner, whose breathing quickened.

Jason forced Tracy's thighs wider apart. He placed her legs over his shoulders and knelt poised above her, wagging the dilated prick in his fist. 'Open your cunt, you randy little bitch,' he shouted. Tracy reached down and tugged her labia apart for him.

At that moment the excitement proved too much. A great sheet of sperm gushed from the head of his cock, darkening the front of her suntop, coating her exposed belly and turning her flaming little bush into a swamp.

'Fuck!' yelled Jason as he collapsed on his polluted bride.

'But it's lovely,' she protested. 'It's such a frigging frill, know what I mean?'

'Frill?'

'Frilling.'

This was all too much for Mark, who tensed, dragged Sophie

back hard against his abdomen and fired shot after shot of hot spunk into her. Almost simultaneously, her response triggered as much by the scene on the beach as by her man's stimulation, the young woman shuddered in a violent orgasm.

The couple down below dashed into the sea to cool and clean off. Tracy had stripped off her soaked top, but instead of hanging around to enjoy the sight of her breasts, Mark surprised Sophie by retrieving the camera and stepping into his thong. He then told the compliant girl to put on nothing but her flimsy skirt and straw hat, and led her back up the woodland track. Warm semen trickled down the insides of both her thighs, cooling and congealing by the time it reached her knees.

Where the path swerved to skirt that large boulder he motioned her to follow him into the thicket. From this position they had a fine view of the path up which the others would have to return. He checked the camcorder and they sat down to wait. While they waited they hugged and kissed, toying with each other's privates but refraining from intercourse. Mark was anxious not be be taken off his guard when the others came into view. That is to say, into his viewfinder.

After some twenty minutes he disengaged and indicated that Sophie should take her hand out of his G-string. They both took cover and Mark grabbed the camcorder. Their hearts were pounding as their quarry approached—at first they could be heard but not seen.

'I tell you it don't matter,' Tracy was saying. 'We got the whole fucking week to get it right.'

Jason's reply was spluttered. 'All that wasted effort. All that wasted spunk. I was supposed to get you up the fucking duff on this honeymoon.'

At this point the couple hove into sight. Apart from his youthful, blond good looks, the boy was nothing special as a physical specimen. He had his green trunks on again, with no sign of turgidity inside them—just a well-proportioned package between his legs. But Tracy was enough to make anyone gasp. Her sex was snug within the tiny white triangle of her thong. A few stray wisps of red hair could be made out around the edges on all three sides. This thong was all she had on. For the first time, Sophie and Mark had a clear view of her beautiful grapefruit-sized titties, jouncing very slightly as she walked. Jason held his beach bag in one hand, but the free one was round his bride's waist, quite high up so that his fingertips just reached the lower slopes of her breast.

Mark couldn't believe his luck when, just where the track came closest to their hiding place, the young couple halted. From the tops of their thighs up they filled his viewfinder very handily. Tracy half turned to Jason. Now it was possible from the side to admire her pretty white bottom as well as one of her tits. She addressed him in a teasing, little-girl voice:

'When we get back to our room I'll let you do me proper.'

Jason already had a hand on her bare behind, and had slid his thumb into the waistband of her thong ready to pull it down.

'Stop that, big boy. When we get back, I said. Well, I'll tell you what. Suppose you get me good and ready for a real fuck. Why don't you play wiv me like you done this morning witv that maid, that Julie—get me all *mushy?*'

Jason moved behind the girl, so that Mark had a direct, full frontal view of her. One hand came round under her armpit to fondle a pert breast. He slid the other one round her waist, stroked it down her tummy and grabbed the triangle of white cloth. She tilted her head back and he slobbered at her cheek.

'Do me—do me good!' she pleaded.

The hand on her vulva squeezed and kneaded it, then tugged the thong to one side. Two fingers could be seen to plunge into the bright red bush, disappearing up to the knuckles. The thumb pointed up and was active at the level of the clit.

Suddenly Tracy fell forward to her knees, panting. Nearly all of her young husband was now exposed. His hairless chest was flushed and the front of his trunks was soaked.

Sophie and Mark lingered on their way back to the hotel to let the others get well ahead as soon as Jason had replaced those trunks with his long 'shorts'. They made straight for a large, airy room overlooking the pool—the Topless Bar, it was designated, and they certainly qualified to join all the other funsters there. Nobody was standing on ceremony: general familiarity prevailed.

Sophie perched on a high stool at the bar. Her wrap-around skirt fell open, exposing a lithe thigh. Someone's casual hand was laid on it, and at first she took no action as she felt sure this was just a lark. When she looked down, though, she was shocked to see her skin partly covered with a lacy white crust. This reminded her of seeing the same thing while making love with Cathy back in Fulham. Mark's sperm it had been on that occasion, too. She pushed the hand away, crossed her legs and adjusted the fall of her skirt.

Cathy? She was sitting over there by the window, talking to Poppy and Tim. All three of them were wearing white shorts—hotpants in the case of the girls and little gym shorts on Tim. Sophie caught Cathy's eye. At the same time Mark excused himself and sloped off to join Rosper and Peter, who were chatting at the far end of the bar.

Cathy detached herself from the exhibitionist couple and came across to Sophie. No words were exchanged. The older woman simply took her friend by the hand and led her from the room. They rounded a corner in the corridor. Cathy opened a narrow door and switched on a light in the dark interior space. It was a large, warm, windowless laundry closet, wooden shelves on one side stacked with clean linen and most of the floor littered with soiled bedlinen, tablecloths and so on.

The horny couple subsided among the sheets on the floor. They kissed long and wetly before clinging together so that their nipples could arouse each other through friction while they still kissed. Then, taking the lead as she had back in England, Cathy unwrapped Sophie's skirt and lifted her own hips to slide off her shorts. A strong female scent quickly overcame the fresh smell of laundered linen. Cathy swung round above her lover to initiate a vigorous sixty-nine.

Once they were both satisfied they shifted to lie side by side, embracing gently and gazing into each other's eyes. 'What's my Peter been getting up to?' Sophie asked.

'You know Pete. He just can't get enough. I really needed a change—just for a bit—which is why I'm so glad of a bit of quality time with you now, darling. We were at it all night long. He wants us to re-enact those times we had at school. He may even get Mark involved, but only if you agree.'

Sophie tried to think quickly, but Cathy had resumed her enthusiastic speech.

'Then we spent the morning on the main beach down here in front of the hotel. Guess what? He actually stripped my bikini bottoms off and screwed me in the water. That Poppy and Tim were splashing about in the nude right next to us, but they just laughed when they saw what we were up to. We had a good long sleep on the beach after that. And Mark? Plenty for him to look at here, isn't there?'

Before Sophie could reply, the door opened. It was the maid or waitress Julie who stepped through the door and closed it behind her. This time she was wearing an upmarket sex-shop's version of a French maid's outfit. In no time at all the white apron and short black dress came off, leaving her in white cap, black garter belt and stockings and instead of that curious spider-like thong just a cluster of soft black hairs. They didn't hide the slit dividing her plump sexlips.

While undressing, she kept up a stream of suggestive remarks, seemingly unperturbed by the sapphic display among the sheets on the floor. 'So glad you found this little love nest,' she chattered. 'I'm supposed to keep it locked, but I only do that when I think people I don't like are using it. All for a bit of fun, me—a bit of hot girl-on-girl action. My boyfriend likes me to join in when I get the chance. Doesn't make me keep my thongy-thingy on when we're all girls together. And that's what we are, isn't it?'

Remembering what fun they had shared with Julie that morning, Sophie hoped Cathy would not object. Three would not be that much of a crowd in these circumstances, surely. A week ago she had never done it with just one woman, let alone two. How things could change when you were having a lark!

Julie threw herself down on her front. She splayed her thighs frog-fashion, twitched her buttocks and cocked her arse up so that her sex was displayed to its fullest advantage. By cramming a bundle of laundry under her she made it possible to maintain this attitude while the others examined her in close detail.

'Look how wet she is!' said Sophie.

'It's practically streaming out of her,' Cathy replied. 'And when I pull the lips apart like this, that looks like a bloke's stuff starting to dribble out.'

It was true, and Sophie blushed as she acknowledged the likelihood of this.

Julie explained. 'Hope it doesn't put you off, darlings. Just come from my boyfriend. Yes,' she giggled, 'that's what it is—his come—plus I've just come from being with him. What am I saying? Sometimes just being with him nearly makes me come. But what I mean is . . .'

Cathy helped out. 'You mean he did you before you came here.'

'But you sweethearts haven't made me come yet.'

She twitched her bottom again and the invitation was taken up. Things were serious now. The two friends went at her in a burst of frenzied activity. Cathy's tongue and lips glued themselves to the leaking vulva while Sophie, a little fastidious when it came to savouring a stranger's jism, covered her teeth with her lips as she bit into the soft buttocks. With her long fingers she reached round Cathy's chin and stroked around until she found Julie's clit, which was already engorged from rubbing on the piled-up laundry.

Soon the maid was quivering and gasping. But the others were not content with pleasuring her in this lavish way. They had been kneeling on either side of her, bending to their tasks. Now, without interrupting this service, they shifted their knees closer to each other until they touched Julie's sides. Julie raised herself slightly and hugged their thighs into the warm nests between her breasts and her armpits. She was now able to reach round to the front and diddle their pussies, though the shudders anticipating her approaching climax made this a rather hit-or-miss operation.

The fumbling was perceived as erotic as much as erratic. Soon the threesome was heaving and thrashing all over the sheets and tablecloths. They climaxed more or less simultaneously. Julie switched off the light and they slept for more than an hour.

After a light lunch Sophie rejoined Mark and they wandered down to the main beach for a lazy afternoon. Although it was far from crowded, this wide expanse of sand, well furnished with sunshades and double loungers, offered plenty to please Mark's ever-roving eye. There was little total nudity—Rosper's restrictions regarding poolside etiquette seemed to be to some extent observed on the beach—but people were uninhibited in their changing procedures, and relaxed about observing the rules while actually in the water. The level of female pulchritude, he remarked to Sophie, was far higher than on your average beach, and the absence of kids encouraged a spirit of fun and games among these young adults.

Except that so many of them, including Sophie and himself, were quite shagged out.

Still, they managed several refreshing dips in the warm blue water. Mark's thong became dark red and sagged down a bit in the front. Sophie's little black bikini retained its sexy elegance, and of course she attracted even more admiring looks from the guys in the water and on the sand when she dispensed with the top. Time passed quickly.

Even more sleep followed when they retired to their room in the late afternoon. Had their flight from England been longer, Mark observed, their condition might have been put down to jet lag. Perhaps, he suggested, it wasn't too fanciful to call it this after all, in view of all the powerful jets he had shot from his penis since their arrival.

As they began to recover, he proposed viewing the tapes he had shot of Jason and Tracy. Sophie was glad to concur; she thought this would give her a bit of a respite from his ceaseless attentions. He switched on the TV and DVD player.

Oh yes. The picture quality was excellent, and the ability to freeze the frame, slow the action and repeat sequences over and over made the experience (even for the novice voyeur Sophie, who lay naked on the bed beside her 'husband') in some ways more exciting than the real thing. After all, they had only been non-combatant viewers when it was happening. Perhaps the only superiority of live over recorded action was the element of spontaneity—the possibility of some unexpected development changing the whole course of events. And this could have had negative consequences.

In many ways the opening sequence was the most breathtaking, maybe because of its tentative innocence and the viewers' knowledge of what was going to happen later. The young couple were shown from behind, lingering on their walk through the pine forest. Jason was quite unremarkable in those overlong shorts, but his bride was delicious. Sophie was reminded of that popular poster Peter had put up in their bedroom at home—the one with a girl tennis-player lifting her skirt to show off her bottom. When she mentioned this now to Mark, she was not altogether surprised to learn that it was he who had given the poster to his friend. In exchange for one of those naughty photos of herself?—she didn't like to ask.

What was so appealing in this short sequence was the sense of sexual tension suggested in the way the boy's hand rested on his mate's bare hip. Little movements that had escaped Sophie that morning now hinted at his longing to let the hand wander down to her exposed backside. And the white string of the thong dipping down out of sight between her buttocks seemed incredibly arousing now that there was time to study it in detail and think about the implications. In front, unseen, the pouch of the thong would have been like a flimsy shield ostensibly protecting her femininity while at the same time the exposure of her bottom offered a most flagrant invitation. Sophie realised her own cunt was oozing as she lay there with her thighs together. Yes, Mark was perceptive: tops without bottoms certainly hit all the right buttons . . .

The scene changed to the orange towel on the beach. Sophie sat up when the lovers flipped over to lie side by side on their backs. The clashing colour contrasts struck her, as they had in the live performance. Strident orange, the towel formed a background to the creamy whiteness of their bodies; the creamy tint was emphasised by the purity of the girl's modest white suntop. Above the straight hem at the top of this, and between the wide white shoulder straps, a sprinkling of freckles echoed those on her cute face, her eyes closed and her teeth biting her pink lower lip in concentration. Half her face was hidden by the profusion of auburn curls, the rest of them tumbling over the towel. And small but dominant, the flaming tuft at the base of her belly formed an almost aggressive foil to the delicate pink of her cuntlips.

Jason's hoarse voice instructed her to open herself to him. She was obviously more than eager to receive him, pulling the elastic leaves apart to reveal the moist, shining inside of her cunt. An attractive and visible detail as she did so was the gleaming gold wedding ring on her finger. Jason leapt into position between her thighs, the head of his cock deep purple and his short, yellowish pubic hair adding the final touch of colour, before his spunk came bursting out all over the girl's belly.

It seemed strange to be fully if casually dressed for dinner. However, Mark found a certain mild thrill in remembering the bodies of all these pretty young women he had observed on the beach, now looking radiant and perhaps a bit embarrassed or maybe flushed with lecherous anticipation as they played respectable and demure. Once again, as had happened the night before and would be the case through the whole week, the guests were served by topless waitresses. Mark and Sophie's table was attended by little Julie, who winked at her new-found girlfriend but gave nothing away to Mark about the action in the laundry closet.

An early night seemed appealing. As soon as they were naked and comfortable on the familiar bed, Mark wielded the remote and brought to life the next episode on his highly successful movie.

The track through the woods was deserted. Jason was heard indistinctly, regretting the fiasco that had so recently prevented the impregnation of his bride. Mark speeded the film up until the youngsters appeared. He then pressed the slow-motion button.

As if drifting through a dream, the pair floated nearer. Tracy's auburn locks were a heavy cloud waving slowly from side to side. But what really caught the eye was the movement of her small breasts, a movement that seemed independent of any gravitational pull. Mark pointed out that you could imagine that invisible hands were massaging them and producing this sensual dance. The bright pink nipples, fiercely erect and surrounded by hardly noticeable areolas, invited you to imagine two sucking mouths on them—his and Sophie's.

Sophie's own contribution to this commentary was to notice that the breasts looked as if they would fit neatly into the hollows of the girl's armpits, one of which was exposed as she brushed her auburn locks from her left eye. This fantasy was unpromising as an erotic stimulus, but suggested a less contortionist one: wouldn't it be a lark, Sophie speculated, to squeeze one of those tits in one of her own armpits? What effect would her damp tuft have on the tender teat and the velvet skin in which it was set?

By this time Mark's attention had wandered to Tracy's scanty white thong. This, as they had realised, was just too tiny to contain every strand of her pubic hair, small though the area was on which the hair sprouted. Small, but plump. Quite a bulge filled out the still spotless white pouch. As she advanced in this dreamlike walk, the movement of her thighs agitated the tight package, hinting at the odd glimpse of a buttock seen through her thightops from the front.

Beside her, her young husband in his green trunks looked very innocent. But when the fingers of the hand he had reached around her back stretched forward far enough for the tips to prod the side of her breast, Sophie noticed two developments. Though he couldn't quite reach it, the nipple became a darker pink and stiffened up still further. And inside the cotton of his trunks there was a slight but definite stirring. Once again the groom was lusting after his fresh young bride.

Mark fast-forwarded a bit and returned to slow motion at the point where the couple was shown from the side. They were now closer to the camera—in what seemed almost shocking proximity, in fact. They stood in a loose embrace. The boy's hand rested on Tracy's bottom, and he was trying to tug the thong down over her buttocks. Her voice came over fairly clearly:

'Stop that, big boy. When we get back, I said. Well, I'll tell you what. Suppose you get me good and ready for a real fuck. Why don't you play wiv me like you done this morning wiv that maid, that Julie—get me all *mushy*?'

And now he turned her to face the camera, almost as if he knew they were being filmed, while he stood behind her. He reached round to grab a tit in one hand and used the other one to abuse her sex, first through the thong and then directly, the shred of white cloth being tugged aside.

Tracy flopped forward in orgasm. Her husband was displayed involuntarily to the lens, his penis still erect inside his trunks, which were dark from the load of sperm he had ejaculated in them.

Sophie could wait no longer. Neither, to judge from the menacing state of his erection, could Mark. He switched off the TV with the remote and jumped from the bed. Out of the cupboard he snatched an item of wedding apparel—Sophie had forgotten about this stuff. It was the headdress, the white, gauzy veil. Mark handed it to his 'bride'. When she pushed her blonde hair back and put it on the veil reached halfway down her back. Just like that bride in the series of photos on the wall, she thought.

Mark stretched out on the bed and indicated what was required of her. Without hesitation, Sophie straddled his knees, bent forward to administer a quick lick and suck, the veil concealing the sight from her man, then, having satisfied herself that the great rammer was at full stretch, sat up again. The veil floated wide as she gave a little twist of her head. She slid forward until her cunt was positioned directly over the bursting plum, from the slot of which a bubble of clear liquor appeared.

Very carefully she lowered her genitals until contact was made. She looked Mark in the eye and extended the tip of her tongue, running it around her teeth. Then, taking the engorged cocktip between a dainty finger and thumb, she began to stroke it up and down through the slippery lips of her sex. Mark reacted by reaching up with both hands and moulding her breasts in his palms. When the teats began to stiffen, Sophie leaned forward so that he could lick and nibble at one of them while pinching and tugging at the other.

And now she was using the head of his prick, slick with her own outflow as well as his pre-come lubrication, to diddle her clitoris. As the lust gathered itself in her loins she sat up straight; her right breast was pulled out into an elongated cone before Mark's lip-sheathed teeth released it. The angle of the penis re-adjusted, she sank down on it with a sigh. It went straight up into her belly and instantly she was stretched with the hot male turgidity she had been longing for.

Mark gazed up, enraptured by the sight of his delicious mock bride. Above all it was that crazy imaginative touch, the tossing veil framing her grin and crowning her nudity, that elevated this from a regular wild fuck to a lifetime's dream realised.

Sophie placed a trembling fingertip on her clit and exploded, collapsing all over her lover and scratching his shoulders. He hugged her and patted her backside.

'Good for you, sweetheart?' he enquired needlessly.

She gasped for breath. 'About as good as it comes. But you

know what? I just wish we could have my Peter and your Cathy with us when we do this. And I'd like to watch them at it. You're not the only one who gets off on watching.'

She could feel Mark's dick swelling inside her. He drew his head back and grinned.

'Funny you should say that. I had a word with Pete and we explained things to old Rosper.'

'What things?'

'Well, like what you just said. Anyway, tomorrow we're being moved to—moved to a double room.'

Mark's muscles went rigid. Sophie felt his balls tightening up against her bottom and then a great flood of hot spunk filling her cunt. She raised herself on her knees and lifted up off the cock before it stopped spouting. A mass of goo slid out of her vagina and spread over Mark's belly. She was furious.

'How could you, you prick! Never, ever, do that again. Not if you're still wanting to get into my cunt.'

'Do what?'

'Arrange things behind my back, without consulting me. I really resent that. You and Peter are absolute shits. You're not having me again tonight.'

She turned her back on him and sobbed herself to sleep. When she awoke in the middle of the night, Mark had a hand on her tit and his prick up her quim.

Monday

'Let's go down to the sauna,' yawned Mark, as his bloated prick plopped out of his surrogate bride's cunt. She had been woken, for what must have been the third time since the middle of the night, by his powerful strokes from behind. Good grief, he must have been up her all night long! His hand had resisted her feeble efforts to remove it from her clitoris and she had shivered into reluctant orgasm just as the latest batch of sperm was delivered into her depths. Now, as her man rolled away from her and rose from the bed, she stretched on her back, grimacing with distaste for her subjection. Yes, distaste rather than disgust was what she felt for Mark's importunity. If she had been disgusted she would have withdrawn from their agreement without hesitation, but as things were she would just punish him a bit by sulking and playing hard to get. As she stretched, a mass of spunk was expelled from her vulva.

After a quick visit to the bathroom, the couple put on white towelling robes and made their way down to the lower ground level. Sophie remained silent, not having spoken since expressing her annoyance the previous night.

Once through the door marked SAUNA they were in a different atmosphere—the outlines of the bright lights were blurred by haloes of steam, and sounds were muffled and deadened. They passed an icy-looking plunge pool, much deeper than it was wide, and Sophie resolved to use the showers rather than submit herself to this torture when she needed to cool off.

The narrow, tiled passage led past several sauna cabins. These had glass doors, through which a vague impression of naked flesh could be gained, shrouded in billowing vapour. Mark opened one of these doors and, gasping in the hot steam, they flopped on to a slatted pine bench with the door on their left.

Sophie flinched away to the right as Mark's thigh pressed against hers. This movement brought her into contact with the left flank of the young woman sitting on her right. She felt a twinge of rejection when this person shifted away from her. How long could she persist in this state of alienation?

At the opposite end a couple could just be perceived through the fog, hard at it. The man was bulky and shining black, with a bald head and large gold earring. His pretty bride, or whatever, had a much lighter skin. She was petite, even fragile-looking; it was really only the mop of frizzy hair that suggested her racial origins. Sophie was concerned that the man would do some damage if he threw himself on her—his erect member looked as thick as the girl's arm. But it was the girl who took the initiative, shoving him down on to his back and leaping into the saddle. She took the entire length in one downward plunge, and battle commenced. How Sophie envied her! The steam grew hotter and denser as the partner of the girl on her right sloshed water on to the hot stones beside the door, and the screwing couple were lost to view.

Mark, who seemed at last to be getting the message, announced that he was going for 'a plunge and look-see' and left the cabin. Sophie was tired. She leaned back against the pine wall and relaxed. Soon she was drifting through clouds and hovering above a sea of naked flesh . . .

Opening one of her eyes she was blinded by a drop of sweat falling into it from the face just above hers. She was being shagged again. All night long her cunt had been stuffed with Mark's manmeat, but somehow her assailant didn't seem to be that particular bastard. He was hard and skinny, for one thing. When her cheek was scratched by the point of a little beard she realised that her shagger was Giles Rosper. Although her legal experience prompted her to accuse him of rape, she realised that he was a valued client of her husband's. In fact, Rosper was their host on Pothos. Perhaps she should just let herself go, and try to enjoy his vigorous thrusting.

Rosper whispered in her ear: 'Would your husband mind?'

She hesitated. Climax was approaching. Sophie was not thinking. 'He's not really my husband—we're just doing a swap for the holiday. Oh shit—I've said it.'

Rosper grimaced. 'Our little secret, dear,' he croaked, clearly intrigued. He bit into her shoulder as he shot fierce streams of semen into her cunt. Then he withdrew and left; Sophie had not yet come.

She found Mark peering through the glass door of another cabin. While she took a cold shower and towelled herself down, he dropped vertically into the plunge pool and immediately bounced out again. Wrapped in their robes and without exchanging a glance, let alone a word, they returned to their room.

Inside they found chirpy little Julie, who had brought their continental breakfast. She was standing at the window and it was obvious that she was displaying herself to Tim across the courtyard. A yellow halter top was pulled up to expose her breasts, and seen from the back her elaborate black thong left her buttocks almost entirely bare.

She turned to face Sophie and Mark. Julie's welcoming grin and giggle went some way towards melting the icy mood restraining the couple (though Sophie was not really quite sure whether Mark had registered her silent sulking at all). Mark helped Julie off with her top, and she removed his towelling robe before turning to Sophie and embracing her.

In a flurry of movement that was both rapid and graceful Julie stripped the girl and stretched her out on the bed. Mark lay beside them and the obliging maid applied one hand to the genitals of each while her lips and tongue darted from Sophie's nipples to Mark's glans and back again. In no time she had worked them both to a high old state of arousal—in Sophie's case this was accomplished almost at once, as she was still itching from Rosper's unfinished attentions.

Julie's next move was to leap astride Sophie facing down her body, the black pouch of her thong brushing damply against Sophie's lips and nose. She wrapped her arms round Sophie's knees and pulled them back to touch the young woman's breasts, forcing them outwards at the same time. Now her tongue flicked against the exposed clit. She hooked her fingers into the blonde labia and opened them as wide as they would go.

Mark got the message at once. He stretched out on his side across the bed so that he was lying at right angles to his 'wife', slicked the head of his stiff cock a few times up and down the open slit and drove it home. The tops of his thighs pressed against Sophie's bottom. Julie allowed the elastic sheath of flesh to close on the intruder and Mark began to pump. 'Go on,' said Julie, 'fuck your wife stupid.'

This engagement had a kind of anonymity. Mark's face was nowhere near her own, and Sophie was very aware of the maid's sex pressing against her mouth and nose while her fingers stimulated her clitoris. Because of this, she was willing to abandon herself to the urgent thumping of Mark's cock in her hungry cunt. At the same time she ran her thumb along the edge of the black triangle embedded against her face. She wriggled her tongue under the elastic. The tip caressed what felt like suede, until it encountered something smooth and moist.

Julie shuddered and came, collapsing forward over the lovers. One of her nipples brushed against Sophie's well-primed clit, triggering an explosive climax. Because of Julie's weight on his hip, Mark could no longer continue his frantic pistoning. Instead, he thrust in as hard as he could and let his prick swell and swell in its tight confinement. Suddenly feeling more sympathetic towards him, the blissed-out Sophie clenched and unclenched her vaginal muscles with a power she was not aware of possessing. She was flooded with a pulsing stream of hot spunk that leaked out profusely from the place of their joining and began to pool on the sheet. The unusual quantity, she supposed, could be partly accounted for by the fluids Rosper had already deposited inside her.

'Don't worry about the mess,' said Julie. 'All part of the service. In any case, you're being moved down to 6B, beside the pool. We'll be taking your things down around lunch time. It's a lovely room. I'll still be looking after you there, unless you fancy a change.'

'No way,' Mark replied. 'I can't wait to get inside that big black spider of yours.'

'Off limits. That's strictly for my boyfriend. And he'll be wanting me now.'

As Julie left and they attacked the breakfast she had left for them, Sophie reflected that what she had just accomplished with her tongue might be considered a slight infringement of that strict rule.

They showered. Mark put on another of the hotel's posing pouches, a black one, and Sophie wore her little black bikini to match him. She now felt closer to him again, almost like a real honeymooner, full of anticipation and longing when she thought of the larks ahead of them. She took his hand and they headed down to the pool.

Along one side of this, impenetrable dark glass sliding doors evidently belonged to a row of rooms, one of which must have been their new one. Yes, 6B was right at the end. This room, like 6A next to it, was twice as wide as the others in the row. Mark tried to slide the door open, but it was locked.

Surprisingly few couples were in and around the pool, presumably having more pressing business to attend to. But Sophie found all the couples who had come out to play extremely attractive. None of the women could have been more than about thirty-five, though some of their men were perhaps a few years older. As for the youngest—well, if they were really married they had to be legal, didn't they?

In a corner facing their new accommodation, Sophie and Mark lowered themselves on to a double lounger. They returned to this after a refreshing swim. Half an hour later they were joined by Cathy and Peter, who also tried to investigate 6B before noticing their real spouses and joining them on an adjacent lounger. Peter wore black posing pouch identical with Mark's, while his supposed bride had chosen to appear topless with a little white bikini bottom.

Sophie felt a bit embarrassed. She was really curious about what the other couple had been up to, and possibly just a little jealous. Closing their eyes and enjoying the warmth in the dappled shade of some hibiscus bushes behind them, they chatted about the hotel's attractions until they were all either dozing or on the point of nodding off. The night and morning had been strenuous for all of them.

Sophie was aware of footsteps. She adjusted her dark glasses and turned her head. At first she thought the blonde girl who had passed behind their loungers and was walking towards the end of the pool was stark naked, in defiance of the house rules. Then she noticed the narrow black tapes, one crossing her back and the other low round her hips. Didn't she recognise that long yellow hair, tied up behind with a pink ribbon? When the girl paused and turned, she saw that, as she had half guessed, it was young Poppy, who approached and stood smiling down at the two couples. In the bright light the freckles round and on her upturned nose were conspicuous. She paused, probably deliberately, long enough for them to take in the details of her shocking pink bikini.

In fact, it was more than a shocking pink bikini—it could be better described as a shocking (pink) one, the design being even more eyecatching than the colour. The actual pink pieces were simply three tiny scraps, bordered by a framework of narrow black tapes. Let into the centre point of one tape, just below her small breasts, was a gold ring, about two centimetres in diameter. The bases of the black-rimmed pink triangles attached to the tape could not have been more than four centimetres across. They narrowed up across her tiny nipples, finally giving way to the black tape that ran as a halter round her neck.

The bottom of the bikini repeated this theme even more brazenly. Three gold rings, about eight centimetres apart from each other, interrupted the line of the tape stretched low around her hips. Only the centre one was functional, supporting the apex of a black-edged pink triangle that cleverly echoed the shape and size of those stretched over her nipples. It was just as narrow as the upper ones, and promised to become still narrower as it worked its way into the split of her sex, the shape of which was quite visible. Most of her plump pubic triangle, of course, was completely exposed. It was also completely smooth and hairless. Poppy's body was very lightly tanned, and the faintest white shadow of a more conventional bikini bottom was just visible. This must have been tiny, but in comparison the shocking pink version was microscopic.

'Mind if I join you?' she asked, winking at Sophie, with whom she had made conspiratorial eye contact the day before as they viewed each other from their respective balconies. Without waiting for an invitation she spread her towel on the tiled floor and sat down facing them. Her legs were spread, and the scrap of pink cloth barely covered the cunt that gaped up at them.

Sophie introduced herself and the others, making out that they were legitimately married. 'Oh yes,' said Poppy, 'I was chatting with your friends on the boat. What a lovely couple they make!'

Then Poppy's Tim arrived, just in time to be included in the introductions. Sophie was struck by the almost girlish prettiness of his features, and the beauty of his white, hairless body. His mop of black hair matched the glossy blackness of his little thong. Tim seemed to combine two attractions very important to Sophie: the appearance of healthy femininity and the undoubted attributes of a lusty male. Maybe they would get it together some time soon.

When Poppy asked what had delayed him, he grinned and admitted that he had been out on their balcony, showing off to 'that little trollop Julie' on the other side of the courtyard. She had been cleaning Mark and Sophie's room—Sophie explained how the two older couples were moving down to 6B. Poppy raised an eyebrow but said nothing.

As if by agreement, all six of them now started applying suntan lotion to the parts they were able to reach themselves, before rolling over to let their partners do their backs.

On the other side of the pool, the smoked glass door of 6A slid open. Out stepped the fair-haired Jason and radiantly auburn Tracy. They looked around rather sheepishly and hurried round the pool, passing behind the three couples now anointing each other. Then they snuggled into one of the double loungers a few metres beyond them. Tracy's attire was that attractive but fairly modest blue one-piece swimsuit, the one that was identical with Sophie's. Instead of his usual green trunks, Jason now wore a pair of very brief, very flimsy and very loose fitting white shorts.

Soon these youngsters were wriggling and writhing on the lounger, their shyness forgotten as they kissed and cuddled. Pretending to be concentrating on the massage she was getting from Mark, Sophie could clearly see that Tracy's hand was playing inside those flimsy white shorts, while the youth had dragged down one of his partner's shoulder straps and was mouthing a small breast. Sophie made sure her companions were aware of these proceedings.

Suddenly Jason stood up and pulled Tracy to her feet. She hastily adjusted the shoulder strap as he led her round the edge of the pool, this time passing hurriedly in front of the spectators. The front of Tim's shorts was tented out with an unmistakable erection. The edge of the nearside leg had been forced up to expose the pink sac. He was also quite unable to conceal his embarrassment. Tracy, too, was blushing. Much of her face was hidden by the copper-coloured curls she had allowed to tumble down, but not all of it. Perhaps she had known all along that their petting had been observed—as she passed in front of Sophie she waved a hand in her direction as if to show off her wedding ring. Sophie couldn't help noticing a wisp of red hair peeping out from the crotch of the blue costume.

Once the pair had shut themselves in their poolside room opposite, they became a topic of conversation. Mark and Sophie described what they had witnessed in the cove and the woods the previous day. The others agreed that the youngsters were fascinating to watch, so naïve and yet so eager.

While they chatted, the three males continued to apply cool lotion to their partners' backs. And their backsides. Then, taking their cue from Tim, Mark and Peter swept their palms up from the backs of their knees to the tops of their thighs and began to work their thumbs against the fabric containing the girls' sex. In the case of Poppy, of course, it was only the slit itself that was covered by the scrap of pink material; Tim's thumbs were playing with the smooth skin of her outer lips.

'Where did you get that bikini?' Cathy asked.

'Made it myself. Tim was looking for this kind of thing and found it on the internet. Trouble was, the picture had a heading: "Prototype bikini—not for sale".'

'Sounds like some secret weapon,' laughed Mark. 'It sure has a devastating effect.'

'Well, once I'd found this hot pink lycra, the black tape and gold rings, it wasn't too hard to copy. And I haven't regretted it.'

'Me neither,' said Tim, whose finger play seemed to be getting more radical. Poppy had closed her eyes and was now panting.

Sophie was aware that Mark was rolling her bikini bottom down to form a tight black band round the tops of her thighs. A finger wormed its way up into her vagina. Another one tickled her love bud. Turning her head sideways, she saw that her own husband was doing something very similar to Cathy, with whom she made eye contact. To her relief, the slight pangs of jealousy were mitigated by the sense of intimacy as the two young women grinned at each other in their erotic bliss. Cathy reached a hand across from her lounger and Sophie put one of the fingers in her mouth just as the finger on her clit brought her off. As if in sympathy, Cathy too shuddered out her climax.

The door opposite slid open. Tracy and Jason reappeared, holding hands. The boy was now wearing his usual green trunks and his hard-on had subsided. As they passed in front of the other couples, Sophie saw that a large damp patch was spreading on the back of the blue swimsuit between the low-cut V and the beginning of Tracy's bottom-cleft. In her dreamy state, Tracy seemed unaware of this.

As soon as those two were back on their lounger, embracing affectionately but no longer furiously snogging, Sophie remarked on the damp patch. They had all been struck by it, and began to reconstruct the events that could have led up to its appearance. All six had observations to make as the pieced together the overall picture. As far as Sophie could tell, it went something like this:

The accident had occurred because of the urgency of the situation—neither of the kids could wait. Jason had thrown Tracy face down on the bed and tugged her swimsuit down to below her buttocks. As usual, he had ejaculated prematurely as he tried to penetrate her from behind. The fact that he had changed into his trunks showed that he must have made this attempt while still wearing the white shorts. Tracy's blissed-out appearance suggested that he had been even more desperate as a result of masturbating her prior to lunging at her with his uncontrollable prick. Mark explained further:

'Look, that's how we know he had her costume down over her bum before this happened. If he'd come on the outside of it while it was still pulled up—well, she would have made him sponge the mess off and she would never have kept the same one on. Not that brazen, is she? No, as soon as it happened he whipped it up again. I suppose she would have been too stunned to realise she had all that spunk trapped inside it, and in any case she must have been distracted by having to put her arms back through the shoulder straps. And now it's starting to soak through.'

'Tell you what,' suggested Cathy. 'Let's make it our business while we're here to help him put it in her properly without spilling anything.'

After lunch on a beachside terrace, Mark and Peter took their brides to settle into their new room. This was very similar to the ones they had spent their first two nights in, but was nearly twice as large, accommodating two double beds instead of just one. Through the smoked glass of the sliding doors the playful occupants of the pool were so close you could imagine you were playing with them. The situation lent itself to close scrutiny of the most intimate activities, the sunbathers not being able to see their admirers.

Along most of the length of the wall opposite the beds was a long shelf, and above it a mirror. Engraved in the glass at intervals were beautiful scenes from what Sophie took to be classical myth. The clever feature of these depictions was that when you moved from side to side they turned out to be, on a much larger scale, rather like the holograms on credit cards or whatever, changing and seeming to be alive if you moved quickly enough. Flimsy garments were snatched from the loins of nymphs. Lovers' lips met in hot kisses. Rough satyrs flung their tender prisoners down to ravish them. Flaccid penises leapt up into erection. Erect penises were thrust into cunts which, modestly closed to begin with, now pouted open to receive them. And as you moved, your own reflection almost seemed to be part of these changing scenes.

The furniture and décor were otherwise identical with those in their old rooms. Sophie was pleased to find that there was even the same gallery of wedding pictures on the wall. This one, though, contained twice the number of photos and featured additional couples. She promised herself that she would view these at her leisure, probably while getting fucked.

There were framed photos on the bedside tables. She was amazed to register that the one next to the bed with 'Mark loves Sophie' on a placard above it showed Mark ramming into her on their bed while pinching one of her nipples and offering up the tip of his tongue to her own. It seemed that there must be hidden cameras in the hotel. Oh well . . . Of course, a similar picture of the other couple adorned the table by the other bed. Sophie decided to wait until later before studying this—her feelings about her Peter screwing Cathy were still a bit mixed up, though she was beginning to realise that once things got going she quite enjoyed the thought (and even the sight) of them larking about with each other.

'Well,' Peter began, 'you ladies got to enjoy yourselves this morning out there by the pool. Now it's your husbands' turn. We need a quick fuck before we do anything else. Isn't that right, Mark?'

'You bet. My balls are bursting.'

In less than a minute all four were naked and embracing on their respective beds. Sophie found that she was already in such a state of excitement that no foreplay was needed to get her lubricated and ready. This was just as well. Mark pulled her thighs apart and with one great lunge drove his prick right up into her belly. At the same time, he took his tongue out of her mouth and his lips battened on her right nipple.

Turning her head to her left, Sophie opened her eyes and gazed at those beautiful wedding pictures on the wall beside the bed. She loved the dark-haired bride shown in one picture completely decent in long white dress, veil and elbow-length white gloves, holding a bouquet of red roses as she smiled up at her respectable-looking groom. Somehow this shot carried a huge erotic charge from its juxtaposition with another one just beneath it on the next row down. Here the post-orgasmic newlywed sprawled on a rumpled bed. Her eyes were closed, one hand resting on a breast while casually displaying her new ring. The other arm she had flung up behind her head. Her nearer leg was stretched out while the offside one was bent at the knee. She was not naked, but retained the veil, now draped across the pillow and her exposed armpit, the long white gloves, a little white suspender belt and lace-topped white stockings. At the very centre of this picture, the bride's hairless cunt drooled with her husband's spendings.

Mark was so stiff and enlarged that his thrusts were almost beginning to hurt Sophie. She heaved her loins up in protest, and at that same moment the hot juice squirted into her in seemingly unending streams. A grunt from the other bed indicated that Peter, too, had discharged.

Both men pulled out and got to their feet. 'Now for a brisk swim,' laughed Peter.

Cathy sat up and pointed at him, then at Mark. 'Better cover up those slimy dicks if you want to show off in public,' she giggled, tossing them a couple of black thongs from a container on the other side of her bed.

The two guys slipped out to the pool. Before Peter was able to close the sliding door completely, a fresh-faced Poppy peeped into the room and blew a kiss to the naked women. She still wore the tiny pink thong, but was topless. As a result of this brief incident, Sophie had the feeling, even when the door was again securely closed, that the scantily clad honeymooners lounging or frolicking by the pool could see everything happening here in their room. But what the hell ...

'Now,' said Cathy, 'I badly need to get the taste of my Mark off you. I enjoy going down on Pete, but the taste is just that little bit different. I'm a connoisseur.'

Grabbing hold of Sophie's feet, she swivelled her round to lie across the bed. Then she opened the legs and let them hang down over the edge. She dropped to her knees and after running her hands up the inside of the girl's thighs buried her face in the exposed sex. Sophie came almost immediately as the tip of a questing nose lifted her clitoral hood. Cathy's tongue entered her love canal and wormed its way around in there. She surfaced, threw herself on to the panting Sophie and kissed her.

A mass of jism slid into Sophie's mouth. Yes, perhaps there was something distinctive about Mark's flavour. A bit sweeter? Less salty?

'Want to compare it with your Pete's?'

Sophie suspected the real reason for this offer was that her friend wanted her own snatch licked out, but this thought was hardly a deterrent. Cathy lay back on the bed and lifted her legs, letting them fall open with her feet resting against her buttocks. Spunk was already issuing from her slit, first a trickle and then a thickish stream that began to form a puddle on the sheet. Sophie's tongue lapped it up, starting down at the pink arsehole and finishing with a little stab to the love bud. Cathy spasmed in response, nearly crushing her lover's head between her thighs.

Certainly Peter's sperm had a much more familiar taste. She didn't know if Cathy, who had been so keen to renew her acquaintance with Mark's, would appreciate a dose of Peter's, but this was not going to put her off. Must keep my mouth shut to stop it running out, she told herself as she mounted the quivering Cathy. The latter's mouth sagged open in exhaustion—all Sophie had to do was hover a few centimetres above her and let the viscous mass drop down, glob by glob, into the waiting throat. Then they kissed. And went on kissing, and using their fingers to fetch up more and more sperm from each others' cunts to add to the shared juices in their mouths.

All four went exploring along the beach, wearing black G-strings and nothing else. It was very pleasant to paddle in the warm water, but they also enjoyed the additional fun of observing attractive young honeymooners sporting in the sea or getting up to the tricks that newlyweds cannot resist for long. The further they progressed from the hotel, the more daring all these couples became. Peter remarked that by the end of the week they would no longer be bothered about where they shagged.

After dinner it was back to the new room for their first night of communal love. A certain shyness surprised them as they stripped off, each couple staying on the far side of their respective beds.

Cathy was whispering something to Peter. She turned to the others. 'We've thought of a little game,' she said. But, Sophie, you've got a special part to play and we need you to hide under the bedclothes for about ten minutes while we get ready.'

Sophie stretched out on the bed and drew a sheet up over her, covering herself completely. She also placed a pillow over her head to muffle the sounds of cupboard doors opening and closing, and whispered exchanges between the other three. She felt both comfortable and excited. But mainly, very tired.

Very soon she was dreaming . . .

Out in the courtyard below their old room, Sophie found herself naked in brilliant sunlight, although the sky was black and studded with stars. She drifted over to the central pool with its rampant Apollo, who seemed to be smiling down at her. Her body was yearning for the obscene intercourse Poppy had indulged in on their first night here. There was something strange about the gleaming god, something different. Yes, that was it—she remembered those statues she had seen on a trip to Barcelona, in the Ramblas. Living people painted white and pretending to be statues, surprising the passing tourists with sudden movements.

As she stood at the rim of the round pool she realised that she herself was completely white. When she tried to lift an arm it was stiff and rigid. On the other hand, the Apollo had now started to move. Still grinning at her, he was masturbating and shooting an uninterrupted flow of spunk almost as far as her side of the pool. Uninterrupted but pulsing, the weakest pulses squirted down to Apollo's feet and the strongest ones splashed the low parapet in front of her. The pool itself was a smooth sheet of silvery sperm, its smell overpowering. If only she could step over the parapet and wallow in it.

But she could. Suddenly her limbs were loosened. She was floating in the warm, viscous fluid, and could feel it forcing its way up into her body. When she closed her eyes she felt as if she was being caressed not by this all-enveloping sperm but by female flesh—thighs, buttocks, breasts and bellies slithered all over her own nakedness, but especially against her face.

Opening her eyes again, she was sorry to see that these bodies had vanished. The lake of sperm had now become clear and bubbling. At first Sophie thought she was floating in urine. But no, the cold liquid was champagne. Apollo had placed a finger over the slot on the tip of his rampant cock, and was directing a fine spray of the sparkling wine over the surface of the pool. The delighted girl opened her mouth and received the spray on her tongue.

And now the smooth-skinned females had reappeared as a flickering white shoal below the surface. They were sliding between her legs and tickling her intimate parts with fingers and tongues.

Or was she outside their new room, splashing about in the swimming pool? This was certainly champagne, but she recognised the familiar couples honeymooning on their loungers. And all the people swimming under the surface and fiddling about between her legs were now guys . . .

'Wake up!' The pillow had been taken from her head, and Mark peeled the sheet down to her feet. Sophie lay there naked apart from the little black thong that had worked its way damply up between the lips of her sex.

For the first time since their arrival Mark was dressed in jeans and a white T-shirt. Peter wore a similar outfit, except that his shirt was red. But it was Cathy's attire that surprised Sophie. Her friend must have brought with her from home her old school uniform, slightly outgrown: a tight fitting white shirt, which hardly contained her bust; loosely knotted striped tie; pleated navy mini- or microskirt (surely the school would have banned this one, unless Cathy had shot up dramatically since her sixth-form days?); knee-high white socks and flat-soled black shoes. Her hair was tied back in a short pony tail and to complete the outfit she wore a maroon blazer and matching beret. This lot must have taken up some space in her luggage. But she had probably not brought much else in the way of clothes. (Later she explained that all this stuff was provided in the cupboard containing bridal finery and other dressing-up gear—it was finding the costume that had given them the idea for the game.)

Mark handed Sophie his camcorder and explained that her task was to film them as they re-enacted and perhaps enhanced a little scene from the past. From their schooldays. She remembered what Cathy had told her about her old association with Peter, and how when he left for university she had been handed over to Mark.

It felt very strange to be operating as an almost naked camera-person while the others were still clothed. Every now and then she glanced at their goings-on in the long mirror and wished that she herself could be included in the film for the sake of this striking contrast.

To begin with, the action was all between Cathy and Peter, while Mark merely looked on, stroking the bulge in his jeans.

The couple hugged and kissed. Strange feelings fluttered in Sophie's tummy as she watched her friend making out with her husband. After all, Peter was her husband in real life, and that fact could not be completely denied. At first the snogging was fairly mild, but Sophie was soon zooming in to focus on the play of tongues.

Breaking away, Cathy shrugged off her blazer and turned her back on her lover. When she turned round again, she had pulled her shirt out of the waistband of her skirt and knotted the front of it up to expose most of her flat belly. Peter dropped to his knees to lick and kiss this flesh. At the same time he spread his hands over her tits and began to knead them through the shirt. Then he stood up to unbutton the white garment.

'Oh, Mark,' he said. 'Come over here, mate, and check her out for me. No touching, mind. I just want you to tell me what colour knickers she's got on today.'

Now it was Mark's turn to kneel in front of her. Cathy parted her feet so that he could peer up under the skirt. He took his time over the investigation and looked up with a surprised expression. 'Not wearing any,' he announced. 'Just asking for it, I'd say.'

So Peter started giving it to her. Motioning Mark over to the side of the room, he made Cathy lie on the floor and got down beside her after removing his jeans and underpants. The girl

raised her knees and let her thighs fall open. The tiny skirt fell back on her belly and her cunt was now displayed with the little triangle of dark hair just above it. Still keeping his distance, Mark undid his zip and drew out the cock with which Sophie had now grown so familiar.

Peter, however, ignored the flaunted girl-sex and straddled Cathy's chest instead. He used the head of his prick, by now dripping clear juice, to paint all over her face and neck until they gleamed. Then he leaned forward and smeared his lips through the slippery coating before planting a passionate kiss on her mouth. Cathy closed her eyes, relishing the taste of her lover.

Peter seemed to be quite worked up, and not just for the sake of the camera Sophie was wielding with a rather unsteady hand. Still kissing Cathy, he unknotted the bottom of her already unbuttoned shirt and opened it wide. Bra-less, the white breasts quivered and their nipples tightened up expectantly.

'For God's sake,' hissed Cathy. 'What happens if a prefect catches us at it?'

'I don't give a toss,' came the reply. 'We're prefects ourselves, me and Mark. And I'm head boy and captain of games. The head boy's allowed a bit of skirt. Last year old Smithers had a whole harem, remember? Had them queueing to do him behind the bike sheds.'

It was now the turn of Cathy's tits to be painted with Peter's lubricant—Sophie had always been amazed at the quantity he produced once he was thoroughly aroused. She herself was used to this form of amusement, and quite liked it. He took his time now, repeating the procedure of letting his lips pasture on the soft flesh and transferring the tangy fluid to his partner's mouth.

'What you want me to do to her?' he asked Mark.

'Fuck her. Give her a hard fucking.'

'That what you want, Cathy?'

'Oh yes,' the girl gasped. 'I need to be filled. Go on, shove it up me. I need your spunk.'

Peter looked across to the masturbating Mark. 'Over here,' he ordered. 'Quick—get her ready for me.'

Mark shifted over on his knees, dipped his head between Cathy's legs and began licking her. He had hardly flicked the tip of his tongue against her clit when she exploded into orgasm, stretching out her limbs in all directions and lifting her hips from the floor. Peter pushed Mark aside and threw himself on her. His engorged prick, pre-come still bubbling from the slit, played for a moment at the girl's gaping entrance before bullying its way in. Cathy was still quivering and the friction of Peter's pubis against her on the inward thrusts immediately brought her to a second climax. Her contractions were having a powerful effect on the cock in her belly.

Suddenly she sat up and half twisted round so that she could grab Mark's erection and clamp her lips over the head. Peter gave one last heave and spewed his cream into her cunt in powerful jets just as Mark withdrew from her mouth and sprayed her face and breasts with thick, hot semen.

Excited but frustrated by the episode she had just witnessed, Sophie felt as if she had drooled a cupful of lovejuice into her thong. She placed the camera on a chair and addressed the others, hands on hips. 'So what's a girl got to do round here to get fucked?' she demanded.

Mark moved to stand behind her. First he rested a hand on her shoulder, stroking gently. Then he ran it down to fondle a breast. His other hand slid over her hip to grope her mound through the little garment. His wet, half-stiff penis nuzzled the base of her spine as he spoke. His voice was quavery. 'That's easy, darling. Normally they just flash their cunt at some fit bloke to show him they need cock.'

'Normally?'

'This is a bit different. You can swap with Cathy—put her school gear on and let her take over the filming.'

Cathy undressed and made herself available as a sexy, nude camera girl. She seemed not to be bothered by the masses of semen now drying into a white crust on her face and chest, or the dribbles that continued to ooze from her vulva and slide, congealing, down her thighs.

When Sophie donned the schoolgirl outfit she found that some parts of it, particularly the front of the shirt, were cold and slimy from the emissions spilt on them. This was not going to put her off, though. She posed for the camera, and for her own satisfaction, as she caught sight of herself in the long mirror. As she twirled around and the skirt lifted, the others noticed that she had retained her little black thong.

They agreed that they would now improvise a scene in which Sophie and Mark had been summoned before Peter, the headmaster, who had caught them fucking. Mark was ordered to stand naked in a corner, watching proceedings with his hands behind his back. The headmaster began to reprimand poor Sophie.

'You have disgraced yourself and let the school down badly, Miss Rogers,' he snarled. 'Unless I am mistaken, you were, er, having relations with this young man, this boy, on the floor of the gym. Perhaps you yourself should suggest a condign punishment.'

'What's condign mean, sir?'

'It means—well, it means the punishment should fit the crime.'

'I suppose at the very least I've got to have my bottom smacked.'

'At the very least. That's what we'll start with.'

'And Peter deserves to be caned, sir.'

'Let me tell you something, Miss Rogers. It's different for males, especially young ones with raging hormones. Just look at his member. Even as it hangs there it's getting bloated and the foreskin's drawing back. You know why? Because he can see you in that indecent skirt and thinks he's going to see you chastised. Boys just can't help themselves when girls flaunt their bodies at them. His only punishment will be to watch you suffering. Indeed, he may even deserve a little treat to make up for the pain it gives him if he's really fond of you.'

Mark made Sophie take off her blazer and lean forward over the long shelf under the mirror. He flicked up the hem of the pleated microskirt, exposing the beautiful white globes with the thin black tape disappearing between them. For a while he stroked and patted them gently, before raising a hand and bringing it down with a resounding THWACK.

Sophie moved her feet apart. The knee-length white socks enhanced the girlish appearance of her slim thighs. Between the tops of these the bulge of her damp pouch was now visible. Three more slaps induced a rosy flush on her buttocks and a full-blown hard-on in Peter's prick, which she could see in the mirror in front of her.

'Come over here, boy,' barked the headmaster.

Peter obeyed. The headmaster tugged at Sophie's thong and pulled it halfway down her thighs. She knew that the inside of the little pouch must now be white with her leakings, and tried to guess what was to follow.

Leaving the waistband stretched across her slightly parted thighs, Mark took hold of the wet triangle and rubbed it firmly into her cunt. He pulled it higher and smeared the oily contents all over her bottom, working the scrap of soaked fabric into her arsehole. In the mirror she saw Peter move even closer. Mark told her to stand up and remove everything she was wearing except her beret, tie, shoes and socks. Then she was made to resume her position bent forward in front of the mirror, supported by the shelf.

The cock forced its way shamelessly into Sophie's anus. She yelped. The headmaster urged Peter on and tried to reassure her. 'You truly deserved this treatment, Miss Rogers. Let yourself go. Enjoy the fruits of your wickedness now. Go on, boy, give it to her.'

As she adjusted to the intrusion Sophie actually did begin to enjoy this violation. It was a mode of intercourse the couple rarely practised at home—perhaps the bizarre circumstances made it more acceptable here. In the mirror Cathy was holding the camcorder in one hand while stroking her cunt with the other.

The headmaster—Mark—had dropped his trousers and was perched on a stool next to her. His prick stood upright from his hairy groin. Sophie swivelled round slightly and moved her hands from the low shelf to his hips. Her mouth closed over the plum just as it burst. A wave of semen filled her mouth and at the same time her husband, her real husband, discharged into her bowels.

All four of them slept soundly that night.

Tuesday

They were still asleep the next morning when Julie brought their breakfast. The first thing she saw was the discarded school uniform on the floor, crumpled and smelling of sex. Before the others were awake she had put it on, everything except the shoes. Then she opened the blinds a little to let in the morning sun. Outside, the pool gleamed blue, glassy and deserted.

Giving a little cough, she paraded between the two beds, at the same time pulling down the covers to reveal sprawled and intertwining nakedness. Julie did a little dance, shucked off her blazer and jumped on to Cathy and Peter's bed. Sophie and Mark, as soon as they had recovered sufficiently to take in what was happening, joined the others.

'These clothes seem to be badly soiled,' Julie remarked. 'No, don't apologise. That's what they're here for. Enjoy yourselves last night?'

'God, we're shagged out,' said Peter.

'Well, they've got to go to the laundry anyway, so let's give them a bit more of a soaking for good measure. Tell you what . . .'

The maid opened her shirt and exposed her small, white breasts. Then she flipped up the microskirt, bringing the familiar G-string into view. The others went ahead with the suggestion she had just made. Mark and Peter got up on their knees on either side of her, and their partners knelt behind them and slightly to the side. While Peter fondled the black package containing her sex, Mark caressed her tits. At the same time, the girls started masturbating their 'husbands'. As climax seemed to be approaching, the men, as if instinctively, turned their heads to enjoy a wet, sideways kiss with their 'wives'.

Mark was the first to explode. Sophie shook his prick fiercely to spray the spurting fluid all over Julia's front. Blobs of sperm were deposited from her forehead to her pubis. Some fell on the white shirt but still more hit her chest and stomach, spreading and running down her sides.

Julia groaned and shuddered as Peter's fingers, pressing the black thong deep into her cunt, brought her to orgasm. Almost simultaneously, his own cock shot hot jets all over her as Cathy jerked him off. The maid now looked thoroughly debauched. The dollops of spunk began to join up with each other on her belly.

Sophie was surprised, though, when she began to button the front of her shirt. Julie explained:

'For my boyfriend. He'll really get off on finding all this goo on me when he undresses me. And he'll be pleased it's not running out of my cunt. Must go to him right away, before this stuff cools down and dries.' She left them, looking like the typical, dreamy, boy-obsessed sixth-former on her way to school.

A couple of hours later, after breakfast and a run along the beach, Mark and Sophie entered the pool area. Peter and Cathy had gone off by themselves to explore the coves on the other side of the island. Not too many people were swimming or sunbathing, and of course there was a welcome absence of screaming kids. A morning to chill and relax.

As well as the double loungers, the management had provided large mats or mattresses under the sunshades. Sophie drew Mark down on to one of these and they lay there sleepily, face down. So many recent memories . . .

A double shadow on the paving stones indicated the arrival of another couple. Tim and Poppy seemed to have decided that they had become friends with the others after yesterday's conversation out here in the same poolside spot. This suited Sophie fine, and she was sure Mark was equally enthusiastic. She patted the mat to her left, inviting the girl to lie down beside her, and Tim got down next to Poppy. It looked as if Mark was going to be restricted to his favourite sport of watching, but at least he would be able to toy with his 'wife' while taking in whatever developed on her left. Perhaps after all he would be able to reach over her back to touch the adorable Poppy, who had discarded that disgracefully provocative pink top and lay in the sunlight naked apart from the narrow black tapes of the thong running across the small of her back and down between her buttocks. On the far side of Poppy, Tim, who also wore a little thong, looked just as naked. What an inviting little bum, Sophie thought.

Julie appeared, unbidden, carrying a tray of drinks which she brought straight to the four friends. She looked pale in a red bikini. Without a word, but winking and grinning widely, she withdrew. From time to time she returned and plied them with more refreshment, seemingly far more attentive to them than to the other poolside guests. On her third appearance she bent down and whispered in Sophie's ear. 'My boyfriend was really turned on by all that stuff he found when he undressed me. And, by the way, I've left a little gizmo in your room that may amuse you.' Then she hurried off, drawing admiring glances from the other men sunning themselves around the pool.

Conversation at first was general. After a bit it became more personal. Sophie and Mark spoke about their background and circumstances but avoided the fact of their pretended marriage. Then Mark asked the younger couple what had brought them on this trip.

'You're wondering how we can afford something like this at our age,' Tim began. 'Well . . .'

Poppy interrupted him. She was very slightly tipsy. 'I did have a part-time job. Modelling work—page three stuff at first, then something a bit stronger but not, you know, the hard end of the market. That's why I had to get rid of my pubes. I had what they call the full Hollywood, and just for fun Tim came along with me and I got them to do him too.'

'But that work wouldn't have paid for the week here,' said Tim. 'Not at the full rate. And my job in a video hire shop brings in peanuts. I only do it to get my hands on their under-the-counter stuff. We love to watch it on wet evenings.'

'No,' Poppy went on. 'My boss, this old photographer, was a friend of Mr Rosper and told me about his island and this competition with a honeymoon as the prize. Well, me and Tim went in for it. Just had to send in some pictures. A portfolio of me by myself and Tim by himself and some of us both together.'

'What kind of pictures?' asked Mark.

Unusually for her, Poppy blushed. 'You know . . . Well, anyway, we were in the top five and there was a tie breaker to decide the winners. We had to go to a studio in Soho—it had a little stage—and prove to Rosper that we could . . . Oh God, I can't say it. Tell them, Tim.'

'We had to show that we could bring ourselves off in public.

As well as old Rosper, there were the other competitors there as audience. Wasn't all that bad—they had to do the same thing, see. Or try to. We were the only ones who managed it, though—both together.'

'Yes,' said Poppy, 'we like showing off in front of other people. Mr Rosper promised we would have a chance to do that properly while we're here. There's going to be a little show tomorrow evening.'

Tim looked across and met Sophie's gaze. 'There's a DVD of our prize-winning performance. Like us to lend it to you?'

Sophie was slightly embarrassed by this bluntness, but Mark accepted the offer eagerly. 'How did you get to know each other?' he asked.

Tim took a draught from his tall glass, breathed deeply and launched into the story of his relationship with Poppy.

He explained that the two of them had grown up in Victorian terraced houses on opposite sides of the same street. They both had bedrooms on the third floor, the sash windows being directly aligned.

It was only when they were well into adolescence that they had really become aware of each other and of this convenient fact. Going to separate single-sex schools they only knew each other by sight, from occasional encounters in the street. Then one evening Tim looked up from his homework. It was growing dark, and the light was on in the room across the road. There was this girl—he didn't even know her name yet—and she was undressing. For a brief moment he caught sight of her small breasts before she put her pyjama jacket on.

From that time on, Tim was constantly on the lookout for repeats of this performance. Often he was disappointed, but every few days something like it would happen again. Sometimes, frustratingly, the girl would draw her curtains at a crucial moment. At other times, though, she would take off her top and walk about her room for a long time, arranging her clothes or admiring herself in a mirror. What she never did was remove her knickers—well, not before drawing the curtains.

Tim, who felt increasingly awkward when they passed each other in the street, grew much bolder up in his room. One autumn evening when, topless, she was preening and playing with her golden hair in front of the mirror, he stripped to the waist, switched on his light and moved tentatively over to the window. The girl went on with her grooming for a minute but eventually turned to the window, covered her breasts in horror and dropped to her knees so that she could crawl over unseen and draw her curtains. Tim was mortified.

The following night was different. He was sitting there in the dark, just in case, when the girl entered her room, switched on the light and started to tug at the curtains. But instead of closing them completely, she stopped halfway and stepped back into the room, disappearing to one side.

Tim tore off his T-shirt and switched his light on.

When the girl came back into view she was wearing only her navy school knickers. She walked boldly to the window and began to stroke her lovely little breasts. She pointed across at Tim, who began to rub his own chest.

The girl shook her head and pointed lower before resuming the massage. Tim dropped his jeans and started to fumble with his crotch through his underpants. She shook her head and made a motion with her hands as if pulling her knickers down.

Tim hesitated.

To his amazement, the girl turned around and lowered the back of her knickers to uncover a white bottom, which she wiggled before pulling the navy garment up again. Turning back to face him, she very slowly lowered the front of her waistband. First a tuft of yellow hair came into view, then an unmistakable slit. She pointed at this, then pointed at Tim. Her meaning was pretty clear.

The boy took a deep breath and lowered his own pants to his knees. Because of his nervousness, the erection that had given him so much discomfort in his underwear now drooped to dangle, bloated, above his balls. He looked up to see how the girl was reacting.

The fingers of one hand were stretched in an inverted V to frame her pussy while the other index finger ran lightly up and down that slit. Briefly she raised this finger, sucked it and pointed it unambiguously at Tim before resuming her gentle frigging.

His embarrassment was rapidly becoming replaced with burning excitement. The dangling prick was now beginning to raise its head. He took it in one hand and shook it demonstratively in the girl's direction. With the other hand he palmed his balls. At that instant a power cut put an end to the show, and his sperm gushed out in the dark.

From now on they didn't just blush but exchanged broad smiles when they encountered each other in the street.

Then came a decisive stroke of luck. Their two schools were to mount a joint production of *Romeo and Juliet*. Because of their liveliness and good looks, Tim and Poppy had been chosen to play the leading roles. So now they became properly acquainted, started chatting and, on stage, kissing. These embraces were necessarily rather restrained, but behind the scenes they found opportunities to indulge in more radical petting and Tim's codpiece was no longer a barrier to his girlfriend's fingers.

On the day before the dress rehearsal the players were given an afternoon off. Poppy brought Tim up to her room and got him to take her virginity. It hurt quite a lot, but this interruption to their fun gave them an opportunity to go through their parts and perfect their lines.

When Poppy's mother found the bloodstained sheets her daughter had been unable to clean or hide successfully, she took her for a checkup and had her put on the pill. The girl was surprised that nothing else was said—maybe her mother didn't want to upset her when it was so important for her to do well in the play.

She did very well indeed. Tim, too, received a standing ovation when he took his bow, and the audience went wild when the couple embraced and kissed.

Both sets of parents were philosophical and allowed the young people certain times when they could be together under fairly lenient conditions. The conditions, though lenient, were not observed. School work was totally neglected; there would be no chance of university places for either of them. They were deemed to be sexually out of control.

A couple of months later, when they were both seventeen and had stopped going to school altogether, the enlightened but angry parents got together to set them up in a little studio flat. The hope was that when they had sated their appetites they would grow tired of each other.

This hope was misplaced. The more they fucked, the more eager the youngsters became to take their mutual lust to new levels.

Tim's narration held the others spellbound. Sophie could tell, from the way Mark's fingering of her bottom became more urgent, which parts of the story particularly appealed to his voyeuristic imagination. Tim had taken her left hand and placed it on Poppy's right buttock as he himself stroked her other white globe. After a while Poppy raised herself on her elbows and addressed Sophie.

'I need to have my boobs played with. They're even littler than yours, Sophie, but they still love lots of TLC.'

'Go on,' said Tim. 'Have a feel, Sophie.'

Sophie half turned on to her side so that she could extend her left hand to cup the nearer of the dangling cones and squeeze the engorged nipple between her forefinger and thumb. The skin of the breast felt like velvet and the nipple like a warm stone. Poppy moaned. Not wanting to be left out of things, Mark reached over his 'bride's' side and ran a caressing hand down from her breast to her crotch. Fingers slid under the waistband of her thong and nestled in her slit.

Tim was now becoming more active. Using one hand to manipulate Poppy's left tit, he ran a finger down under the tape that disappeared between the cheeks of her bottom. He pulled the finger back for a moment before plunging it down and out of sight. Then he began a whispered running commentary on what he was doing. Though this was for Sophie's benefit, she knew from the increased liveliness of Mark's marauding fingers that he too could hear the boy's words.

'I've got the tip of my thumb on her arsehole. She likes that, as long as I'm gentle. My first finger's just playing with the lips of her pussy and getting them to open up for me. God, yes, it's sliding right into her. She's so hot and wet. And now my next finger's reached up to her clit. It's so big and ready. Want to have a feel of her bottom, Mark?'

Mark pulled his hand out of Sophie's thong and leaned across her to smear her female juice all over the beautiful buttocks Tim had offered him. They quivered.

'I want it—inside,' said Poppy.

Tim now pulled her legs apart and got on his knees between them. She lifted her behind. Between the tops of her thighs, the beginning of the narrow pink pouch of her thong came into view. Tim eased it aside

At that instant a stern voice blared out from speakers around the pool. It was Rosper's. 'Guests are reminded of the rules displayed at the entrance to the pool area. For health and safety reasons no running, no diving, no total nudity and no full intercourse.'

Poppy rolled over and laughed. 'That's what I meant when I said I wanted it inside. In our room, you silly.' The young couple got up and left the pool, Tim chasing Poppy and flicking her with a towel.

Mark and Sophie lay there panting. Then Sophie noticed Poppy's shocking pink bikini top discarded on the mattress beside her. 'Let's give it back to her,' she said.

Mark was delighted. 'Tell you what, why don't you put it on to surprise them.'

Sophie did so and Mark said it didn't look bad with her black thong. They hurried from the pool area, finding their way to the courtyard with the spouting Apollo. Nobody was about. Working out which was the right staircase, they crept up to their friends' balcony. The door was open and they stepped into the room.

At first, Tim and Poppy were too busy fucking to be aware of the intruders. They were doing it dog style, kneeling on the

bed, both of them naked, their thongs tossed on the mattress beside them.

Mark placed a palm on Tim's bottom and curled his fingers under to give his balls a little squeeze. He couldn't help finding the hairlessness a bit of a turn-on. The boy yelped and knelt upright, his member pulling out of its sheath with a plop. When Poppy looked round and saw what Sophie was wearing, she giggled.

'You forgot your top,' said Sophie. 'Want to take it off me?'

She threw herself down on her back at right angles to the girl who, instead of feeling for the clasp at her back, dragged the narrow pink triangles to the sides to uncover Sophie's swollen teats. One of these she took into her mouth.

By now, Tim had regained his cool. 'Don't mind us,' he said. 'In fact, you can be our guests. We like an audience.'

Poppy stuck her behind up again and he mounted her. She continued sucking on Sophie as he resumed his interrupted fuck. Sophie realised that Mark was being left out of the party, although she knew he would have been well enough pleased simply to be a spectator. But she was getting highly aroused and felt an urgent need for a cock. She parted her thighs.

Mark stripped off his diminutive garment and threw himself on her, pulling her black thong to one side and driving his prick straight into her open cunt.

On the point of coming, young Tim pulled out of Poppy and aimed his spouting semen horizontally forward. It squirted parallel to Poppy's belly, between her little titties and landed in successive pulses on Sophie's face. Some of the spurts were slightly off-target and caught his own partner's breasts. Both girls squealed, and Mark, overcome with the excitement, shot his load into Sophie.

When they had recovered a bit, Tim took control of the situation. 'I guess we need to liven ourselves up before we can screw again. At least, me and Mark need to. Tell you what. Let's swap partners for the foreplay. When we're stiff again I'm going to give Pops a good seeing to and Mark can do Sophie.'

Lazily and a little shyly at first, but gradually working themselves up into a frenzy, Sophie and Tim started to stroke each other. Sophie now discovered for herself the pleasure Mark had experienced momentarily when he fingered the boy. The complete hairlessness of Tim's body made her think of the beautiful statues in the hotel. But this one was warm, alive and far from bloodless. Her fingers and mouth lingered lovingly around those parts from which all traces of hair had been removed—armpits, lower abdomen and the whole pubic area down over his balls to his pink arse. Skimming over the smooth skin, she caught herself thinking of Cathy.

Tim was enjoying this leisurely examination. His own hands wandered all over Sophie's shoulders and back. They worked their way down to her bottom. After gently kneading the firm flesh he stroked a finger along the groove between her buttocks until he came to her little hole, which he began to tickle. Unused to this kind of treatment, Sophie found the sensation exquisite and did the same to him. His response was to ask her to suck his cock.

She didn't take it into her mouth immediately, but lay there playing with it and wondering at its boyish vulnerability, sprouting as it did from a perfectly smooth and innocent-looking pubis. It was not yet stiff, neither was it completely limp, but just lively enough to have lifted up off the testicles. The blue veins stood out slightly with their promise of the refreshing, stiffening blood that would soon be streaming through them. Sophie could see and feel the outline of the swelling plum, and the foreskin was just beginning to retract, its frilly cuff opening to allow the slit to peep through. She ran her fingers up from the base to the tip. The lad's cockskin was still slithery with Poppy's cuntjuice. Sophie ran the tip of her tongue up the lengthening stem, relishing the tang. Then she sleeved back the foreskin and clamped her lips over the purple fruit. Looking up she saw that Poppy had just about reached the same stage with Mark. The two girls, each sucking on their stiff-standing lollipops, winked at each other. Sophie loved this sense of shared intimacy with near-strangers.

Suddenly Tim pulled away from her, his face flushed bright pink. He elbowed Mark aside and got on his knees between Poppy's legs. (The shocking pink thong was now draped around one of her ankles.) Before he could go further Sophie bent down over the girl's tummy, taking the hot cock in one hand and opening the fragrant, hairless cunt in the other. As she guided the stallion into his mare, Mark took her from behind. In a matter of minutes both girls were lying back with their men's seed dribbling from their pussies.

Everyone was hungry. Mark and Sophie went off to find some lunch. Tim jumped up and gave them the unmarked DVD he had promised to lend them. And Sophie remembered to take off Poppy's shocking pink bikini top and leave it on the bed.

At lunch they met up with Peter and Cathy. All four of them were tired, so they took their little mats down to the beach and dozed side by side with the sound of the lapping waves and the happy squeals of honeymooners soothing them. This lazing about continued right through the afternoon, alternating with dips in the sea. Sophie loved being looked at by the young men showing off their muscles, but felt no need to be fucked by them or anyone else just yet.

After dinner they retreated to their room, meaning to take things easy. All four got naked and sprawled on their beds to relax and reminisce about their day. When the business with Tim and Poppy had been related, Sophie reminded Mark about the DVD Tim had lent them. He got up and fed the disk into the player.

'This is supposed to show the audition they had with Rosper. They had to masturbate in front of an audience. That's how they were selected to come here—they said they were going to give a show tomorrow evening,' he explained. He flopped back on to the bed, clutching the remote control. The screen flickered and the semi-professional movie began.

A briefly displayed title: YOU SHOW ME YOURS AND I'LL SHOW YOU MINE. POPPY & TIMOTHY DO THEIR THINGS FOR YOU. First a panning shot of an audience of about a dozen young couples. A few were clothed, but those who had already performed sat there naked and dazed. As the houselights dimmed the camera swung round to take in a small stage area. Spotlights illuminated a wide couch. Other spotlights picked out Tim and Poppy as they advanced towards the couch from the wings on either side. From now on the single camera moved around discreetly, showing all the hottest action, often in close-up.

The girl wore pink pyjamas. Her yellow hair was tied in two plaits and she was holding a rag doll by one of its feet. Tim's body was concealed by a blue dressing gown, but he stepped to the front of the stage and discarded this at once. The audience gasped at the sight of his completely hairless groin. His dick hung innocently over his ballsack.

Rosper's voice was heard. 'You know the rules. No touching except of yourselves, but show each other as much as you like. Oh, and don't forget the audience. And the camera. Our friends at home will want a good view. Poppy, dear, I'll know if you fake it. And Timothy, remember you've got to shoot it over her body—if you can get that far. The other blokes just couldn't make it, could they?'

The screen dimmed and the image was replaced by a rapid sequence of shots showing the failed attempts of previous contestants. Pricks were frantically frigged but remained limp. Others rose to their full height but exploded prematurely. Cunts were rubbed to frustrated soreness. None of these kids had the right qualities for a public performance. One after the other they returned to their places in the intimate auditorium. The screen dimmed for a second time and the action resumed.

'Get on with it, my little beauties,' called Rosper.

Tim strolled forward to the edge of the stage again, grinning rather nervously. He stroked his penis and wagged it at the audience. Nothing happened. Some of the girls giggled. He retreated and sat on the couch at the far end from Poppy.

It was now Poppy's turn to give one of these little pre-arranged displays. She skipped to the front of the stage and at first just stood there sucking her thumb. Then, thoughtfully, she began to unbutton the front of her pyjama top. Easing the jacket to one side, she would have exposed a breast—except that the doll was hiding the nipple as she pretended to suckle her baby. Her free hand dropped to the waistband of her trousers and disappeared down the front. She hurried back to the couch and the two youngsters sat eyeing each other intently.

Tim slid his bottom forward on the couch, leaned back and heaved his slightly swollen prick up to tempt his partner. In response, she shrugged her pyjama top off one shoulder and started stroking the white breast with its little pink nipple. Tim's prick swelled up further. He sat up and stretched out on his stomach, his face not much more than twenty centimetres from Poppy's nipple. His tongue made little licking motions as if being flicked across the hardening bud it was not allowed to touch.

Poppy uncovered her other tit and applied the 'baby's' mouth to it. She was careful not to conceal the one she was stroking from Tim's wide-eyed gaze. The audience were silent and enthralled.

Next she knelt up on the couch facing her partner and bent forward. Without touching the youth, she pulled at the waistband of her pyjama bottoms so that, although the sight was denied to the audience and the viewers of the movie, he could see right down inside. He grinned and licked his lips. She shifted around so that her back was towards him and pulled the bottoms down over her buttocks. Tim stretched forward and could only just stop himself from making contact.

When Poppy resumed her posture on the couch, half sitting and half sprawled, her bottom was still bare but the waistband was now level with the top of her slit. Before anyone could really make out just how much of the slit was visible, she covered the whole crotch area with her hand and started to frig herself through the trousers.

Tim sat up again and rose to his feet. His cock was hugely

erect. Poppy opened her mouth wide when she saw this, but Tim ignored her and advanced once more to the front of the stage area. As he had done at the beginning of the performance, he shook his prick at the audience. Everyone could see the glistening pre-come forming at the tip and being tossed in all directions in silvery strings. The delicious obscenity of this exhibition was heightened by the smoothness of the skin surrounding his sex. When he had finished, the strands of lubricant amalgamated into one viscous thread which swayed lazily from side to side and finally clung to the length of his right leg. He turned his back on the audience, bent down and let them view his bursting pink scrotum from behind.

'Don't forget your girlfriend,' called Rosper's voice. 'She wants to see how much stuff she can make that cute cockie of yours dribble by showing off to you.'

Tim now stood behind the couch looking down at Poppy. More lubricant drooled from his pisshole as the girl eased the trousers halfway down her thighs and displayed her bald cunt. He moved forward so that his thighs pressed against the back of the couch and the length of his prick extended over it. Poppy leaned her head back. She stuck out a flat pink tongue.

A thin column of clear fluid slowly descended from the cocktip and began to pool on her tongue. And now she pulled her legs right back and tugged her cuntlips apart as Tim stooped to gaze in wonder and lust. As if in sympathy with his juicing prick, his mouth dribbled clear saliva down to coat her pubic mound and run into the channel Poppy held open for him.

Rosper's voice: 'Remember the old song?

She'll be wearing pink pyjamas when she comes,
  When she comes,
She'll be wearing pink pyjamas when she comes;
She'll be wearing pink pyjamas,
She'll be wearing pink pyjamas,
She'll be wearing pink pyjamas when she . . . '

He paused for a beat and the audience roared out: *COMES!* just as Poppy's legs flashed out straight in front of her, the pyjama trousers round her thighs, and her bottom lifted from the couch, tense in orgasm. Tim, who had been furiously fisting his dick, now held it firm to take aim. Streams of thick cream gushed from the inflamed head. The first hit Poppy's pussy and masturbating hands; the second splashed all over her tummy; the third, which Tim directed from side to side, coated her tits; the copious final spendings flowed straight down to drench the girl's face and hair. Lazily she raised a hand to her chest and swept the palm down her belly, gathering a mass of spunk as she did so. This mass she transferred to her still quivering loins, and forced as much as she could into her cunt.

Tim stepped round the couch, took one of Poppy's hands and led her to the front of he stage. Both kids looked a bit groggy as the shockingly hairless lad raised her hand over their heads to acknowledge the applause and catcalls and to proclaim their victory in the competition. Her exposed underarm was shiny with sweat, but not as shiny as her face and the front of her body, which were dripping with semen. Beside her, Tim's pale skin was almost like sculpted marble—shining, but not wetly. The girl's other arm was still in the sleeve of her pyjama top, the rest of the jacket hanging down behind her. The trousers were round her knees. Her baby seemed to be forgotten.

Sperm oozed from the sex of both of them, but especially from Poppy. So much bubbled from her quim that one might think she had just been fucked by her boyfriend's smooth genitals.

The four of them had been lying naked on their beds watching the show. Sophie's hand lightly cupped her mound with the fingers curled down to plug the opening and prevent the flow of sexjuice from puddling the sheet. Mark and Peter were hugely stiff and made no attempt to hide the fact.

As the movie came to an end, the men threw themselves on their surrogate spouses, who were more than ready to receive them. The fuck was brief and powerful. Life was so good, Sophie felt, as she and Mark hit their peak.

He rolled off her and reached for the remote on the bedside table, meaning to switch off the TV. But pressing the ON/OFF switch had no effect. When he held the little black device under the lamp he saw that it was not what he thought. He dropped it and got up from the bed to switch the TV off manually. Peter reached over from the other bed, where he was still encunted in Cathy. He took the strange remote and considered it, explaining what he found to Sophie.

'It's got five buttons. This one's easy: ON/OFF. The other three are marked NO WAY—what the fuck's that?—ONE WAY and TWO WAY. The there's a SOUND ON/OFF. What do you think all that's about?'

'Obvious, isn't it?' Sophie answered. 'This must be the gadget Julie said she was leaving in our room. Give it here. Look, it's set to OFF now. I'll switch it on. There. The display says NO WAY. Right, let's hit ONE WAY and see what happens.' Pressing the button, she pointed the device at the wall opposite. Or, more to the point, at the long mirror running the length of that wall.

The mirror seemed to melt away, leaving the holograms, those lewd scenes of copulation engraved on the glass, seemingly suspending between the two rooms. For this had indeed become a one-way see-through mirror, and the foursome were looking into the softly-lighted room next to theirs—into 6A, occupied by Tracy and Jason. It was a double room, literally the mirror image of their own, and like theirs was equipped with two large beds.

As they watched, Tracy emerged from the bathroom, which was away out of sight over to the right. She had a towel wrapped round her hair, which she must have been washing. Her nipples were puckered and almost orange in their engorged state. A white silk scarf was tied around her hips. It was about twenty centimeters wide, just wide enough to make a pretence of covering most of her bottom and sex. Because it was knotted low on her left hip, the scarf narrowed from its deepest point on her right flank, tapering to the little knot from which it hung down to her knee. This meant that the crease of her left groin and a small patch of bright red hair were left exposed.

Mark groaned and moved to sit on one of the four stools in front of the shelf with the mirror above it. The others did the same. They were all keen to see what would happen next. Or, in Sophie's case, just to admire young Tracy's pretty body even if nothing actually happened. To begin with, all that happened was that Tracy removed the towel from her head and began to dry her tousled mane of copper-coloured hair. She bent forward as she did so and her small breasts hung down, shaking with the motion of her drying. She turned her back to the mirror and as she bent again the lower edge of the silk scarf was pulled up just a fraction. The whole of her left buttock was uncovered and her red-fringed sexpurse pouted back between her thighs.

Jason wandered in from the bathroom side of the room. A white towel round his waist was tented out in the front by his erection and he looked slightly embarrassed. His close-cropped blond hair was damp from the shower. He said something to Tracy, who nodded and sat on the end of the nearest bed. When she lay back and parted her knees the spectators had a clear view of her sex.

Her young husband dropped his towel and stood there as proudly rampant as the satyrs depicted in the engraved holograms quivering between him and the four voyeurs. His light tan, and the little bush of damp yellow hairs at the base of his belly, made him look very different from the other youth whose antics they had just been enjoying, but no less appealing. Tracy was speaking. Peter suggested pressing the SOUND ON button on the remote.

'. . . in me mouth,' Tracy was saying, her voice relayed loud and clear through several hidden speakers. 'Then, just before your stuff comes out, shove it real quick up my cunt and squirt it in there,'

She sat up and Jason stood in front of her. He held his stiff pole horizontal and the girl's lips closed timidly around it. Gagging noises bubbled from her nose but she endured her ordeal bravely. Suddenly Jason's buttocks clenched. Sperm was forced out of the corners of his bride's stuffed mouth.

'You stupid cow,' he moaned. 'Made me come before I was ready. Well out of order. Don't swallow—don't you fucking dare. Want you to blow that load into me mouth so I can try to spit it up your snatch.'

He sealed his lips around hers and sucked the juices from her mouth. When he pulled back the wretched girl sobbed. 'Couldn't help it,' she wailed. 'There was so much of it. Come on—fuck it up me with your tongue.'

She fell back on the bed and Jason dropped to his knees. His head went between her legs and loud slurping noises issued from the speakers. The movements of his head and the flailing of Tracy's legs became more and more frantic. Suddenly Jason stood up. His face was red. It dripped with spunk, while the whole of the girl's pubic area was similarly drenched in whitish goo.

Furious, the boy addressed her. 'Fucking bitch! How was I supposed to get anyfink in there when you hadn't even popped your cherry like what I told you?'

'What you mean? You never said nuffink about that. We was supposed to be saving ourselves up for our wedding night.'

'That was Saturday, you cunt. I told you to use one of them plastic things in the drawer over there. That's what they're for, innit?'

The poor girl wailed and crawled into bed as her husband stomped off towards the bathroom. Peter pressed the OFF button and the disappointing image was replaced by the viewers' own reflection.

Things now moved to a rapid and satisfying conclusion. Cathy strapped on a pink dildo she found among the sex-aids provided by the hotel. She drove it into Sophie's wet pussy as Peter and Mark watched and encouraged the violation. Soon the men grew impatient and pulled the girls apart. Peter ripped the dildo from Cathy's loins, breaking the strap in his haste, and started to fuck her with long thrusts. At the same time Mark plugged Sophie's cunt, which had been stretched wide by the dildo and was more than ready to take the river of spunk he now shot into her.

All four of them were asleep before they could disengage from each other.

Wednesday

J ust as the previous morning, they were woken by Julie bringing their breakfast. Even before he pulled out of his partner, Mark insisted on the maid lifting her little apron and showing him the spidery thong. But today she refused to let him have a grope.

'Sorry. I need to go and see to your next-door neighbour. He seemed a bit down when I took him his breakfast just now.'

'Neighbour? What about his wife?'

Julie was vague. 'Oh, she's not there today. Don't worry about her—she's being taken care of. Did you have fun with the mirror?'

As soon as she had left them, they activated the see-through button on the remote. The blinds in the next room had been partially opened, so there was a good view. Jason was sitting up in bed with a tray on his lap, looking sorry for himself. Sophie wondered if Tracy had walked out on him, angry at the way he had treated her. He perked up when the maid entered and shucked off her uniform. With a bound he was on his feet and had her on the bed, her knees up and apart. Standing over her, he lunged forward. What had happened to his shyness, Sophie wondered.

'Look,' Cathy gasped. 'He's fucking that thongie thingie right up into her. Won't it be ruined?'

Jason's position, with his legs slightly bent to bring him down to Julie's level, must have been uncomfortable. He stood back and his cock, wetly shining in a ray of morning sunlight, snapped up against his belly. Julie now looked almost naked, most of her thong having been pushed up into her vagina—only the web of narrow black straps securing the little pouch remained visible. She looked up, smiled and winked, no doubt guessing that the others were watching through the mirror.

She seemed to know what to do, and rolled over. Up went her white bottom and down came Jason's hand in a succession of blows, somewhere on the higher end of the scale from semi-serious to serious. A pink flush spread over the maid's buttocks.

All at once the boy stopped his slapping, which could be heard really clearly now that Peter had switched the sound on. 'Oh shit!' he cried. 'I need to do it in your mouth, innit. Turn round.'

Julie got to her feet and began to kneel. She opened her mouth, but before Jason could insert the purple knob his whole body jerked and he spouted his seed all down the front of her body.

'At least none of it went on my thong,' she laughed, pulling the pouch out of her cunt. It might have escaped the deluge of sperm, but it was soaked with her own juices and badly in need of rinsing out.

Cathy led Sophie into the bathroom and turned on the shower. The two girls embraced under the flow of warm water and their perky nipples rubbed together. Soon Cathy's fingers were scrabbling at the younger woman's cuntlips, seeking out the entrance to her body.

Two lusty males stepped into the shower cubicle, which was not wide enough for all four to stand in it without touching.

Sophie felt soapy hands lathering her back and bottom—soapy Sophie, she thought—and another hand slipping between her tummy and Cathy's. She also felt a stiff rod of flesh digging into her side, and didn't care whose it was. Quite a lark! Cathy plunged her tongue into her friend's mouth.

'We want our cocks sucked,' said Peter. 'Isn't that right, Mark?'

'That's what we want. You can go back to each other's mouths after that, if you must.'

Putting their hands on the girls' shoulders, they gently pushed them down on to their knees and presented their hard, upstanding dicks. Sophie was desperately eager to get back to kissing Cathy, so she took Mark's tool to the back of her mouth and let him fuck it into her throat. The other couple were not far behind. Mark was saying something to Peter but the noise of the shower drowned his words. Peter had obviously understood. Both men withdrew and pulled their partners to their feet.

'Now we want to fuck you standing up,' he said.

When the girls parted their legs, it turned out that Mark and Peter had slightly divergent ideas. Peter turned Cathy round and made her bend down, her hands on her knees and her head dripping outside the shower tray. He grasped her hips and drove his soapy prick into the channel that gaped to receive it. Mark, on the other hand—and Sophie was thankful for this— bent his knees to bring himself down to the right level. She helped by tugging her pussy lips apart for him. The head of his cock slipped in easily. Sophie wound her arms round his neck and he hoisted her up so that her legs embraced his thrusting hips. She felt his hands supporting the tops of her thighs as he straightened up, the long fingers reaching up into the crevice of her bottom. When he kissed her, she reflected that she was getting on much better with him now. Perhaps not the most considerate lover, but certainly a fucking powerful one . . .

Peter collapsed forward on Cathy, pushing her right out of the shower cubicle. He had spent a pretty massive load, as Sophie saw when he rolled off sideways and the thick fluid flowed out of the girl on to the tiles. But her own shagger was now shooting his stuff into her. And if Cathy had taken an unexpectedly heavy charge, it felt as if even more had been injected into her own body, and was still being injected. The semen was streaming down her thighs well before Mark had finished pumping it up her.

The men cleaned themselves under the shower and tactfully left their girls to finish each other off. This was easy, as they were both on the point of no return. Mark and Peter had got carried away with their own excitement; untypically, they had neglected their partners' final satisfaction. Cathy and Sophie stood under the shower once more and kissed. When their fingers penetrated their cunts, well stretched by the fuck they had just been given, they found them swampy with sperm, which made the frotting and frigging they now delivered a smoothly delicious luxury.

The men put on little shorts. The girls decided to wear almost decent, pale blue bikini bottoms. Sophie opted for a little white halter top, but Cathy preferred to go topless.

Instead of leaving through the pool area, they used the corridor running behind these rooms. It lead them out into a small courtyard through which they had passed on their first day, the one with the well. The Bridewell, Sophie reminded the others, pronounced bridal, which sounded the same as *bridle*. This morning a little group of honeymooners stood peering down into the well. They made room for the newcomers.

Down below, the iron grid was illuminated by flaming torches. Far below the grid, fiery points were reflected in the water. Spreadeagled on the iron bars, her wrists and ankles chained to them, a naked girl was writhing. Although a black blindfold covered much of her face she was easily recognised from the auburn hair streaming out behind her head and shimmering like fire in the torchlight. It was Tracy. A narrow black gag stuffed her mouth. A fat, black dildo projected from her sex.

Out of the shadows at the circumference of this small torture chamber a black-clad ruffian stepped forward, hooded and masked. He started ramming the dildo in and out of her. Sophie felt a hand on her shoulder and someone's breath on her neck.

'Don't worry, dear,' said Rosper, who had joined the group. 'Her husband had her taken away for correction. Works wonders, as a rule. She'll soon see sense.'

Sophie replied indignantly. 'But that's really, really cruel.'

'He won't hurt her. Strict guidelines, see. No marking of skin, no blood to be drawn. In any case, it's consensual. He made her sign a form of consent before she was taken.'

'That's crap, though, what you say about letting blood. I can see bloodstains on the poor girl's thighs, can't I?'

'Doesn't count. It's just virgin's blood. You just missed her being broken with that whopping great toy. It's a toy, see— they're playing games.'

Sophie was not altogether convinced. Games, as she remembered from school, could often be cruel. Some of the other bystanders were laughing, possibly at her anger, and she

was glad to get away when Rosper led the four of them, whom he seemed to consider his special guests, to a door marked PRIVATE and down a spiral staircase. They now found themselves in the gallery that ran round the circumference of the well-shaft at the level of the grid. Openings in the wall all the way round gave them clear views of the proceedings.

The torturer was stooping over his victim, who struggled against her securing chains. Black, studded gauntlets added menace to his hands, but their roughness contrasted with the implement he was wielding. It was a feather. First he tickled her armpits. Then her nipples, circling around the breasts before homing in on the engorged buds. When she seemed on the point of passing out, he traced a trail down her belly and stopped just above the furry red triangle.

Tracy went rigid as a gauntleted hand gripped her sex. Its evil-looking fingers parted the outer lips and pulled back the hood protecting her clitoris. With the other hand her tormentor applied the very tip of the feather. She was screaming into her gag, so the sound was no more than a muffled wail, which rose to a peak as she climaxed. As her muscles clenched, the fat dildo was expelled from her cunt. It fell through the bars of the grid to splash echoing in the water below.

The man in black unchained her ankles and raised them above her shoulders, fastening them to the grid so that she was now bent double. Her arse was up in the air and was subjected to stinging swishes of a thin cane that left red lines criss-crossing the flesh.

'Not allowed to break the skin, see,' said Rosper. 'That cane's nearly as gentle as the feather.'

All at once the torturer unzipped his costume and removed the gloves, hood and mask. It was Jason, who now stood there black-booted and erect. On the boat out to the island, Sophie recalled, these newlyweds had seemed to be so much in love. What had happened? Jason crouched over his shuddering wife and lunged forward.

'He's got it right in at last,' Sophie exclaimed, joining in the applause of the spectators up above and genuinely pleased that these dreadful proceedings had led to a successful outcome.

Rosper grinned cynically. 'Yeah, but he's using the tradesman's entrance. No class, that lad. Only here because his old man won the lottery.'

They took it fairly easily for the rest of the day as far as sex was concerned. To tell the truth, Sophie felt a little shocked after what she had witnessed in that Bridewell. Excited, but shocked. She thought that when she did it again it would be with renewed passion, but she needed time. When she mentioned this to the others, they agreed.

Until lunch they paddled and lazed on the beach. In the afternoon they wandered up the track that sloped up to the highest point of the island, from where they had a distant view of Skiathos, shimmering beyond an expanse of deep blue. Although they had encountered a few lovestruck couples on the way, they had the summit to themselves. Without discussing what they wanted to do, they stripped off their light clothing and got down in the shade of some olives. But instead of a fierce fuck they simply lay there cuddling, enjoying the companionship of their partners and stroking each other into a state of semi-arousal. And much of the time they dozed.

For the way down the men put their shorts back on and the girls their pale blue bikini bottoms, but Sophie decided to be like Cathy and go topless. It was in this state—topless and hungry—that they entered the dining room, and looking around them they had no reason to feel underdressed. To be sure, auburn-haired Tracy on the far side of the room was wearing a flimsy skirt (to cover the marks on her bottom?), but her pretty breasts were displayed without inhibition.

Giles Rosper made an announcement over the sound system. 'Ladies and gentlemen, I hope you've not forgotten about the show we're laying on for you in our little theatre tonight. No, ladies, I'm sure you haven't or you wouldn't be listening to this announcement—you'd be screwing your husbands.

'What I need to say is this. For a rather special reason I must ask you all to dress modestly for the occasion. Nothing too hard to get out of in a hurry, mind you. But just a suggestion of decency, please. Enjoy!'

Back in their room they tried unsuccessfully to guess why they were supposed to dress up rather than down. Mark and Peter thought their skimpy shorts and scarlet vests ought to pass as modest enough. Sophie opted for a lightweight black cocktail dress reaching less than halfway down her thighs, with a rope of chunky red beads round her neck. A pair of hold-up black stockings and red high heels completed the sophisticated get-up. The guys whistled when she stepped in from the bathroom. Cathy, not attempting to compete, chose a denim microskirt with a gold-sequined boob-tube that left her tummy bare. The foursome grinned at each other and made their way to the theatre.

This turned out to be a small, intimate, steeply raked auditorium with elaborate rococo décor, especially around the gilded proscenium arch, on which all kinds of sexual licence was depicted under the cover of mythological allusion. A heavy curtain at the front of the stage was painted to represent the portico of a Greek temple. The architectural style, according to Peter, was Doric—'simple and chaste', he said. A banner draped across the pediment read TEMPLE OF HYMEN. The hum of the air conditioning was soon drowned out by gentle, exotic flute music. A topless girl showed the little party to their seats. Peter explained that in cinemas in the old days there used to be girls like this, but in non-revealing uniforms, to show the punters to their seats. They had big flashlights. He thought the girls were called usherettes.

Sophie was not particularly interested in this information—it was so like Peter, who could be a bit pedantic, a bit nerdish, to be explaining what you either knew already or didn't need to know. She took the opera glasses from the back of the seat in front of her and surveyed the audience.

A couple of rows down she saw Jason and Tracy, who now seemed to be getting on surprisingly well with each other. The boy wore jeans and a white shirt, his bride a blue and white checked gingham sun dress. They were canoodling and gently snogging, any animosity seemingly forgotten. Even from behind, Sophie could see that Jason had a hand inside the front of Tracy's dress.

From the side of the stage an almost impressive figure entered. It was Rosper. A golden wreath crowned his head, and his lean body was robed in purple inwoven with gold. He stood behind a lectern made, as Peter pointed out, from half of a Corinthian capital, and spoke.

'Ladies and gentlemen. Oh, and boys and girls.' He leered in the direction of Jason and Tracy. 'This is Honeymoon Island. As you know, our entertainments are devised with the interests and needs of newlyweds in mind. Occasionally we discover we have admitted an unmarried couple, and when this happens we always try to do something about it. Sometimes the unhappy pair are sent packing with their tails between their legs. But when they are as young and attractive as the couple in whose honour we meet together this evening, we take a more positive line. You have been invited here to witness a marriage ceremony celebrated according to the ancient rite. On this island of Pothos it has absolute validity, and also in all other places when the couple are in bed together. My friends, you are welcome to the joyful and wanton nuptials of Poppy and Timothy. They will re-enact the *hieros gamos*, the sacred marriage, of Hymen and Priapus. Let the bridegroom approach the temple.'

Sophie guessed that Peter would be fuming at the dodgy legality of this transaction.

A spotlight swept up the raked central aisle and picked out Tim, who was descending with a firm stride. Sophie turned her opera glasses on him. He was got up to look like some youth from those Greek myths, she thought. On his head sat a little garland of ivy leaves. A tunic of white muslin hemmed with gold hung to some way above his knees. It was fastened on his left shoulder, falling diagonally to his right hip. A golden girdle round his waist held this garment together—though not quite, as the front and back were separated by a wide expanse of bare flesh. As he progressed down the aisle, Sophie could see the muscles of his thigh and buttock rippling under the spotlight. To complete his outfit, Tim wore classical-looking sandals of soft white leather with thongs criss-crossing up to his knees. Peter expressed doubts as to whether these could be described as buskins or *kothornoi*, but Sophie was not too interested in his footwear. She noted, however, that he carried a wand round the stem of which a spiral of little rosebuds had been wound. The tip of this wand was adorned with what she first took for another rosebud. In fact it was a crimson cockhead. Know-all Peter reckoned the wand was a *thyrsus*, whatever that was. Tim mounted the stage, where Rosper directed him to wait on one side.

A reverberating organ struck up Mendelssohn's wedding march, and all eyes swung round to the top of the auditorium to watch the bride's entrance. Poppy was radiant in the spotlight that followed her as she processed towards her groom and the robed celebrant. She held a bouquet of red roses. Beneath her head-dress of white flowers—orange blossoms?—and a gauzy veil that hung to the small of her back, she was draped in a loose white robe with a train. This was held up by two pretty children, a bridesmaid and page. Their attire was less modest than the bride's: apart from the flowers in their hair, they wore nothing but low-slung, multi-layered white frills round their loins. These frills concealed their genitals, but as they moved down the sloping aisle it could be seen that they left their bottoms bare. The frills were supported by narrow white tapes running round their hips and fastened at the back with bows that dangled down to tickle their clefts. Sophie averted her eyes and tried to blot out the memory of Tracy telling Jason that his premature ejaculation on her belly in that little cove had been a 'frigging frill'.

The bridal party mounted the stage, and Tim moved to stand beside his darling as she faced the audience. The congregation. Poppy's attendants had clearly been well briefed. The girl undid the clasp on Tim's shoulder and eased his tunic out from the girdle securing it. He was left with this length of gold braid round his waist; attached to it, a small square of white silk hung down to conceal his manhood. The silken scrap was not hanging straight down, and there was a hint of some movement behind it, this movement emphasised by the jiggling of a little golden fringe along the bottom edge.

At the same time, the page boy relieved Poppy of her gown. Her remaining outfit now, although shocking, was no more extreme than what could be seen any day beside the pool without much comment. It was the context of a supposedly sacred ceremony that made it seem outrageous, Sophie reflected.

That gauzy veil, full but light as gossamer, still floated from the headdress of white flowers. At her throat a little triangle of pearls set off the delicate hue of her skin. Elbow-length white gloves gave a touch of formality, but Sophie was interested to note that they were fingerless mitts—she could easily imagine why this was. Her white bra was semi-transparent. The cups were decorated with a diamond-shaped pattern of white threads, and tiny pearls winked at the intersections. Matching the bra she wore a thong that would have allowed any pubic hair she had to show through. As it was, she looked quite innocent, though the ripe bulge was full of promise. A chain of little diamonds was draped round her loins and crossed the bulge suggestively; from a clasp at the side an extension of this chain hung a little way down her thigh. Finally, her sheer white stockings were topped with broad welts of patterned lace, almost as high as the creases of her groin. The spectators applauded. After all, they were not in church. But Sophie found the wolf whistles some of the men let rip quite inappropriate.

Rosper addressed the bridesmaid and page boy. 'Right, kids, thanks for your help but this is where you have to leave us.

What these folks are about to see and hear is not suitable for innocent eyes and ears.' The blushing pair hurried back up the aisle, accompanied by continuing applause and playful slaps on their bottoms.

Rosper stepped out from behind his lectern and spoke confidentially. 'They insisted on taking part. They're with a little group who came out here to model for some more of my statues. Have to be kept segregated. You can see now, folks, why you were asked to dress decently, can't you. You can loosen up and get more informal now. And the kids' places will be taken by our temple maidens and youths. They're legal. Just. They serve the goddess as sacred prostitutes.'

Mark's hand went to the zipper at Sophie's neck and ran it right down her back. He reached round under the loosened dress to palm a breast. She tugged the hem of her skirt up to her waist, enjoying the feeling of the velvet seat against her bare behind. Glancing down, she admired the pallor of her loins between the dress and the tops of her black stockings. Her pubic tuft winked blonde in the dim lights of the auditorium; she was glad she had not worn knickers.

All around them people were making themselves comfortable. A couple of rows in front of the foursome, Jason had unfastened and lowered Tracy's dress, which was bunched around her waist. Her copper-coloured tresses hung over her shoulders and down her white back, untouched by the morning's ordeal in the Bridewell.

The curtain rose, revealing what was meant to be the scarlet-draped interior of the temple. The upstage area was dominated by a huge golden phallus standing in a round basin. Every now and then a spurt of water issued from the tip, surely using the technology that had been developed for the sculptures around

the hotel. Taking up most of the centre of the stage was a large circular bed covered with purple sheets.

From one side a young couple made their entrance, and then another couple from the other side. These were the temple youths and maidens Rosper had mentioned, Sophie decided, turning her opera glasses towards them in turn. The athletic-looking youngsters were dressed exactly like the page boy and bridesmaid they had replaced. All four of them bounced across the stage, reversing positions. As they passed each other they executed cartwheels and handstands, letting their frills flip up as they did so. To Sophie, both the youths and the maidens looked well fit. Unlike the girl they replaced, the females had proper breasts, which jiggled enticingly as they cavorted.

Sophie felt Mark's teasing of her pubic tuft as he whispered in her ear that he had noticed a costume just like Poppy's in one of their cupboards. 'Can't wait to see you in it,' he chuckled.

Poppy and her bridegroom were standing side by side at the front of the stage. At a nod from Rosper the four attendants surrounded them. They detached the square of silk from the strip of gold braid round Tim's waist and Poppy's bra and thong, but nothing else. It was only when the youths and maidens went twirling back to their corners that Sophie got an unobstructed view of the bridal couple, both their bodies completely free of hair.

Tim's prick stood up proud and trembling. The opera glasses picked out sharply a bead of pre-come growing on the head. It got larger and began to snail its way down the rigid stem. His bride looked lovely. One side of her veil had fallen over her shoulder and half covered the breast. The nipple winked out through the gauzy material. Her other tit was fully exposed, as was the pretty mound with its pink slit disappearing down between her thighs with their white stocking welts.

Rosper made the couple stand facing each other in front of him, and began intoning an obscene litany:

'Dearly beloved, we are met together in this consecrated place to join you in body and spirit as man and wife.'

The audience had been murmuring but now fell silent.

'Do you, Poppy, take this lusty and rampant youth, Timothy, to kiss and caress you on mouth, nipples, bottom and cunt, to finger your most intimate places until you cry out for fucking, and to shag you untiringly until the spunk boils in his balls and jets into your tight, rippling young sheath?'

The bride looked down bashfully. 'I do.'

'Do you, Timothy, take this fresh young beauty, Poppy, to kiss and caress her on mouth, nipples, bottom and cunt, to finger her most intimate places until she cries out for fucking, and to shag her untiringly until the spunk boils in your balls and jets into her tight, rippling young sheath?'

'I do.'

The couple now repeated, sentence by sentence, the celebrant's next words.

'I, Poppy, promise to open my body to you, Timothy my darling husband, and to your fingers, tongue and prick. And I will lay it open to all whom you invite to partake of the sensual feast. My tongue will explore and delight each opening of your male flesh. And I will roll your balls on my tongue and suck your soft cock to raging hugeness so that you may thrust it deep into my cunt to spout there until the sperm flows down my thighs. And when my lusts are sated I will refresh myself to renewed lewdness while you enjoy the lively young cunts I shall procure for your use. So will I serve you as your wanton wife.'

Sophie was shocked but excited. So were most of the audience. The ceremony continued.

'I, Timothy, promise to hold my cock and balls in constant readiness for you, Poppy my darling wife, to quench the thirst of your cunt whenever you so desire. I will keep the channel of that dear cunt always flooded with my spunk. And I will kiss your breasts, bottom and thighs, lick your eager clit and lap up the sperm as it runs down your legs from your overflowing cunt. When your desires are sated I will quench my own raging lusts on the youthful bodies you procure for my delight. And when my prick droops from overspending, I will furnish lusty cocks for your use and enjoyment until once more I am stiff and bursting with lewdness. So I will serve you as your lecherous husband.'

The two temple maidens stepped forward. Julie, naked, held a little purple cushion, which she handed to Rosper. A pair of rings winked on the cushion. Julie now knelt before Tim, whose prick arched out semi-erect. Sophie thought the girl would suck him, but instead she hefted his testicles in one hand and gently frigged him with the other. Soon clear fluid was seeping from the cocktip. Rosper held out the cushion, Julie took one of the rings and slid it about in the juice. Still on her knees, she shifted over to Poppy, frotted her vulva, slipped the other ring into it and slowly drew it out. Glistening wetly, both rings were returned to the cushion and Julie withdrew.

The rite proceeded with Poppy's declaration as she placed the appropriate ring (Sophie hoped it was the appropriate one) on Tim's finger:

'Timothy, my dear husband, I slip this ring, slick with the juices of my longing cunt, on to your finger with a loving pledge that I wed you with it and will worship you with my yielding body, and that soon I will welcome your cock as it follows that finger through the tight ring of my vagina.'

Tim took the other ring.

'Poppy, my darling wife, I slip this ring, slick with the oozings of my yearning prick, on to your finger as a loving pledge that I wed you with it and will worship you with my rampant body, and that soon my cock will follow my own probing finger through the tight ring of your vagina.'

As the congregation gasped expectantly, Rosper spoke:

'I pronounce you man and wife. You, Timothy, may kiss your blushing bride, Poppy, on her mouth, nipples, bottom and cunt. And you, Poppy, may return your husband's kisses.'

Mark's teasing of Sophie's sex became more insistent and he laughed. 'Sounds like she's going to be everybody's bride, wouldn't you say? A regular fuckfest.'

The bridal pair lay down on the mattress and engaged in the ritual of kissing as just prescribed. Soft flutes struck up a jig and the four young servitors began to dance around them. A lewd dance, with much flipping up of their frills. Before long the dance became almost stationary and the four were masturbating each other indiscriminately, with no distinction of sex, but avoiding climax.

Suddenly the music stopped. The two temple maidens dragged Tim away from his bride and writhed lasciviously over his body and limbs. From time to time a gap was left between the bodies through which the boy's raging erection was seen. Mark explained that the girls were rubbing their wet pussies against his skin. 'Oiling him up for her,' he said.

At the same time the youths were kneeling one on each side of Poppy, wanking the cocks that had lifted their frills until they rained down on to her pale body. They used their palms to spread their spendings over her skin without rubbing it in, making it as slick and shiny as Tim's. The maidens reached a screaming orgasm; all four attendants rose from the bed and withdrew to the sides.

It was now time for the consummation of this highly irregular marriage. Poppy opened her legs and pulled her labia apart. Tim mounted her missionary-style and plunged his stiffness into her depths. She groaned.

Because the youths and maidens had made such a good job of lubricating their whole bodies, Tim was able to slide and slither all over his bride as he pumped and pumped. The picture was greatly enhanced by the way the skimpy garments Poppy still wore—her veil, gloves, stockings and the narrow chain—contrasted with Tim's almost total nudity: he was bare except for the wreath of ivy leaves still perched on his head, his strappy sandals and the belt of golden braid round his hips. Through her opera glasses, on each upstroke Sophie could make out his swinging balls.

After a few minutes of this fucking the couple froze. Tim's buttocks clenched, hollows forming in his flanks. Then Poppy's white-stockinged legs flashed up in the air and her arms waved about on either side as she beat the mattress. She howled out her delight. Tim's balls bunched up in readiness to shoot their load; he made a final thrust and collapsed, gurgling, on her breast.

To entertain the onlookers while the newlyweds recovered, the youths and maidens did another little dance, which included licking, sucking and penetration, both boy-girl and boy-boy, but again no ejaculation. Mark's hand was now romping freely over Sophie's sex and she reciprocated by reaching into his shorts.

Rosper stepped forward and drew Poppy and Tim to their feet. They staggered to the front of the stage, still shining with sexjuice. More recent liquors streamed down Poppy's thightops to stain her stockings. It was clear that they had been coached in this part of the service, as they were able to say their words without prompting from the priest. The bride spoke first, her voice hoarse and slightly tremulous:

'Sated and overflowing with his sperm, I now seek lively young cunts for the use and enjoyment of my darling bridegroom until my own body is refreshed and lewd for renewed fucking with him.'

The temple maidens approached Tim as he stood there while they began to service his mouth and prick. The priest spoke:

'We already have two. To make up the mystical number three, let us find a fresh-cunted young lady in this congregation. Examine your tickets, gentlemen, to see if your good lady is going to be the winner.'

From behind the lectern he produced a golden bowl. He held this out to the trembling Poppy, who looked away and drew a counterfoil from it. Her voice was almost inaudible, so Rosper repeated her announcement.

'Number seventeen. Lucky for some!'

Seventeen happened to be Peter, who lifted Cathy to her feet. Edging past the knees of Sophie and Mark and detained momentarily by the latter as he ran his free hand up under her denim microskirt, she passed between applauding spectators and mounted the stage. Rosper directed her to strip. Her skirt fell to the ground. When she had successfully struggled to take off her gold boob-tube over her head, her only garment was a small, lime-green G-string. This she peeled down her legs, kicked it off and got down on the edge of the bed, her thighs wide open for the delighted view of the audience.

And of Tim, who pulled out of the maiden servicing him in a standing position and threw himself on this new quasi-sacrificial offering. He had no difficulty in flooding her with come, though Sophie was not sure that her friend could have achieved full satisfaction in such a short time.

Tim extracted his dripping prick from Cathy, who was about to return to her seat. Rosper placed a restraining hand on her forearm and made her sit on a little stool to one side. Groggily, Tim addressed the audience:

'Sated and with drained bollocks, I now seek lusty cocks for the use and enjoyment of my darling bride until my own tool regains its vigour.'

With a feeble hand Poppy was about to draw a number from the golden bowl, but she had evidently forgotten the order of service at this point. The priest pushed her to the front of the stage. The two temple youths moved to stand on either side of her. Their frills were pushed up against their bellies by their hard-ons. Rosper spoke:

'To find a well-hung stud to make up the mystical number three' (he pointed at Cathy), 'let us ask this lovely volunteer's husband to present himself.'

Mark pulled four fingers out of Sophie's sopping cunt, licked them and rose eagerly from his seat, only to be pulled down again by his partner. 'Other people mustn't know she's really married to you,' she whispered. So it was Peter who came forward and got up on the stage. While he stripped, the youths pushed the veiled Poppy back on the bed and began to fuck her mouth and cunt.

As soon as they had finished, they stood by her head and

raised her white-stockinged legs, parting them widely. Sophie squinted through her optical aid and just had time to make out the semen oozing from the corners of the bride's mouth and the distended opening of her love-channel before Peter stooped on bent knees to ram her and complete her ecstasy. What a lark! After a brief pause, he straightened up. The three studs now stood over the girl they had pleasured so efficiently and squeezed the last droolings from their cocks to dribble down and puddle on her nipples and cuntmound. When they were drained they pulled her to her feet. Poppy and Tim joined hands and stepped forward to take their bow to thunderous applause.

The husband's ivy wreath now sat on his dark locks at a jaunty angle. His golden girdle intersected white skin gleaming with dried girljuice. Although his dick drooped from its efforts, it already seemed to be thickening up in anticipation of further conjugal treats behind closed doors.

In contrast, his wife's body was wet and streaming with the spendings of her servitors. Sophie loved the way she still maintained the image of the radiant bride with her stockings, gloves and veil. A travesty of the conventional image, to be sure, but still lovely and still blushing.

Peter and Cathy returned to their seats. The curtain fell and the house lights came up. All around was a scene of embarrassed debauchery. While some of the spectators remained brazenly exposed and engaged in sexual activity, others scrambled to force pricks into trousers and to cover tits and pussies.

It was easy for Sophie to pull the hem of her dress down, but the back was still unzipped and, as they moved towards the exit, Mark slipped a hand into it. The hand stroked over her side. He leaned close to her and stretched round to fondle a breast.

In the crowded aisle they found themselves next to Tracy and Jason. The girl had left the bodice of her blue and white checked dress bunched round her waist, and her auburn tresses offered very inadequate cover for her pert charms. Jason looked at Cathy, who was naked and carrying her clothes.

'Nearly come in me pants when they did you,' he offered. 'That's what I call a fuck, innit.'

'A shag, even,' Tracy added, giggling. 'Not enough shag on them two, though—Tim and whatsername. I like it a bit rough.'

Mark, Sophie, Peter and Cathy returned to their room to fuck and shag until they fell asleep all over the beds and floor.

Thursday

'This is hen and stag day, friends,' announced Julie as she delivered their breakfast. 'No sex before you leave, if you don't mind. You'll need all your energy when the fun begins.'

As if to underline the message, she was wearing full maid's uniform. The only indecency in it was the open bodice, which she had shrugged off her left shoulder, allowing her left breast its freedom. The nipple peeped out between the black dress and the edge of her little white apron. She explained that separate events were being mounted for the guests at the two ends of the island: females to the north and males to the south.

'What should we wear?' asked Cathy.

'We've got special outfits for you when you arrive,' Julie replied. 'Wear whatever you like on the boat. Girls and boys will be going separately, if that affects your choice. You won't be seeing your partners again till this evening, but then you can get together at our bottomless ball. The girls' boat leaves from the jetty at half ten and the boys' at eleven fifteen. I'll be in charge of the girls, so you'd better behave.' She swept out of the room.

Sophie and Cathy slipped into simple, well-cut bikinis, Sophie's red and Cathy's black. Their men opted for the skimpy black thongs that had become their habitual attire. All four put on dark glasses and the wide-brimmed straw sunhats provided by the management. They slid open the sliding door and flopped on to the nearest poolside loungers to relax while waiting.

By ten-thirty the jetty was thronged with excited young women. When the honeymooners had boarded the launch that brought them over from Skiathos five days earlier there was only just room for all of them, and most had to stand, squeezed against each other. Sophie realised why they were now so cramped—the honeymooners, men and women, had been ferried to Pothos in three boatloads, and now half that number were crowded together for one trip. Such was the sense of cameraderie and intimacy generated by the island experience, however, that everyone seemed to be happy with the arrangement. But how would the boys feel about this proximity, Sophie wondered. Her Peter had a horror of male-on-male contact, or at least he claimed to have.

On the jetty she had noticed young Tracy, who seemed more relaxed than usual. She was wearing a close-fitting T-shirt with red and white, centimetre-wide horizontal stripes. The small mounds of her tits pushed out the front of the shirt, and the enlarged nipples were very evident. Lower down, the striped cotton hugged the slight swell of her tummy in front and the roundness of her bottom at the back. The garment was almost a mini-dress rather than a shirt: its hem just covered the V of Tracy's crotch, but only just. In fact, when she moved it looked pretty much as if the apex of that inverted triangle of russet fuzz could actually be glimpsed. And when Sophie had followed her as she clumped up the gangplank in chunky white trainers to board the boat, the undercurves of the younger girl's soft buttocks were very inadequately covered. Thin, faint pink lines criss-crossed the upper thighs and quivering cheeks, evidence of her ordeal in the Bridewell. Nothing like the boldness of the red stripes on her T-shirt in their rigid parallels, but a pleasing echo of these striations nonetheless.

Apart from the colour of the shirt, it reminded Sophie of the vests worn by Russian sailors. This nautical impression was strengthened by the peaked yachting cap perched on her auburn curls and bearing the legend *HMS LOLLIPOP*. Cathy pointed out that lollipops were for licking and sucking. Sophie now found herself brushing against the girl, who looked up at her with wide green eyes.

'Awesome last night, that wedding,' Tracy remarked.

'Quite a lark. You enjoyed it, then?'

'It was good to see them kids doing it. They're about our age—mine and Jason's, I mean—and it kind of helped me forget our own problems.'

'What problems are they, then?'

'Well, you know . . .'

'You mean he comes too quickly?'

Tracy blushed. 'Well, yes, I spose he does. And he don't always, well, you know . . .'

'Doesn't always bring you off?'

'Sort of. How did you know?'

'Oh, that's very common with inexperienced young men. I've read about it and, well, I've come across it myself, when I was younger. You must let me and my Pete, I mean my Mark, give the two of you some tips and, er, practical guidance.'

The girl's blush deepened. 'Well, I don't know about that.'

During this shouted conversation (the boat's engine throbbed powerfully and the girl chat on board was shrill and lively, as was the accompanying clamour of sea birds wheeling over the launch) Sophie and Cathy, as well as Tracy, had been forced over to the rail on the far side as more and more of the women crowded on to the deck. Cathy sat on a bench with her back to the water, while Sophie fell back on to her lap, straddling her left thigh and leaning against her bosom. The chattering throng forced Tracy forward until she was standing with her feet parted and her knees on either side of the seated girls' legs. To stop herself falling over she leaned forward, reaching over her friends' shoulders, and placed her hands on the rail. Her cheek rested against Sophie's, whose ear was tickled by warm, intimate breath. Was this an invitation?

Partly to find out, and partly because it was the natural thing to do, Sophie ran her hands up the backs of Tracy's thighs until they slipped under the shirt and palmed the cheeks of her bottom. The teenager gasped into her assailant's ear and straightened up. Had she gone too far?

This question was answered when Tracy's hands came down to the hem of her shirt and lifted it just enough to expose that flaming little mound with its pouting lips. She was so close to Sophie's face that nobody else could see what was going on. Oh yes, thought Sophie, it's true—lollipops are for licking and sucking. A truly fragrant aroma issued from the girl. What did Peter call this smell? Oh yes, something like *odor di femina*. When Sophie had given Cathy oral sex there had always been at least a residue of male discharge, and sometimes much more than a residue, but now there was no trace of that Jason's pathetic activities. Bending down, she stuck out her tongue and went straight for it, her nose and forehead pressing into the soft belly with its red and white stripes.

Although her view of the proceedings was obscured by her friend's back, Cathy was well aware of what was happening. Moving her hands to Sophie's lap, she started stroking her upper thighs and tummy, working closer and closer to the skimpy red bikini bottom until one hand cupped the plump triangle and the other one sneaked under the elastic.

As Sophie slurped the juices the point of her tongue had got flowing from the younger girl's cunt, she once more ran her hands up the back of those slender thighs to enjoy the firm but yielding flesh of her buttocks. By this time, her own sexlips had been eased apart and two fingers were probing the channel of her vagina. She parted her legs wider, easing her right one up and over Cathy's, so that she was straddling both of her thighs.

The boat rode the waves of the Aegean. Sophie and Tracy mounted the same crest, which burst in a mind-shattering orgasm.

They had to slip off their footwear—in most cases sandals— and paddle through delightfully warm water to get to the beach. This place certainly looked like an earthly paradise, Sophie reflected. Beyond the white sand of the cove, the ground rose gently towards a cone-shaped hill. The lower slopes were largely given over to olive groves, their leaves shimmering in the light breeze from the sea. Interspersed among these, dark cypresses punctuated the rocky higher ground like exclamation marks, or upside-down exclamation marks without the dots—whatever.

Julie, now wearing a simple white one-piece swimsuit that had become wet and transparent when she took a tumble disembarking from the launch, led the party up the beach and out of the hot sun. A few metres into the shade of the olives they came to a moss-carpeted clearing bright and fragrant with the wild flowers that flourished profusely on the island at this time of year. The girls sat in a wide semicircle facing down to the beach, while Julie remained standing and addressed them.

'Right, ladies, this is your special day. At last a chance to get away from those husbands of yours—who *hasn't* had enough of them by now?'

Every hand went up and they all laughed.

'Put it another way, then. You've all had your fair share of cock. Who'd refuse a bit of variety at this stage?'

No hands were raised. There was an expectant hush. Sophie, who was sitting near one horn of the semicircle, glanced round the nervous faces. Opposite her she saw young Poppy, seated a few places away from Tracy. Tracy had her knees apart and her feet crossed in front of her. The hem of the stripey T-shirt was quite unable to hide her fiery sex, no doubt relaxed and moist after its recent tongue-lashing. Poppy was sporting the top she had shown off at the swimwear ball on their first night, with its the two little daisies just covering her nipples. To complement this she had chosen a tiny red skirt of a soft material. She sat there hugging her knees. Noticing Sophie's friendly smile, she shifted slightly so that the skirt, which had fallen right back to expose her flanks, formed a scarlet foil for her bare buttocks. The purse of her hairless sex pouted lewdly in the dappled sunlight. Recognising Sophie, she grinned.

Julie continued with her welcoming speech. 'For those of you so inclined, and those who would like to experiment and fool about a bit if you haven't done so before, what about some girl on girl action? You can have yourselves some mini orgies if you like. But our main attraction's something a tad meatier—and I don't mean the barbecue we're laying on for you. Now, you're all brides here on your honeymoon, right? My boyfriend tells me the ancient Greek word for bride is the same as the word for nymph. You're going to play at being nymphs for the day. And what happens to nymphs, eh? Well, they get chased and ravished by the fauns and satyrs—satyrs are the older ones—who live in the woods. Predators, all of them, and they won't take no for an answer.'

There was an audible gasp and the women in the semicircle stirred, some in fear and some with anticipation of the fun to come.

'Not real fauns and satyrs, of course. Local lads who work for us on the island. A bit rough and ready, some of them, but others are proper smoothies. No goat legs or horns or tails, I'm afraid, though some are quite shaggy. And horny. Some of them can manage a bit of English, but it's more fun to think of them as dumb beasts. Most of them will go straight for you and do you before you know what's hit you, but some may behave as if they're more interested in each other. What they call Greek love. Up to you to offer your own bottoms and lure them away from their boyfriends. See it as a challenge. Oh, and as it's the lads who do the barbecue, you won't get to feed till at least some of them have been satisfied. Now, if any of you good ladies don't feel up to it, there's no compulsion. All you have to do is come to me and ask for one of these red scarves to give you immunity. You can still enjoy watching the others at it, of course.'

There were no takers, though some of the women seemed to be tempted.

Next, Julie handed out costumes supposed to be appropriate for nymphs. All of these were of gauzy white muslin, some with gold or silver trimmings at the edges. None of them offered much in the way of cover. Though most of the women stripped off without inhibition to change into these outfits, some were shy and tried to conceal their charms like kids on an English beach. Some even slipped into the undergrowth for the sake of modesty.

Sophie quickly worked out what to do with her flimsy garment. This was no more than a scarf-like scrap of gauze. She fitted it over her hips, securing it with a knot between her belly button and her pubis, so that the narrow strip hung down not quite to her knees. Her bottom was covered but the front of this improvised skirt hung open to show off her sex. Looking around, she could see that the others had adorned themselves in a variety of ways, making the most (or, more precisely, the least) of the bits and pieces they had been given.

Cathy was relatively modest, in an outfit worn by quite a few of the women. It was a simple tunic, held in at the waist with a silver girdle. A clasp held it up on her left shoulder, leaving the right breast exposed. The skirt was as short as it could possibly be, and only concealed her privates and buttocks when she stood still.

The slim, black woman Sophie had seen in the sauna looked striking in a much longer white robe, slit down both sides from armpit to hem. The only other person in a similar costume was Julie. Like Sophie, all the others were displaying far more gleaming flesh as they moved about nervously under the olive trees.

Where was little Tracy? Sophie turned round, and there she was, tripping towards her with a broad smile on her face. She had a scarf similar to her friend's, but instead of fixing it as Sophie had done, Tracy had fastened it round her chest. From the knot between her tiny, firm breasts the gauze hung down so that its silver-fringed end just tickled her mound of Venus with its flame-coloured curls.

The two of them were joined by Poppy, in one of the tunics worn by Cathy and others. The nipple on her bare tit stood up proud and pink; a shaft of sunlight striking through the leaves illuminated it and cast a long shadow down the curve of her white skin.

Well, thought Sophie, there's safety in numbers—let the fun begin. Her mates must have been thinking the same; Poppy immediately grabbed Tracy and wrestled her to the ground to smother her body in kisses. Cathy did the same to Sophie, and the two couples rolled about like kittens.

Soon the older women's posture stabilized itself, with Cathy flat on her back, the skirt of her tunic whipped up over her stomach, while her partner straddled her in a fevered sixty-nine. Sophie's raised behind quivered as a pointed tongue searched the folds of her sex. Her nipples grazed over Cathy's belly as she eased apart her friend's thighs and lowered her mouth to the oily entrance.

Just as Sophie approached her climax, a searing pain pierced her bowels. A well-greased prick drove up into her and a pair of rough hands forced their way between her chest and Cathy's belly, to pinch the nipples. Clinging to the thighs in front of her, she strove to keep her tongue working on Cathy's clit while the deeply embedded prick pistoned in and out as if its owner had been celibate for God knows how long. And this movement, this earth-shaking vibration, had the merit of rubbing her own cunt backwards and forwards over Cathy's tongue-tip. The pain in her gut had eased. The sense of overpowering fullness was now racked up, literally, to overflowing as her brutish violater discharged his seed into her body. He withdrew and disappeared into the woods, unseen by his victim. Sperm streamed from her abused opening to flood Cathy's tongue. Both women were racked with the spasms of satisfied lust and collapsed exhausted.

Lying there side by side, they gazed lazily at the younger

couple. Tracy and Poppy had probably only seen each other from a distance previously, Tracy being so retiring and Poppy so extrovert. Yet they were certainly hitting it off now, even if the redhead was still a bit shy. She sat propped against the base of a tree while her partner knelt beside her, kissing her tenderly with an arm supporting the girl's head. From the waist up, the appearance of these lovers was almost chaste. They might have been painted by Lord Leighton or some such—he was one of Peter's favourites. Tracy's breasts were bound by the gauzy scarf, and only one of Poppy's was exposed along with a white shoulder. The suggestion of chastity, though, was deceptive. Poppy's other hand rested lightly on that coppery cuntmound, and Sophie could see that Poppy had a finger well up her. The shuddering of Tracy's thighs indicated that the penetrating finger and pressuring palm were giving her continuous low-level thrills. *Frills*, she would have called them.

Suddenly another of the naked predators came dashing in from the undergrowth. He was young, dark and good-looking in a boyish way. No more than seventeen, Sophie reckoned, though she had the impression that in these parts the guys could be quite a bit younger than they looked. His penis was long and slim, standing out horizontally from a small cluster of tight black curls. Stooping, the youth placed his hands on Poppy's shoulders. Not her boobs—he appeared to be showing her some respect. Reverence, almost. Then, instead of tipping her rudely on to her back, as might have been expected, he knelt and lowered her quite gently. Tracy, left to her own devices, used her own finger to prolong the pleasure the bolder girl had been giving her.

The dark-haired lad ran his eye down the body of his pretty captive, but refrained from touching her. This encounter even had a hint of romance about it, thought Sophie. He stooped to kiss the girl, who responded by allowing her thighs to fall open in invitation. Without removing his tongue from her mouth, the 'faun' placed his knees between her legs. The tip of his slender tool slipped up and down her opening before bursting all the way in.

He lay there on top of her and continued kissing her in a leisurely fashion. Her thighs came up; she locked her legs around him. Sophie and Cathy now had a good view of the boy's full ball sack. Cathy winked at her friend and got up on her knees. Then she rested one hand on his bottom and with the other one cupped those testicles. He reacted instantly, driving his prick even further up Poppy's love channel.

Cathy addressed Sophie. 'Fancy a go?' she asked.

Of course she did. Cathy moved aside to give her mate access to the now rhythmically pumping buttocks and jiggling scrotum. Fondling the soft white globes of his bum, Sophie lowered her head. The point of her tongue homed in on the lad's balls, and after tickling them a bit she took the whole of his purse into her mouth. The testes now rolled about on her tongue. The pleasure she was delivering was obvious—the speed of the already rapid fucking increased dramatically.

Cathy now made her own contribution to the action. As Sophie went on with her tongue play, the older woman ran a well-licked finger down the boy's bottom-cleft. She pulled the cheeks apart and dribbled into his anus before penetrating it with the finger.

The effect was immediate. Poppy squealed as the prick was thrust right up her to the limit of her vagina. Sophie felt the balls harden and tighten up. The boy's buttocks and flanks clenched and quivered as he injected a pressurised stream of semen into his partner's cunt.

At the same moment Tracy, who had been frigging away steadily as she watched this operation, wailed and thrashed about in a magnificent, unashamed, self-delivered climax.

The youth pulled out of Poppy with a sigh and trotted off up the hill. Considerate though he had been, Poppy had not been brought to the point of orgasm and was panting with unsatisfied desire. Sophie felt sorry for her, and immediately brought her mouth down to her gaping, spermy snatch. The *odor di* whatever—*uomo? semina?*—smelt heavenly, and Sophie sucked in a long draught of the foaming liquor before attacking Poppy's stiffened clit with her tongue-tip. The teenage bride came almost at once. Now all four had been taken to the heights and after a brief rest were ready for more fun. They got up and wandered down towards the beach.

But before they had gone far they encountered a refreshing stream. Splashing water on their faces and cooling their feet, they decided to follow this watercourse upwards into the woods. As they advanced, high-pitched whooping and screams could be heard from the hill. The commotion soon died down, followed by nervous laughter and giggling, and these sounds became louder as they ascended the course of the stream. Rounding an outcrop of rock they entered a large, sunlit clearing. At the centre of this was a pool, fed by a waterfall that poured down from a towering crag. The margins of the pool presented a colourful picture—billowy masses of white flowers (jasmine?), spilled over into the water, interwoven with what might have been yellow celandine and some delicate, mauve, bell-shaped ones. An earthly paradise and no mistake.

This paradise was populated by a large contingent of nymphs, perhaps two-thirds of the party. Some were splashing about in the pool, some were playing under the waterfall, some were scattered about in twos or threes on the flowery banks around the circumference, but most were congregated in one patch of sunlight. Looking at those enjoying themselves in the water, Sophie was reminded of another of Peter's favourite Victorian painters, with the appropriate name of Waterhouse. A poster of one his paintings, showing nymphs bathing, adorned their bedroom wall at home.

Sophie gasped. 'Look, girls,' she said. 'There must have been a raid.'

And indeed, the disposition of the group in the sunny patch suggested that a party of marauders had swept through the gathering, ravishing everyone in their path, before disappearing into the woods. This was evident from the disarray of the women's scanty garments, some of which had been ripped to afford free access to the desired parts when these were not already displayed for all to see. Moreover, where the raiders had passed through, their victims were sprawled in all manner of lewd attitudes, spent and gasping. Spent, Sophie reflected, was probably not the word. The only spending seemed to have been done by their attackers, the fluid product of whose depredations could be seen everywhere—in their hair, on their tits and bellies, their thighs and pubic mounds. And, as the newcomers watched, it began to seep, trickle and gush from the orifices in which it been deposited. Mostly, but not exclusively, the honeymooners' cunts.

As they slowly recovered, these violated ladies began, almost automatically, to give each other the relief their fuckers had denied them, sobbing in each other's arms. The four friends picked their way down to the water, carefully stepping over the bodies of these ravished brides, and agreed that what they needed was a cooling dip.

The pool was deep enough for them to float and swim. Soon they were splashing and squealing under the waterfall, their little white garments soaked and completely transparent. Suddenly, Tracy took Sophie's hand and looked at her pleadingly. She seemed to be a bit nervous as she led her through shallow water across to the far side of the pool. They climbed up on to the mossy bank, Tracy leading the way and almost shoving her wet, white bottom with its faint lines from her whipping into Sophie's face as Sophie followed her. If she had been a man up as close as this behind the tempting young thing . . . Once out of the water, the girls stood facing each other. Yes, Tracy was shy, and Sophie found this rather charming. The girl spoke.

'What you did to me on the boat. That was fuckin awesome. I really got off on that, know what I mean?'

'You mean feeling your bottom . . .'

'Yeah. And, and . . .

'And licking your cunt? No need to be coy with me, dear.'

'Yeah, licking me. Absolutely awesome. Can we . . .'

'Do it again? Let me tell you something, you little darling. It was lovely for me, too. I'd love to do it again. We've got a bit more room to manoeuvre here. Get down. Oh, and I want to suck those little titties as well.'

Tracy lowered herself to the cool moss. Sophie knelt over her and untied the strip of white gauze round her chest. Because it was wet, the knot between her breasts was quite difficult to loosen. By the time Sophie was able to peel it away, Tracy was in a fine state of arousal. Since she was lying on her back, her scarcely developed chest was almost flat. By contrast, her little areolas, puckered from both the cold water and her lust, were crowned with teats that stood up proud and stubby. They gleamed in the sunlight with a kind of orange translucency, as if associating themselves with the carroty hairs at the base of her belly.

Sophie was charmed. Or rather, she had no time to be charmed, but went straight for her prize, twisting one of the nubs between her fingers while she clamped her lips over the other one. The youngster stiffened and Sophie ran her free hand down her stomach to cup and squeeze the damp sexpurse.

After a minute or so of this rough treatment, she rolled Tracy over and began to apply much gentler touches to her bottom. She soothed the faintly visible weals with fingertips and tongue, licking along the creases demarcating the buttocks from the tops of the thighs and then up through the central rift. As she made this pass she kneaded the girl's soft globes and pressed them together. Her tongue was held captive, tickling the anal opening.

Sophie needed to breathe. She drew back and gloated over her partner's behind. Then, lovingly, she stroked the backs of those slender thighs and gently pulled them apart. Yes—there, where they almost joined, a line of reddish hair drew her gaze to the thin lips of her sex. Once more she plunged the tip of her tongue into the cleft of Tracy's bottom. This time, she ran it right down until her nose was jammed into the arsehole and the stiffened point of the tongue was enjoying the roughness of those short hairs. Soon the hairs parted and the tongue encountered silky, wet skin. The skin parted and the tongue slipped into the girl's opening.

And now young Tracy took the initiative. Heaving up her

bottom, she shook her lover off and rolled over. Now she was on her back again, but this time she opened her legs wide and pulled them right back against her chest. Her succulent cunt gaped open, the wispy red hair fighting a losing battle for attention with the juicing pink of the love channel. Sophie was beside herself with lewd desire. She stroked the labia with one finger, applying more and more pressure until the tip was sucked in and the whole length of the digit slid along the tight sheath.

'So you've really and truly never had a cock up here?' she enquired, wriggling the finger from side to side and producing squelching sounds.

'No, never. Well, not right up. A few kids might have frigged about just at the opening, like, but I never let them like pop my cherry, know what I mean? I was saving meself up for me wedding night—that's a joke, innit.'

'And these men. Did they actually come?'

'Wouldn't call them men, most of them. Boys. Didn't know no more than me. Yeah, they used to squirt their stuff in there. But they wasn't in far enough to do no harm. It used to pour out of me while they was still coming.'

'How would you feel about getting fucked today by one of these Greek hunks?'

'No way. I'm not on the pill or nuffink. Jason's dad's really keen for me to fall pregnant. He won the lottery—otherwise we wouldn't be here. It wouldn't be no good if the baby wasn't as fair-haired as my Jace.'

'Or as red as your pussy!'

The girl blushed. 'And anyway, I really want Jace to be me first. Kept meself for him.'

'I know. For his exclusive use. We must make a big effort

to get the two of you fucking like stoats. I'm sure you can manage it.'

'So I'm quite scared that these Greek blokes are going to—to take advantage of me today. I was lucky they went for you and that Poppy. But how will it be next time, know what I'm saying?'

'Why didn't you ask for one of those red scarves? We could still get you one if you feel that way.'

Tracy whimpered. 'No, I couldn't do nuffink like that. Don't want to make meself ridic . . . conspicuous, like.'

'Well, you could try to keep a finger jammed up yourself—no room in here for a prick as well. Even without the finger, some of the big ones might have a problem sticking it in. Otherwise, you must just do your best to suck them off, or tempt them to do it up your pretty little arse. I think Julie's right—that's what they mean by Greek love, unless that's the same as the love that dare not speak its name.'

'Same difference, innit,' Tracy interjected.

'Right. Oh, and me and Cathy can do our best to entice them away, though I can't think they'd prefer us to a poppet like you. But don't worry too much, love. It may never happen.'

She squeezed Tracy's clit between her thumb and the finger sheathed in her cunt. The girl's blush deepened and spread from her face, down over her neck and right across her chest. Her nipples were almost bursting—she moaned and came, throwing her arms around Sophie and kissing her with real passion.

A whistle blew, and Julie's voice was calling. 'Barbie time! Everyone down to the beach!'

A naked contingent of shaggy satyrs and smooth, olive-skinned fauns were busy with the barbecue. Everyone was hungry and thirsty; paper plates and cups were provided; meat, salad and chilled retsina were doled out in abundance. Most of the nymphs seemed by now to have lost or discarded their scraps of white gauze, but the boys serving them were too busy to take much notice. They were probably doing their best to stop their dicks getting the same grilling as the sausages they resembled.

It was just as well that the sand of this little cove was scattered with flat rocks and great logs of sunbleached driftwood—the girls were able to sit and lie on these without getting uncomfortably silted up. Sophie and her three friends withdrew to a stone slab at one end of the beach, under a cliff that provided some shade. When they had eaten, and decided they could do without second helpings, Tracy stood up and sipped her drink, gazing out at the sparkling waves. The rough sandstone of the cliff contrasted strikingly in colour and texture with the soft smoothness of her body. The girls were joined by Julie, who offered them more wine. She screwed up her eyes and looked at Tracy, whose face as usual was half masked by her coppery curls. The even more vivid hair at the base of her belly did rather less to hide the slit that was still slightly open after the fingering Sophie had given her up by the pool before lunch. Julie took a deep breath.

'Unbelievably fuckable,' she sighed. 'Could be fresh out of the convent. Maybe the nearest thing to undamaged goods you're likely to find on this island. Just look at those titties—what a little angel! Bet my boyfriend would love to give her one.'

Sophie wondered if the girl was a catholic. Fresh out of the convent? Was Julie thinking of nuns or schoolgirls? Predictably, Tracy blushed and giggled, turning away to hide her face against the cliff.

'And what a pretty bottom you've got, dear. Can just imagine your cute husband playing with it. Would have a go myself if I wasn't doing the rounds with the retsina.' Julie ran a hand lightly over the white cheeks and moved off to look after other groups of women on the beach.

Even after licking their own and each other's fingers, the friends still felt a bit sticky from all that chicken, sausage and lamb, so Poppy suggested a dip in the sea. Quite a few of the others were already splashing about and trying to duck each other, and their hysterical voices were getting louder and shriller. Wading out until the water was level with their waists except when a wave would lift their tits before dipping down to sex level, Sophie found herself grabbed from behind, and at first feared one of the Greek love boys had insinuated himself among the crowd of females. But it was only Poppy, who started nibbling her neck. The teenager reached round Sophie with both hands, took a breast in one and used the other to squeeze her pussy. A finger overcame the tightness caused by the salt water and stabbed into the hot vagina. As it wriggled around, stimulating a flood of juices, Poppy's thumb attacked the clitoris mercilessly. With her other hand she twisted a swollen nipple, and at the same time nipped the skin of her neck with sharp little teeth. Sophie squealed and came. The two of them collapsed into the cooling water.

Half an hour or so later nearly all the women were paddling, swimming or generally messing about in the sea. Suddenly there was a great roar from above the beach. Hordes of swarthy males swarmed out of the shadows, stampeded down across the sand and flung themselves into the waves. The major assault had begun, at 14.35 hours precisely.

Sophie's first reaction was to float on her back with her

legs parted in anticipation. But then she remembered poor Tracy. It seemed very important to preserve the kid's quasi-virgin status for her husband's pleasure. She had more or less promised, hadn't she? Abandoning her abandoned pose, she gathered the others around her and explained her strategy.

The attackers had swum out to sea and formed two groups, swooping inwards to trap their prey in a pincer movement. At the same time, another detachment of invaders charged down the hill and deployed themselves on the beach to cut off any attempted retreat to the woods. Things were looking dangerous.

Sophie, Cathy and Poppy clustered together hugging, with Tracy in the middle. They did their best to keep her youthful beauty concealed and protected. Sophie thought they must have looked something like the three graces trying to hide something. But the impression they created must have been much more exciting than any representation in white marble—their wet breasts with proud, crimson teats, their dripping locks, blonde, dark and, in Poppy's case, lighter blonde, Tracy's copper-coloured tresses being hardly visible. And whenever a trough between larger than usual waves exposed them, three lovely, shining bottoms completed the effect of an animated sculpture. All four bent their knees and ducked low in the water, making themselves as inconspicuous as possible.

They were surrounded. The four brutes who pawed and mauled at them were able to take their pick, and it was partly luck that protected Tracy's pussy from this first attack. Sophie, Cathy and Poppy confronted the guys with open arms, mouths and cunts, but their arses seemed to be the preferred mode of gratification for this lot. There was so much flailing about in the water that it was hard to make out exactly what was happening. All Sophie knew was that she was gagging on a mouthful of cockmeat forcing its way down her throat while a second intruder burrowed into her vagina. She could just make out that Tracy was getting it up the behind, thank God. Oh well . . . As for the other two, they were hidden in a turmoil of spray and hairy limbs.

When this lot were through, the girls rubbed seawater on their violated parts and tried to recover their breath before being forced to submit to the next assault. All around them were scenes of debauchery—few of the females seemed to be putting up much of a resistance. Some were getting fucked and gangbanged in the sea, but in other instances the Greeks would sling selected beauties over their shoulders and carry them to the beach or higher up among the olives to screw them.

Suddenly four guys who had been cruising under water like submarines broke the surface between the friends' legs and grabbed them round the waists, easily breaking up their protective huddle. They dragged their prey, protesting, up to the beach and threw them down on the damp sand. It now looked as if poor Tracy was bound to get it up her unused cunt.

Sophie saw that the immediate objective was to prevent a regular pairing off. She seized the ankles of two of the men and brought them down with sudden tugs. Her lips clamped on the bloated cock of one of them, and she was able to prise her fanny open and shove it at the gentials of the other one, who was into her in a jiffy.

Cathy and Poppy knew exactly what was required. Cathy got up on her hands and knees, presenting her bottom and the choice of two entrances. It was impossible for Sophie to make out which of these was being abused, but she herself was taking such a ramming from her two satyrs that she didn't give a toss.

The fourth assailant was familiar. Yes, he was the smooth-skinned young lad who had humped Poppy in that rather gentle way in the first action that morning. And Poppy was building on that encounter by flaunting her hairless, wet sex at him as she sprawled on her back. But the youth had taken a fancy to the 'unbelievably fuckable' Tracy. Still trying to distract him, Poppy knelt up with her knees on either side of Tracy's terrified face. She stroked her own tight nipples and pushed one into the boy's mouth. But this only heightened the fury of his lust for the squirming Tracy.

His tongue and lips slobbered their way down Poppy's front and, as he gripped her roughly by the hips, he began chewing and sucking at the puffy cuntflesh. At the same time, without letting up, he scooted back on his knees and advanced the head of his prick to the mouth of Tracy's reluctant channel. It was about to be flushed out for the first time with a discharge of male seed.

A shrill blast from Julie's whistle signalled the arrival of the launch. Everywhere fauns and satyrs were pulling out of their nymphs and heading off into the woods. The one Sophie was fellating whipped his meat out of her mouth. As he turned to make his escape, the pent-up sperm burst out of the purple plum and coated the otherwise unviolated Cathy. Sophie's vagina actually received a heavy load before her shagger popped out of her and loped off.

And as for Tracy, the faun's shiny helmet just made contact with her pouting sexlips as, at the blast of the whistle, it shot wads of thick cream all over her private parts and belly. The little triangle of red hair was soaked with so much spunk that it was almost invisible. 'Oh Jace,' she moaned deliriously. 'You done it again.'

Back in their room, Sophie and Cathy showered off the male spendings that had dried on their skin and in their hair, along with the itchy sand stuck to them. Then they relaxed and dozed on their beds.

It was not long before the men returned with their account of proceedings at the other end of the island. Peter did most of the talking, with Mark filling in the odd detail, mostly of a visual nature.

Jason and Tim had teamed up with Mark and Peter on the strength of their new acquaintance. On landing, Rosper had persuaded everyone to strip naked. Quite a few of the men had been inhibited about this—sporting minuscule thongs was one thing, but flaunting their mostly flaccid dicks and hairy ballsacks to their peers was a bit different. For an exhibitionist like young Tim this was no problem. His hairlessness attracted plenty of curiosity, although most of these guys, who had enjoyed the wedding show shamelessly from their darkened seats last night, pretended not to notice it. Jason, on the other hand, was always covering himself with a hand, or turning his back on anyone who got close to him—until he realised that he had admirers whose interest in his tight buttocks could not be concealed.

Under Rosper's direction, the order of play was not quite the same as that experienced by the girls. To get things going, all the men sat in a large circle in a grassy clearing. A ghetto blaster provided exotic music as a crowd of nymphs clad in wisps of gauzy muslin tripped out of the woods and entered the circle to perform a dance. Among them Mark had recognised the two temple maidens who had done the honours (or some of them) on stage the night before. These two seemed to be the most adept dancers, and the others took on supportive roles, cavorting around them or adopting more or less stationary poses, often in pairs or little groups with a lesbian orientation.

(At this point in Peter's narration, he paused to quote:

The isles of Greece, the isles of Greece,

Where burning Sappho loved and sung . . .)

Mark then took up the description, focusing on the lewd performance of the two principal dancers, who were soon naked apart from chaplets of flowers on their heads. These must have been secured with pins or something, as they stayed in place even when the girls turned somersaults or stood on their heads. While in this latter position they made vigorous cycling movements before letting their legs fall wide open, exposing gaping cunts. When this happened, little queues of nymphs formed beside them, and in rapid succession the girls stooped to stick their fingers and tongues into the pink gashes before hopping off and pirouetting around in the circle of spectators. Some of these were unable to stop themselves coming as they watched the action with hands on cocks.

The music fell silent and all the nymphs, including the temple maidens, sank down limply. Rosper stepped into the circle and addressed the crowd, explaining that this performance would be followed by a barbecue. 'And after that,' he said, 'you're all invited to be lovesick shepherds. It's going to be a nymph hunt. A cunt hunt. Chase these lovely young things and give them what they've been dreaming about all night. They're well up for it. We kept them away from their regular mates, who are seeing to your good ladies at the other end of the island.'

And so it happened. After half a dozen scantily draped nymphs had dished out their lunch, which was wolfed down impatiently—most of the guys were fairly well behaved under Giles Rosper's strict eye—, the party broke up and prowled off in all directions looking for sport, in particular for the splashes of white muslin among the foliage that would betray the presence of their prey.

Peter had notched up four conquests and Mark six, although they admitted that Peter had only achieved four orgasms and Mark three. With the remaining girls it had been a matter of flirting, smooching and feeling. One of them Mark had pleasured orally, then penetrated, but pulled out to save himself up for later. Some of the nymphs had played hard to get, running away and then deliberately stumbling to allow themselves to be taken. Others lingered under shady trees, sucking their thumbs and cocking their hips in invitation.

Cathy then told the guys what had happened at their end of the island. Her account was slightly edited, and Sophie added nothing to it. Still, this edited version was enough to get pricks stirring, but they all decided the sensible thing after those multiple performances would be to wait until later. So they slept.

After dinner they returned to their room to prepare for the bottomless ball. What would they wear? From the fancy dress cupboard Peter chose a black leather jacket with silver zips, along with a peaked cap. This outfit made him look wickedly gay, and he hoped no one would get the wrong idea. Mark opted for a plain green T-shirt.

There was such a choice of female attire that girls had possibly more scope for inventiveness. Cathy went for a little black waistcoat or bolero with silver embroidery. A silver chain linked the two sides of it at the top, below the neck, allowing the garment to hang open and expose the curves of her breasts and her belly all the way down to the dark triangle between her thightops. When she twirled around glimpses of her nipples could be seen. And of course, even when she was standing still her pubic fuzz and pretty bottom were on view. Sophie tried on a number of costumes, becoming increasingly frustrated, until Mark encouraged her to go for a simple gingham blouse in white and blue check. He showed her how effective this could be when she added a broad blue ribbon to tie back her ponytail, and white ankle socks with white sandals.

'Not just cute,' he observed. 'Positively indecent. She looks illegal, don't you think, Cathy?'

'I don't think you'd let me out on the street like that back in Fulham.'

'No, but I might get you to try something of the kind in our bedroom. And out in the garden.'

The banner over the door read 'WELCOME TO THE HONEYMOONERS BOTTOMLESS BALL', the lights were dim and the music issuing from the sound system was swoony and seductive. Before they could claim one of the tables around the edge of the floor, they were caught up in the swirl of dancers. Being packed fairly tightly together, these looked innocent enough at first. All the men had shirts or other tops of various kinds, and the most revealing female garments seemed to be bikini bras. Many of the women were far more modest, in polo-necked sweaters, high-buttoned shirts or the like.

But when the music paused and couples began to retreat to their tables, the scene changed. Sophie was immediately struck by the bare behinds of both sexes revealed by the coloured strobes—behinds mostly, rather than fronts, since their owners were withdrawing to the sides of the ballroom. Those of the women who just wore little bikini tops or something similar could almost have been nude. It was hard to decide which seemed more transgressive: these near-nudes or those of both sexes whose conventional or even fashionable upper wear contrasted so starkly with the bareness of their bottoms.

As they reached the edge of the floor, the foursome were beckoned over to a table occupied by Tracy, Jason, Poppy and Tim, who wanted them to join their party. The boys were in plain black vests, while their girls had retained the outfits they had worn on the boat. Tracy's appearance sitting at the table, though pretty enough, was tolerably modest—as well as that red and white striped T-shirt, she wore the *HMS LOLLIPOP* yachting cap at a rakish angle. And in this artificial light she had swept her hair back so that the whole of her freckled face was on display. Poppy's chest was more provocatively adorned with the two daisies adhering to her nipples.

Each table was laden with champagne flutes and three ice baskets with bottles of something sparkling though not necessarily very expensive. The four couples toasted each other, enjoying the scene around them. As her eyes became used to the strobing gloom, Sophie realised that the tables were arranged round the floor at wide intervals. Between them were couches draped in scarlet. Their intended use was fairly obvious.

It was hard to make conversation against the music, but Jason was unable to curb his enthusiasm. 'Them nymphos was awesome, right—know what I'm saying?' he began. 'One or two of em nearly got me to cheat on my Trace. Told em we was newlyweds, but they didn't speak English all that good.'

The music stopped and Rosper addressed his guests over the sound system. 'Good evening, friends. Hope you're not totally totalled after today's fun and games. You'll be needing a bit of bounce in your muscles to enjoy the dancing and whatever at this ball. More bubbly at the bar. Couches laid on to be laid on, but only one pair at a time, please. The covers on them are disposable in case you're anxious about that, ladies. Some of the activities may be filmed for training purposes, but you should take that as a compliment. Hey—enjoy!'

The volume of the dance music was turned up and couples started to get to their feet. This time men and women were facing in all directions, so it was not just their bottoms that were exposed. Sophie felt her juices beginning to run at the sight of all these young wives dressed more or less respectably down to their waist or thereabouts but with smooth white bellies and thighs and the well-furred or shaven love nests on lewd display. One or two of them seemed to be looking at her with disapproval—her girlish top, the ribbon in her hair and the little ankle socks could have been too much for them, she supposed. The outfit was certainly having a devastating effect on the men. Sophie gasped at the sight of a sophisticated-looking woman dressed (up to a point) in pale blue. She was wearing a feathered hat, elbow-length gloves, a satin basque with slender suspender straps holding up sheer stockings, all of the same delicate colour. In the centre point of the whiteness between her basque and stocking tops a dark, wonderfully luxuriant bush flaunted its invitation. As for the husbands of these women, their position, Sophie reckoned, had to be more embarrassing, as there was no hiding the fact that they were either drooping limp amid all this temptation or ramping into horizontal or near-vertical erection.

As she stepped on to the floor, she felt hands patting and fondling her buttocks. Why not? She let her own palms glide over all the passing bottoms of both sexes within easy reach. Because they had just left their table, this meant that with a little manoeuvring she soon had her hands on Poppy and Tracy, while she was aware that the cleft of her own arse was being tickled by Cathy, who was running a sly finger down it. Rather like when they had formed that three-grace-like grouping (or groping, she thought) with Tracy in the middle on the beach, her friends gathered tightly round Sophie, hugging her and titillating each other's intimate places. The upper garments combined with partial nudity proved quite a turn-on, and she had almost forgotten the ostensible purpose of the ball—to fuck and get fucked by their menfolk. She ran a hand up over the satin back of Cathy's little waistcoat, then over a shoulder and down to the breast which she uncovered by peeling back that side of the top. She squeezed it, provoking the intrusion of her friend's finger into her back passage. Turning her attention to Tracy, she stroked the back of her soft, striped T-shirt, moving firmly from the girl's shoulder blades down to the hem, which she lifted so that her fingertips could play over the delicious cheeks she had caressed so tenderly earlier in the day. Sophie was tempted to imitate Cathy's assault on her own anus, but instead bent her knees sufficiently to allow her stroking hand, now turned edgeways with the thumb up, to sneak between the teenager's thighs. The thumb penetrated Tracy's vagina with ease. With a half-turn of the wrist she brought three fingers into action all over the lightly fuzzed lips, the plump little mound and the swelling bud of her clitoris. While all this was happening, the near-naked Poppy was getting herself off by working her smooth, moist cunt up and down Sophie's left thigh.

Suddenly their little huddle was surrounded by Peter, Mark, Jason and Tim, who prised them apart. And now the girls found themselves in the arms, not of their husbands or pretend-husbands but, in Sophie's case, of Tim. She was drawn into a loose clinch as the lad swayed against her. The looseness allowed her to reach down between them and feel the lovely smoothness of his pubis and scrotum as his prick filled out and mounted to flounder about against her tummy. A tongue snaked into her open mouth and a finger invaded the outer reaches of her quim. Some lark, this! What a long way she had come since poor little Sofe had been the sixth-form wallflower, since bookish Sophie Rogers had never been up for much time for socialising at uni, and even since buttoned-up, efficient Miss Rogers had kept things running smoothly in Peter's office. She felt so sexy now in her semi-nudity, and had done ever since she stepped into the ballroom. The way all eyes dropped from her pretty face to her exposed parts, the way casual hands brushed 'accidentally' against her buttocks or tempting bush . . .

The music paused and Tim's place was taken by Mark, the hairiness of whose limbs and sex made an almost brutal contrast with the smoothness of the suitor he had displaced. When the dancing resumed, Mark twirled her round, hoisted her over his shoulder as if he had been one of the predators on the beach, and caressing her exposed bottom carried her across the floor to one of the couches. This one turned out to be already occupied by a rutting couple, as did the next three or four they passed. Sophie found the spectacle arousing. Because of the dress code on this occasion, it was like coming across bosses furtively fucking their secretaries at an office party, or something of the sort—the experience was not unfamiliar to Sophie, who had sometimes both seen and been seen at the little parties Peter gave for his staff.

At last Mark found a couch just being vacated by none other than Jason and Tracy. The youth looked glum as he rose from between his 'unbelievably fuckable' wife's slim thighs. She grinned sheepishly. Her striped T-shirt was up almost to her little tits. Semen had pooled on and around her ginger pussy and was dripping down to form a spreading puddle on the sheet as Jason helped her to get up. But, far from feeling disgust, Sophie flushed with excitement when Mark lowered her bottom into the warm spunk and began to fuck her silly.

On returning to their room, the four exhausted honeymooners fell into a profound sleep.

Friday

A fully dressed Julie brought in their breakfast and explained that if the boys wanted to go scuba diving they would have to be down at the jetty in twenty minutes. 'Some beautiful coral out there,' she declared. 'Oh, and you might get to see some of the nymphs that entertained you yesterday. I love the way their hair waves about in the water. Even when it's really short and curly. By the way, talking of entertainment reminds me that there's something special laid on for your last night. Mr Rosper wants to throw an intimate party, just for you and a few other favourites of his.'

Sophie couldn't help blurting out: 'What about . . .'

'Hold on, Sophie,' Peter interrupted. 'We're the guests here. It's up to our hosts to invite whoever they like.'

Julie reassured her that the four young people they had befriended would also be there, as well as another three hand-picked couples. She advised them to take things fairly gently for the rest of the day. It could be a demanding evening. They were to select suitable costumes from the fancy dress cupboard in their room.

When she had left, her advice about taking things easy was followed until the lads had set off for the jetty. Cathy then moved languidly into Sophie's bed, and for a while they simply lay in each other's arms, drifting in and out of slumber. When Sophie moved a hand down to free a few strands of pubic hair gummed to her labia by sperm that had seeped out in the night and dried, her friend mistook this action for an invitation to play. But they were both still a bit tired. With a finger in each other's cunts they enjoyed another little nap.

They both felt refreshed after this, and began to chat. Sophie wanted to know about Cathy's first honeymoon, the one with her real husband, Mark.

'You know what my Mark's like,' Cathy began. 'He got me to go with him on a photography course on, what's the island near Ibiza—oh yes, Formentera. No traffic, loads of lovely, deserted beaches and some great accommodation for us. He paid extra for that. And there was a studio in a converted windmill, though a lot of the photography was out in the open and in our own room. What I hadn't bargained for, though, was that this was all about *erotic* photography. With proper old-fashioned film. And that I was going to be his model.

'Every morning he'd go off for instruction up in the windmill while I lazed about or wandered down to the beach. When he got back he would work his way through a list of poses he'd worked out on the basis of the kit we'd brought with us. I can remember most of them. He took a whole roll of film of me in my white baby-doll nightie, pretending to be coy. Then we had some outside ones that I thought were going to be quite innocent: I was in a small, blue top, just a kind of vest, with little white shorts. But he got what he wanted by making me slip the strap off one of my shoulders and pull the top down to show off a boob. And then, of course, the shorts had to come down. Halfway down my thighs, in fact. The next set was the same, except that instead of the shorts I was wearing white knickers. I had to yank them up behind to show off my bumcheeks, and then turn round to pull the front down just far enough to uncover my pussy bit by bit. He enjoys colour contrasts, and did a series on our balcony with me in a cute white top and blue silk panties. This time the front of the top was opened little by little till it was pulled right back. He licked his finger and got my nipples to stand up to full stretch, taking shots to show every stage of them growing. The top came off and I posed in the panties. Next I was wearing that blue vest again, but nothing else. I remembered that one last night at the bottomless ball. What else? Oh yes, face down on the bed in a black G-string. I took that off and he got me to stand in the doorway to the balcony so that he could get shots of me nude from outside—I had to make as if I was inviting someone in. Like a whore. Down at the end of our nearest beach we found a spot where a rocky headland ran down into the water. I had a large, transparent chiffon scarf or shawl thing, patterned in mauve, white and blue. Mark posed me in all sorts of ways, in the sea and on the rocks, completely draped in the scarf, showing off various bits he thought would be attractive for the guys who did the processing up in the windmill and finally, with me holding it up behind with my arms stretched out level with my ears, using it as a lovely background. I looked like an unwrapped present, Sophie. He still loves those pictures. Always wanking over them.'

'Doesn't that ruin them?'

'He always calls for me so I can finish him in my mouth if I'm not ready for him in my cunt.

'Still, this wasn't just a fashion shoot, was it? It was supposed to be a honeymoon, so we made sure that each of these sessions ended with him fucking me till we were worn out. If we had any energy left we went exploring on the bikes we had hired, and kept finding other couples from the course doing the same sort of stuff. What about you, dear?'

Sophie was dreaming, imagining how it would have been if she had been Mark's model. Still, her own honeymoon had been a wonderful introduction to married sex. In fact, her previous experience had been so limited and unsatisfactory that the honeymoon had almost been an introduction to sex full stop. Her memories of it came flooding back, and she poured them out to her eager listener. As she began, she slipped a second finger into Cathy's love hole.

Peter had hired a narrow boat on one of the canals. The weather had been sizzling, so it was great to have the option of lying in the shady interior of their boat or taking dips in the canal. Most of the time, though, they were either just idling along with the throbbing engine pushing them lazily forward, or working up a sweat in the bursts of activity involved with negotiating each lock. Peter's habitual dress on board was a pair of tight white shorts, and Sophie's a skimpy purple bikini.

She would sit on the little platform at the front of the vessel reading and showing herself off to guys on the towpath and passing boats, while her husband stood at the other end—the stern, he insisted—controlling the tiller to steer a straightish course. 'Youth on the prow and Pleasure at the helm,' he kept shouting, to impress passing crews, quoting the title of a painting by another of his favourite Victorians. Sophie was embarrassed.

When the sun was not too dangerous, Sophie liked to stretch out on the flat roof. Lying on her tummy, she undid her bikini top and eased the bottoms down to just below the beginning of her cleft. When this presentation provoked whistles from strangers, she would rise up on her elbows, pretending to have forgotten that her breasts were bare, before hurriedly dipping down and refastening the top. Peter encouraged and loved to watch this behaviour.

When they came to a lock she would have to jump ashore and work the gates. Because she was so alluring in her bikini there were always guys around eager to help her with the donkey work. Peter enjoyed easing the slender craft into the narrow locks with their slimy walls, which he said was like sliding his cock into a well-lubricated cunt. And the rushing of the water through the sluices reminded him of orgasms . . .

But in the hottest part of the day he got her to go down into the cabin and lie naked on their bed right up at the stern. By leaning slightly to the right as he steered, he could see her lying there, her legs apart and her sex fully visible. He watched as she fluffed up her hairs and masturbated for him. Although Peter was unable to leave the tiller, Sophie still had to relieve the painful erections she induced in him, and she did this by crawling up to where he stood, pulling down the front of his shorts, and hoping that no one spotted her as she sucked him off.

'Well,' she said after a pause, 'maybe I didn't care too much if they did see me, and I'm pretty sure some of them did. By this time I was getting a bit more confident.'

'Or brazen,' said Cathy.

'Brazen, yes. I loved it, though, when we tied up for the night and stripped off down there in that long cabin—these boats are twice as long as a bus, you know. We would cook and eat in the nude, and romp about on that bed till Pete was drained. What a honeymoon!

'We used to moor at canal-side pubs for lunch. At one of these we picked up—well, Peter picked up—a pair of American girls. Backpackers they were, identical twins, Marylou and Sissie. Said they'd just graduated high school. I didn't make a fuss about it because they didn't want to go all that far and offered to do the hard work getting through the locks.

'If Peter had been hoping to screw them, he was disappointed. Guess what? They were into each other, big time. But they said they'd no objection to both of us getting off from watching them at it.'

'Well, they could hardly afford to object if they wanted the ride, could they?'

'I suppose not. Anyway, when they told us this we felt a bit embarrassed and weren't quite sure whether to believe it. We didn't react, really. Pete was careful not to touch them too much when he was teaching them how to work the lock gates and use those crank handles to raise and lower the things that let the water through. Paddles, they're called. Sissie and Marylou were fast learners, and pretty strong, which you need to be to push those huge lock gates open and shut. Worked up quite a sweat. The backs of their checked flannel shirts got soaked. And the fronts. Their short, mousey hair was sticking to their foreheads. Their thick woollen socks had fallen down round their ankles, and I don't know how they managed to survive in those heavy hiking boots and knee-length khaki shorts.

'Anyway, as we got to the seventh lock they were managing by themselves. We were gobsmacked to see them strip everything off, right down to little, pale green thongs. Pete stopped the boat in front of the gates, and they jumped off regardless. I got off too, not to help this time but to watch. And I wasn't the only audience: there were lots of walkers and cyclists on the towpath, and another boat was waiting on the far side of the lock.

'I was afraid someone would call the cops, but they all seemed to be keen on watching the show, even the middle-aged couples. When Marylou worked away at the crank handle to let the water gush through from the higher part of the canal where our boat was waiting, her biggish tits bounced up and down with sweat dripping down between them and her bumcheeks tensed and untensed rhythmically. And when Sissie leaned back against one of the massive gates to push against the weight of the water, it was not just her nipples thrusting up that caught your attention, but the green bulge between her straining thighs. There was polite applause when she got the gate to move. She shifted round to the other side of it to push it all the way open, and this time her white bottom was on full display. A volley of wolf whistles replaced the polite applause.

'This was the last lock we had to go through that day. We tied up. Pete opened a bottle of wine and I made a simple pasta dish for the four of us. The Americans slipped out of their thongs, which they said were too damp to sit in. To even things out we undressed too.

'When it got dark we put some cushions on the floor up at the dining end, so that one of the girls could sleep down there while her twin used the comfortably upholstered bench that ran along the side of the boat. Me and Pete could be fairly private up at the other end on our big bed, which was hidden from our guests by the well-equipped bathroom and what Peter called the galley. We decided to put off fucking until everything was quiet, and meanwhile tried to fall asleep.

'Peter had been snoring for some time and I had just dozed off when there was an almighty rumpus up at the other end of the boat. The dining area light was on. We found the twins fighting fiercely over who could sleep on the bench. This was the first time I'd seen naked girls wrestling, and it was awesome, as Tracy would say. They were rolling around with their limbs locked together. Sissy had grabbed a great hank of Marylou's hair and Marylou was twisting one of Sissy's nipples really hard. I thought someone was going to get hurt quite badly—they were both squealing and shrieking like fighting dogs.

'Well, we pulled them apart and took them into our own bed. Plenty of room for four. Marylou stretched out on her back to our left, and Sissie immediately got on top of her in a sixty-nine position. After a couple of licks at each other's slits, they shifted so that each of them had a hard nipple nuzzling against her sister's clit. Peter was certainly getting it on watching this performance. He made me get up on all fours beside the twins so that he could see and slobber over the action when he rammed his swollen tool up my cunt and started to fuck. And I must say, the sight was exciting for me, too. Those teats got bigger and bigger, and so did the clits they were—what?—frigging? Kissing?

'Me and Pete came at least three times before we collapsed and fell asleep, but the girls kept on and on. When we woke up late the next morning there was no sign of them. No note or anything. Just the two green thongs, stained and smelling of girl sex. I've still got them, and like to wear them sometimes.

'The rest of the trip, when we weren't doing the locks, was one long, leisurely fuck. So that's my first honeymoon for you.'

Having fetched each other off with fingers and tongues, the girls felt more than ready to take cock. They decided to give their men a little treat on their return from the scuba diving ('muff diving more likely', as Cathy put it). Sophie remembered that Mark had expressed a wish to see her wearing the duplicate of Poppy's wedding outfit he had discovered in one of their cupboards. This was easily found. At Cathy's suggestion, Sophie agreed to leave the bra off, but otherwise got herself up to look pretty much like the other night's bride: headdress and veil, elbow-length fingerless gloves of white satin, white stockings, the silver chain round her waist and the little lacy thong. Unlike Poppy, of course, she boasted an attractive blonde bush. This could be made out through the gossamer-like fabric, and stray hairs peeped out round the edges.

Cathy picked out something more revealing though not really more provocative. A wreath of peach-coloured artificial blossoms adorned her head, with a pair of ribbons of the same colour hanging down behind. Her mittens were of white lace, but only reached halfway up her forearms. Sheer white stockings were held up by a white satin suspender belt; her bottom and sexmound were bare. The two friends admired each other, admired their own reflections, and sighed.

They had hardly completed this toilette when Mark and Peter returned. Mark's first reaction was to grab his camera and get the two 'brides' to pose together. But Peter had no time for this fooling about. He pushed Cathy back on the bed, plunged his tongue into her slit while mauling her breasts, and then rose up to throw himself on her. She tugged at the zip of his jeans and pulled out a stiffening prick, which she guided straight into her love channel.

Mark, who had captured this action with his digital camera, slipped out of his own clothes and approached Sophie. Even as he did so, he kept glancing over at the arousing sight of his real wife getting fucked by his best friend. Sophie was aware that this had been a huge turn-on in those early days at school she had heard about and which they had re-enacted a few nights back. She didn't really care who or what was causing the monstrous erection that wagged above his swinging balls—all she wanted was to feel it filling her.

In a jiffy he was on her. He tugged her thong to one side, snapping an elastic leg band in the process. Sophie was already so wet and loose from her lovemaking with Cathy that nothing impeded his smooth entry. Smooth, but brutal in the power he brought to bear on her cunt. As he got into his stride, he buried his face in the crushed veil that fanned out from her headress on one side. At the same time he caressed one of her forearms through the satin glove and made a big thing of rasping his hairy thighs against her stockings.

Sophie felt ecstatic; though a little sad to think their honeymoon was in its last day. She lay there, a fragile-looking bride, as her temporary husband performed his conjugal duty by drilling away at her with his massive tool. Suddenly she tensed in all her muscles and shrieked out her lust. At the same moment Mark poured streams of hot sperm into her spasming cunt.

As soon as he had recovered his breath and pulled wetly out of her, he reached for the remote control and clicked to make the mirror transparent. 'Let's see if those two kids are there and what they're up to,' he suggested. Cathy and Peter, who had completed their frantic fuck just before the others, were keen. All four sat on the stools ranged along the length of the mirror with its distracting holograms. Cathy and Sophie used towels to protect the seats from the spunk dripping out of them.

There on the bed in front of them sprawled Jason and Tracy, propped up against their pillows. The boy was nude, but Tracy was wearing an elasticated yellow boob tube. It was hard to tell if this clashed with the red of the hair on her head and pubis or set it off rather piquantly. The only contact between the youngsters took the form of Jason's right leg being casually thrown over Tracy's left thigh, and their right feet playing with each other. The real business, Sophie realised, was that they were masturbating themselves with some eagerness.

After a while, Tracy appeared to be saying something. Mark clicked the audio button, and the end of what she said could be heard. '. . . Each other, innit. That Sophie said she was going to try and help us, know what I'm saying? No sign of it yet.'

Without replying the boy took his hand from his cock and reached across to place it on his 'unbelievably fuckable' but hitherto unfucked bride's cunt. Her own hand wrapped itself around the well-primed prick and began to jack it up and down. Jason's groans could now be heard, loud and clear. He used the tip of a finger to tickle the top of Tracy's slit in a way Sophie found surprisingly sensitive until his whole body stiffened and he dug the finger in with so much force that it skidded down the trench of the sex and stabbed into the vagina. Tracy yelped and came, just as Jason's upright cock fountained over her hand and his own stomach.

As the day wore on all the honeymooners on the island became more and more concerned about making the most of their remaining time, Sophie found herself hugging, kissing and petting almost everyone she encountered, most of whom she recognised only vaguely. But her mind was not really on these men and women, attractive though they were. She was thinking about the party.

They had been asked to find 'suitable' costumes for the

occasion. The dressing-up cupboard in their room contained more than enough to choose from. Sophie went for a simple but striking purple bikini in shiny lycra, its halter top comprising two triangles hardly more generous in their coverage than Poppy's shocking pink one, while Cathy opted for nothing more than a black G-string. As for the guys, Mark's choice was the same as Cathy's—he said he wanted his hairy chest to be on full view. Peter got himself up more modestly in a maroon vest and little white shorts.

At the appointed hour the four presented themselves at Rosper's penthouse suite. They were received by Julie, who immediately supplied them with canapés and champagne. In spite of her role, she was not dressed in her waitress gear. Her hair was adorned with a tiara of pearls. She wore a long, black, velvet dress. It was backless, but its most striking feature was that it left both her breasts bare—a narrow rope of pearls around her neck held up the centre of the top part almost as high as her throat, but the velvet curved down on either side to expose the gleaming white globes with their perky teats. When Julie moved, Sophie noticed that the long skirt of the dress was slit up both sides as high as the hips. An elegant leg came into view, sheathed in a sheer black hold-up stocking, which drew attention to the whiteness of the upper thigh and flank. The curtains of the room were drawn, but outside the sun was low over the western horizon, and a golden beam slanting through a gap momentarily illuminated this flesh as well as the exhibited breasts.

The newcomers circulated, at first as couples but soon breaking away from their partners to get acquainted with the other guests or to renew their acquaintance with the four they already counted their intimate friends. Soft background music encouraged a certain amount of dancing, but mostly people just smooched around or chatted, much as they would at any party at home.

Sophie sized the others up as she circulated, glass in hand. Because of her eye-catching bikini, she had the feeling that she was being thoroughly sized up herself, especially by the guys who hadn't met her yet. And she wasn't only being *sized* up—casual hands kept making contact with the skin of her belly, thighs and bottom, and the lycra covering her boobs and cuntmound.

Poppy was immediately noticeable. She had chosen a school uniform identical to the one Cathy had worn when they played that game in their room—beret, blazer, striped tie, tiny skirt and knee-high white socks with white trainers. Being young and slim, the girl looked extremely convincing in this role. Another sure winner was Tracy, whose slight but fuckable figure was displayed in one of the ever-popular bridal outfits first seen on the stage the other night. She had done the same as Sophie earlier that day, omitting the bra from the costume. The little ginger triangle of hair could just be made out through the diaphanous thong. As for their husbands, Jason wore a pair of shiny yellow bathing trunks while Tim, bold as always, had turned up completely nude, his hairless body attracting strange looks from everyone to whom this was a novelty.

The others were a mixed bunch. A guy in black biking leathers topped up Sophie's glass, introducing himself as Seb. He seemed a bit rough, she thought, and she was glad when he was drawn away by his wife, whom he called Karen. Karen was a classy Scandinavian type. All she wore was a pair of pink satin hotpants. Her medium-sized, firm mammaries looked irresistible. Sophie felt easier doing a little dance with a dark-haired younger lad named Roger, who seemed to have disregarded the dress-code for the party by turning up in jeans and a roll-necked green sweater that looked a bit warm for the occasion. He said his young bride was Linda, a pretty girl in a black microskirt and a high-necked broderie anglaise blouse, white with pink trimmings.

More unconventional and party-like was a tallish girl in a pale green harem outfit embroidered with motifs in gold thread. This outfit consisted of flimsy, low-slung, loose-fitting trousers of semi-transparent muslin, showing off the shapely legs of a ballerina, and a sleeveless top of the same material. This top was a little waistcoat reaching to just above her belly-button, the two sides linked by a couple of gold chains that stopped it from falling right open to expose her nipples. The shape and size of these, however, could be seen where the flimsy top was stretched over their stiffness. As for her pussy, that appeared to be confined in a dark green thong. When she twirled round on her upcurling green and gold slippers, the lovely curves of her bottom shimmered through the gauzy fabric. Speaking through the little veil attached below her eyes to hide, rather ineffectively, her nose and mouth, she told Sophie her name was Sloan, and said she 'belonged' to a youth called Clinton (though Sophie suspected this was an attempt to make a monosyllabic 'Clint' sound a bit more sophisticated). Clinton looked somewhat unappealing with a shaven head, unshaven chin and jowls and a knee-length blue silk dressing gown that stressed the hairiness of his legs.

Having made her rounds, Sophie returned to Mark and had just started to dance with him when the music stopped and their host, Giles Rosper, stepped forward to speak. To Sophie's taste he was definitely unappealing in a pin-striped waistcoat (his only upper garment) and three-quarter length tartan shorts. His thin goatee did nothing to improve his appearance. She cringed as she remembered her encounter with him in the sauna.

'Welcome, boys and girls,' he began. 'You know what kind of party this is going to be, don't you? It's an intimate party. An adult party—though there's no lower age limit, and I don't have any issues with the little redhead there—Tracy, is it?—even if she does look a bit young to be a bride. Well, just to start things off and get you all in the mood, me and my girlfriend want to give you a swift showfuck. Draw up chairs to make a semicircle for us to perform in.'

Girlfriend?

Sophie was not all that surprised when Rosper beckoned Julie over from the side of the room to join him in the little arena. So what they were about to witness, presumably, was the kind of thing Julie had been holding herself back for whenever Mark or Peter had tried to get off with her on her morning visits to their room.

Rosper kissed Julie fiercely, pinching her exposed nipples before turning her so that her back was towards the audience and he was standing facing her. He drew aside the skirt of her dress to reveal a beautiful, knickerless bottom, which he now stroked and gently slapped while she continued to kiss him. With gentle pushes he edged her back until her stockinged legs were almost touching the knees of the seated spectators.

'Have a good feel, everyone,' Rosper hissed. 'Be my guests.'

Hands, both male and female, reached out from both sides. By leaning across or kneeling on the floor everybody was able to reach the white buttocks, which they petted and mauled. Sophie was tempted to slip a finger into the dark cleft, but Clinton got there first with a jabbing, hairy hand. She contented herself with running the tips of her fingers up the back of one of the stockings, pinching the firm muscles and moving up across the welt to fondle the creamy flesh of Julie's upper thigh.

Rosper pulled his girlfriend back, away from her admirers. The back flap of her skirt dropped as he released her and stepped out of his silly shorts. His scarlet-headed tool was released, curving up like a scimitar. Spinning Julie round to face the audience as he stood behind her, he now raised the front panel of her dress. She took the hem from him, being careful to fold the panel so that her bosom was not concealed. When his hands went to her breasts, he too avoided completely covering them from view. Her head flopped back to rest on his shoulder, and he winked at the spectators before dropping those bony hands to her sex. She gasped.

The fingers of both hands scrabbled about in her pretty bush, parting the hairs. They dragged aside the plump lips to show off the pink petals of moistening girlflesh. Most of the men applauded or whistled, but Sophie was just a bit embarrassed. Then, winking again, Rosper spoke. As he did so, he walked his girlfriend forward in little steps until she was as close to the semicircle of chairs as she had been when her bottom was on offer.

'Contents of this juicy package reserved for me, mind. But the outside's fair game if anyone's interested. And I call the game clickety clit. Just the tips of your tongues, folks. Everyone gets to have a go. She likes to come like that—just loves it.'

He moved the young woman slowly along the line of seated

guests, each of whom seemed very willing to indulge her. When it came to Sophie's turn, Julie's cunt was already drooling, and the tangy freshness of the juices showed that they were not just saliva. Previous lickers had opened the inner labia to their widest extent as Rosper held the outer ones back. And the hood of the clitoris had retracted itself so that the sexbud stood out, proud and glistening. Sophie tickled the tip with her tongue, closing her lips over the small but eager protuberance. Julie squealed, and Rosper moved her along to the next person, who happened to be the naked and erect Tim.

Suddenly Rosper dragged her away from her admirers and pushed her down on the thick carpet, sideways-on to the viewers. He made sure the front of her skirt was well out of the way, eased her legs apart and knelt between them. Keeping an upright posture, he hefted her bottom up off the floor and drove his tool straight into her. She winced. He began to fuck. Her expression changed and a pink flush spread from her cheeks down over her bosom and, after moving unseen down the few inches of her dress, to her bare belly.

Rosper's head went back so that his beard pointed up and his eyes rolled in their sockets. He drew his dick out, gleaming with sexual fluids and seemingly twice as thick as when it had penetrated his partner. Mark nudged Sophie.

'Now we're going to get what they call the money shot,' he whispered.

'What's that?'

Before Mark could reply, their host leaned forward over Julie, supporting his weight on one hand while grasping his cock in the other one. A torrent of spunk gushed from the inflamed tip, pulsing all over the girl's abdomen and pubis. He collapsed on top of her, and Sophie was able to make out rivulets of the sticky goo trickling down Julie's side as it escaped from between the squashed-together bellies.

While the couple recovered from their 'showfuck', the honeymooners, rather quiet and subdued, moved about the room again and refreshed themselves at the buffet-cum-bar. The only penis on display, Tim's, stood out rigid and horizontal.

Soon Rosper was back in action, but with his shorts on again. All Julie had to do to recover a semblance of decency was to stand up. The dress now covered the site of her violation, although her breasts, of course, remained delightfully bare, their nipples apparently in a state of permanent arousal.

Rosper clapped his hands and spoke. 'Another game now, my friends. Form a circle round that laundry basket. Boy, girl, boy, girl. That's it. Boys stand still, but when the music plays I want the girls to weave around them in a clockwise direction. Take the boys' hands to help you find your way: your right hand takes his right hand, then your left takes the next lad's left one. Walk it now to make sure you've got the idea. Good. When Miss Maddingley stops the music, you stay where you are. Got it?'

Miss Maddingley?

Well, obviously, thought Sophie. It was Julie who stood by the CD player and set the music going. But did Julie have any connection with the erotic novelist of that name whose books were to be found in the hotel rooms?

Things went fairly smoothly. The men stood dumbly holding out a right hand, then a left one, as the girls threaded their way in and out in their clockwise progress. Sophie was reminded of the country dancing they used to do in junior school, especially as she recognised her favourite melody of those days, a repetitive, jolly tune called Dargason. Judging from the way the guys squeezed her hand and wobbled about as she passed, Sophie's little bikini seemed to be a big hit. When the music stopped, she found herself face to face with Jason. On the whole, she was glad to be with one of their own little group. Rosper spoke again.

'Down on your knees, ladies. All I want you to do now is strip off your partner's shoes, pants, and anything he's wearing below the waist. Chuck the things in the basket. When you've done that you can kneel there and enjoy the sight until the music starts again, but no touching, right? Then it'll be the boys' turn.'

Sophie glanced up at the fair-haired Jason, whom she caught gawping down the cleavage of her purple, halter-top bikini. She ran her hands lightly over the back of his yellow swimming trunks. The boy flinched. Next she let her cheek rest against the bulge in the front of the trunks, where the shape of his softish cock could be seen (and now felt) resting on the warm ballsack. Her hands slid up a little, into the soft fuzz on the small of his back. Hooking her fingers into the waistband, she now eased the garment down little by little, until she had uncovered the top half of his buttocks. As she did this, she felt a sudden jolt against her cheek as lustful blood began to pump into Jason's prick.

Trapped in the trunks, the hardened member must have been pretty uncomfortable, so Sophie grabbed the front of the waistband and eased it down. Because the elastic was tight, she was unable to pull it forward enough to release the prisoner. Above the yellow fabric the small cluster of slightly darker yellow curls decorated the base of Jason's belly, contrasting nicely with the light tan of his skin. The danger, of course,

was that he would shoot off prematurely—Sophie needed to hurry. Rosper had said touching was forbidden, but perhaps this didn't count. She saw no alternative. Dipping a hand into the trunks she took the penis between her fingers. With the other hand she tugged the waistband out as far as it would go and let the prick spring up against the lad's belly. It was now an easy task to slip the yellow garment down to his ankles so that he could step out of it.

Rosper clapped his hands. All the women stood up. It was now the turn of the males to dance in and out of the circle, this time anti-clockwise. Dance? Actually they lumbered, and their progress kept being held up when one of them was reluctant to move on from the girl whose hand he was holding. When the music stopped, Sophie found the appalling Clinton dropping to his knees in front of her. She looked up to avoid the sight of his shaven head as he undid the bows securing the sides of her bikini and dragged it rather roughly out from between her legs. Luckily it had become too slippery with her exudations to cause any real discomfort as it was dragged through the folds of her labia—in fact, the sensation was pleasurable. But she was glad that their host once more clapped his hands for the men to stand up before Clinton was able to do more than snatch a glance and a quick sniff at her blonde pussy.

Rosper explained what was to happen next. 'One more round, please. This time girls and boys must both dance. Try not to make it too chaotic. When the music stops, I'll ask Miss Maddingley to do the honours. She has a nice touch when it gets a bit more intimate.'

The music started, but stopped after just a few bars. Sophie's partner was now the completely nude Tim. Julie entered the circle and spoke in silky, seductive tones: 'The next bit's to get you completely ready and in the mood for the real game. Grab your partners and hug them tight. That's it. Now, while the music's playing this time, I want you to feel each other up and try to get yourselves and each other as turned on as you can. Ready for instant penetrative sex, but be sure you hold yourselves back from climax.'

Sophie reckoned she understood *penetrative* as well as the next girl, but what was meant by *instant* in this context? She noticed that Tracy was looking pretty miserable.

The CD player resumed its pulsing beat, pumping out the recurring rhythms of that infuriating Dargason, and she was very conscious of the rapacity of Tim's exploring fingers over her bottom and between her legs. In response, she cupped his balls and rolled them gently in her palm. With the fingers of her other hand she squeezed his glans through the foreskin. Her engorged nipples bored into the fabric of her bikini top. The boy's tongue shot into her mouth, but she pulled her head back to take in the scene around her.

Just to her side stood the tall girl—Sloan, was it?—in the little pale green bodice of her harem outfit. Her tightly packaged breasts seemed to be straining against the two delicate chains that kept the two sides from opening completely. Her yashmak had vanished, and her mouth was sagging open, the pink tongue peeping out lasciviously between orange-painted lips. Her bottom and long legs were bare. The luck of the draw had thrown her together with Roger, who was swaying against her. His chunky sweater, a darker green than his partner's top, reached to just below the undercurves of his buttocks, but Sloan had hitched it up. With one hand she stroked and patted his bottom and with the other Sophie reckoned she must have been playing with his prick. Roger leaned to his right as Sloan worked him. This allowed him to reach round the young woman's left buttock and upper thigh and thrust a scrabbling hand into the dark dampness between her legs.

Sophie groaned as a long finger entered her. Tim's cockhead had swollen up so much that she was afraid it was about to explode, so she moved her fingers from it to wander over the smoothness of his hairless parts. Over to her left her eye caught Jason and the Scandinavian-looking Karen. As they had both been topless before their lower garments were removed, they now stood side by side in total, dazzling nudity, smiling at her. Jason turned to Karen and clasped her to him, ravenously plundering her mouth. She raised herself up on the toes of her right foot and, with Jason's help, lifted her left leg so that it rested on his right hip. His stiff prick stuck out beneath her trembling bottom. Was it about to squirt?

Cathy, too, had made the mistake (if you could call it that) of coming to the party topless, so she contrasted sharply with Karen's husband, Seb, who had retained his black leather biker's jacket. As he mauled Cathy's breasts and fingered her belly, the shiny leather and the black hairs on his hands, legs and lower body looked like a real menace to her white innocence. Innocence? But more menacing than the general effect was the huge, scarlet-knobbed phallus around which the poor girl could hardly close her fingers.

The pattern of nudity was reversed in the next couple to catch Sophie's attention: Roger's pretty little bride Linda was still wearing her high-necked broderie anglaise blouse, and her private parts were being fondled by none other than Mark, stark naked. As Sophie watched, he stooped and thrust his hips forward to brush the head of his rampant cock against the pink moistness Linda held open for his attentions.

Unfortunately, Sophie's view of Mark and Linda was now obscured by the muscular and well-endowed Clinton, whose silk dressing gown hung open to show off a massive erection. As he swaggered across the floor, he dragged with him Poppy, tugging on her school tie. Her maroon beret had been knocked sideways. Clinton forced her to her knees and made her suck his cock to even fuller hugeness while he doubled forward to delve between the cheeks of her upturned bottom and down into the lewdly displayed fruit of her sex.

Where was that unbelievably fuckable young bride, Sophie wondered. She pushed Tim over to the side. He seemed to take this manoeuvre as just a sign that she needed a bit more action, as indeed she did—she was dying to have her cunt crammed full of cockflesh—and jabbed another finger into her, at the same time stiffening his tongue and worming it under the triangle of purple lycra that covered her left tit. The lowering of his head made it easier for Sophie to see what she was looking for. Wow! The lovely auburn-haired Tracy—this literally blushing bride—was being squired, as Sophie found herself putting it, by dear old Peter. He, of course, was naked, while Tracy looked glorious in all her bridal finery except bra and knickers.

Catching his real-life wife's eye, Peter moved the girl into a good position, unobstructed by any of the other couples, and got her to stand beside him for a moment. He whispered in her ear. She blushed an even deeper pink, grinned shyly, tossed back the veil that had fallen over one shoulder so that a pert breast was no longer obscured, reached downwards and sideways, opened her hand and let the fingers left free by those long gloves go spidering all over his genitals. The brand-new gold ring winked as she cupped his balls and squeezed the prick protruding between two of her fingers. Peter bent his knees, thrusting his loins forward against her hand and at the same time reaching his own fingers between her legs from behind until Sophie saw them curling up in front and poking into the red-fringed cunt. Tracy squirmed.

During this lubricious interlude, Rosper and Julie Maddingley had been rearranging chairs. They were ordinary wooden, straight-backed kitchen chairs without arms. Six of them had been placed in a line, facing in alternate directions. The seats projected out from the aligned backs, three on each side.

The music fell silent and the guests reluctantly ceased their activities to listen to Julie's next announcement. 'You've guessed,' she began, though Sophie certainly hadn't, her head still in a turmoil from Tim's manipulations. 'It's going to be musical chairs, though possibly not as you know it. First I want the girls to wait quietly while the boys dance clockwise round the chairs we've set out for you. Seven boys, six chairs. Get it? When the music stops, one of the boys has to drop out. Let's do that bit now, shall we?'

Round and round trotted the males, their stiffies wagging in front of them. Dargason broke off. After some rough jostling, Peter had to withdraw to the sidelines. The others sat there expectantly, some of them using their hands to try to conceal the pricks sprouting rudely from their lower bellies. Julie spoke again.

'Right. That's the easy part, the part you all know. Now it's your turn, girls. It's the boys' laps you've got to sit on. Seven girls, six boys, so one girl will have to drop out. Never mind—I'm sure all the dropouts in this game can have fun with each other in a relaxed way when they're out of the competition.

See those great stiff spikes sticking up? You know where they have to go, I hope, girls. Sit facing them. If any of you don't get it in you, your partner's out of the game. Got that? And boys, that goes for any of you who squirt your spunk while it's happening.'

Tracy looked extremely worried, and was about to speak, but Sloan interrupted. 'Please, Julie, how do we know if someone's cheating? You won't be able to see who's got it in properly.'

'No, but Peter here can make himself useful by helping me to check you all out. He'll be on one side of the chairs and I'll be on the other. We'll have a good feel between all of you and maybe give a bit of a commentary on the situation. Off you go, now.'

When the music resumed the young women began their giggly dance round the seated guys. The giggles became screams as they dived for the waiting laps. This time the loser was the naked Karen, who moved away from the row of chairs. Was that a tear on her cheek? The others gasped and sighed as they impaled themselves. Sophie effortlessly sheathed Clinton's spike, hoping the ordeal would soon be over. Clinton's chair was in the middle, with Tim on his left and Seb on his right. Over her partner's shoulder she could see the back of Mark's head. He was nuzzling Sloan's neck.

Peter was already refereeing over on that side. Sophie grinned at Cathy, who was on Jason's lap, to the left of Mark and Sloan. Peter's examination of their joining passed without comment. Was it only with his wife, Sophie wondered, that Jason had those problems?

Julie reported on proceedings between Seb and Tracy, to Sophie's left. 'Here's a reluctant bride,' she announced. 'But let's give her the benefit of the doubt. Scoot forward a bit, dear, and lift up so you can get it in properly. Not shy, are you?'

Quivering, Tracy shunted just a bit forward and pulled a sour face. 'Won't go in,' she sobbed. 'Much too big, innit.'

When Sophie peered down into Seb's lap, this assessment turned out not to be just an excuse. His knob was indeed obscenely big. Resting his hands on Tracy's stockinged thighs, he pleaded with Julie. 'If I let her bring me off first I bet I can shove it in while it's shooting.'

'Well,' Julie replied, 'we've got to get on, I'm afraid. You know the rules. Seb—you're lucky not to be out.'

This exchange had given Sophie an idea she thought might come in handy later. The young man snorted in disgust and moved away, leaving Tracy to sit on his chair trying to control her tears. Julie now confirmed that Sophie was properly joined to Clinton, allowing a soft breast to rub against Sophie's cheek as she did so, and then turned to Linda and Tim, on the next chair. 'Lovely,' she said.

By now Peter had satisfied himself regarding Mark and Sloan and Roger and Poppy to their right, but was taking his time over the latter couple. The combination of a knickerless 'schoolgirl' and a boy whose heavy sweater made his white thighs—Poppy had raised her own legs up his sides—look attractively youthful seemed to be irresistible to Peter, whose hand was lingering illicitly down where Sophie could only imagine the delights it was abusing.

Julie ordered the girls to stand and hustled them off to one side. She removed one of the chairs, leaving five. Rosper restarted the music and the six lads rose to jog jerkily round and round. Their pricks gleamed with the girls' fuckjuices. With the sudden stopping of the CD, it was Clinton who failed to secure a seat and slunk off, frustrated. The side with three chairs now accommodated Tim, Jason and Mark, who sat with their backs to Roger and Seb. The ladies did their nervous dance round them, and this time Cathy had to withdraw disappointed. Maybe she would get it off with Clinton over on the sidelines.

Sloan and Poppy had landed in the laps of their previous partners, Mark and Roger. Sophie was really pleased to be able to spear herself on Tim, whose smile showed he was just as delighted. The slim cock felt incredibly stiff as it screwed around in her vagina. By chance, Tracy was now with her real husband, Jason, between Sophie and Sloan. Looking over Tim's left shoulder, Sophie was confronted with Linda's pretty face. Catching Sophie's eye, she grimaced to hint her distaste at having impaled herself on the leather-jacketed Seb. And further over to the right, Roger was feverishly unbuttoning Poppy's white shirt while leaving the school tie in place. Her beret had been pushed even further awry, and one of her plaits was coming undone.

Peter didn't take too long checking that his own real-life wife was properly sheathing Tim. He moved on to the young bride straddling her naked groom, and stooped to reach down into their laps. He froze.

'Fuck,' he choked. 'It's splashing up my arm. Off you go, son.'

Tracy got up. Blushing, Jason hobbled off, his prick still enlarged but now semi-flaccid and dripping. This was the second time poor Tracy had lost a partner. Instead of crying, though, the girl just grinned sheepishly at Sophie as she turned to sit in Jason's place. She crossed her legs. The tiny ginger fleece was almost but not quite hidden between the tops of her thighs, the creamy smoothness of which invited

Sophie's wandering hand to move up across the lacy welt of her stocking. Her tummy was all wet with a discharge that was now trickling down to soak into what could be seen of the pubic tuft. The salty smell was fresh and seductive.

Peter winked at his mate Mark. A quick visual check was enough to convince him that he was satisfactorily encunted in the gorgeous Sloan. He murmured some words of encouragement and Mark opened the clasps securing the two gold chains holding the sides of Sloan's bodice together. Mark dipped his mouth to a ramping nipple.

By this time Julie had satisfied herself that Linda and Seb were sexually joined, and was monitoring Roger's busy petting of the little, cone-shaped tits he had freed from the shirt of the flustered 'schoolgirl'. She shared her findings with the other contestants.

'I love doing this. I'm wriggling my hand down between their tummies now. Oh, yes. All this wetness. And I can just feel the root of Roger's fat cock, with her cuntlips stretched round it. It's pulsing quite strongly—hope he's not going to burst.'

The music resumed and the girls pulled themselves off the erections they had been enjoying, to dance off to the side. Since Jason had already been eliminated, Julie removed two chairs, leaving just two on one side and one on the other, between them. The four surviving lads, Mark, Roger, Seb and Tim loped rather wearily round these chairs until the music stopped and a wild free-for-all ensued. All four seemed to be contending for just one of the chairs.

At first it looked as if they had all been accommodated—an impossibility. But it immediately became clear that, in the mad scramble, Seb had hurled himself into Tim's lap. He yelped and sprang up off the involuntarily buggering prick, out of the game.

When the girls did their dance and got themselves seated, the loser was Linda. Sophie was a little disappointed to find herself harbouring the familiar prick of her temporary husband, who had landed on the solitary chair between the two facing the other way. To her left, Sloan was straddling Roger; to her right was Poppy, who must have overtaken Sloan in the dash for laps, and was now with Tim. The 'schoolgirl', her shirt wide open, pressed against the naked Tim's smooth chest as they trembled in a close embrace. Roger was still wearing his sweater, but Sloan's green top had come right off, so she was getting the points of her small tits massaged by the chafing wool.

Julie inserted a hand between the bellies of the first couple she tested; Roger winced as she did so. She deliberately let her left nipple brush across his lips as she leaned forward and addressed the little crowd: 'You know, folks, I reckon I could tell which of them's which from the texture of the hair, though that could just be because the back of my hand's more sensitive than the palm. Rodge, yours is quite wiry. Sloan, darling, yours feels much finer. Quite silky.'

As she said this, Sophie was aware of a sudden enlargement of the prick she was sitting on. Mark crushed her against his hairy chest and gasped as a flood of his semen burst into her stretched cunt. She pushed back from him enough to whisper in his ear. 'Look, if you can manage to keep it up, maybe you can stay in the game.'

'Oh, I can keep it up,' he replied. 'With you I can keep it up forever.'

But it was not to be. Julie had overheard the exchange, and ordered Mark to withdraw, both from Sophie and from the contest. Meanwhile, Peter had approved the congress of Poppy and Tim. It was agreed that, since the end was in sight though no one really wanted it to end, only one chair would now be removed. The two lads were allowed to stay seated where they were.

The dance resumed and Sloan was the frustrated one this time, but only after a struggle. She and Poppy both landed on Roger's knees. Julie pulled them off and they fell to the floor. At first they lay there on their backs, astonished. Sloan was stark naked, while Poppy was still half dressed in beret, tie, unbuttoned shirt, long white socks and trainers. The legs of both girls were apart, displaying pink cunts ripe and slick with lustful seepings. A moment later they were at each other, wrestling, pinching, biting and tugging at each other's hair. Suddenly Poppy contrived to break free, bounce up and hurl herself on to the slender but rigid pole the eager Roger was holding in readiness for whichever girl claimed victory. It was her third time with him.

Sophie hoped she and Tim might be able to stay the course. He was hugging her so tightly to him that Julie, who had by now taken over all the refereeing, could hardly work her hand between their bellies to check the conjunction. To Sophie's surprise, she announced a failure to engage. When her body had slammed into Tim's, it had trapped his ramrod up against his stomach, and the closeness of their embrace had allowed this to go unnoticed.

Poppy and Roger were declared winners, a highly successful and popular outcome, as Julie remarked. 'Well,' she said, 'the young man gets to go first. Choose whichever lady takes your fancy, and give it to her on that bed over there. When you've finished with her, it'll be Poppy's turn.'

Gallantly, she thought, Roger selected Sophie and led her across the floor to the bed. But before he got down to business, he had a special request, which Sophie considered no less gallant. He asked Julie if it would be all right for him to be kissing his wife while fucking Sophie. Julie was delighted to allow this, and everyone applauded. How would the threesome be managed?

Roger lay on his back, stroking an upright dick which, if he had carried on, would have shot his spunk all over the front of his dark green pullover. Sophie squatted over him and let herself down slowly, until he was fully encunted and she could see her blonde hairs tangling with his dark ones. When he reached up to fondle one of her breasts, she pulled it free from the bikini top to give him access. Meanwhile, Linda, her pretty blouse now hanging wide open, was kneeling beside her husband's head. She trailed the tip of her tongue along his lips—his own tongue darted out to meet hers and soon their mouths were clamped together.

Sophie moved languorously up and down, varying the posture of her trunk to let her feel Roger's rigid stem massaging the walls of her vagina from different angles. Moving in this way also encouraged him to play with her exposed tit more imaginatively. And this in turn gave her the idea of reaching forward to find his wife's right breast, which was just concealed by the right side of her open blouse. As Linda became aware of the warm hand cupping the boob, she shifted round so that, while she was still kissing her husband, her raised bottom was just touching Sophie's left flank. Sophie reacted in the way she supposed Linda wanted: she stroked the white buttocks lightly before running a finger down the cleft, teasing the little pink hole and then probing further down. She penetrated the love canal with her thumb and used her finger to tickle the girl's stiff clit. At the same time she returned her right hand to the breast she had been fondling. Both hands occupied, she increased her bouncing on Roger's prick, every now and then pausing to squeeze it with her cunt muscles.

A stabbing pain in her nipple caused Sophie to lean back, tearing the teat out of Roger's pinching fingers and inevitably pulling her hands away from Linda and bringing them up to soothe the abused breast. By leaning back she unintentionally allowed the young lad's cock to escape the grip of her sex. He groaned. The green sweater was coated with pearly white as the thick member throbbed and spasmed. Well, it was just a lark, wasn't it?

Everyone clapped and hooted. Julie announced that it was now the turn of the other winner, Poppy, to take her pick of all those potential partners. The 'schoolgirl' surprised everyone by declaring that she couldn't make a sensible choice and wanted to be gangbanged. 'Even the girls can join in,' she added. 'I love everyone here. Oh, and one other thing. Because I adore my husband so much, I want him to be last so he doesn't have to make way for any others.'

Julie wondered aloud how Tim would feel about this arrangement.

'That's fine,' he said. 'Was going to suggest something like that myself. The guys can give her everything they've got. That's something I learned here on Pothos: just love to slip my dick into a spermy cunt.'

Mark nudged Sophie, who stood trembling beside him, her boob still looking perky with its purple covering pulled to the side. 'Remember what I said at their wedding?' he chuckled. 'Seems like she really does want to be everybody's bride.'

Poppy threw herself back on the bed, flinging her arms out to the sides. She had discarded her shirt, but the striped tie was still loosely round her neck. She had pulled the maroon beret firmly down on her head, as it had almost fallen off. One of her plaits was completely undone, the other one beginning to unravel. Her feet, in white trainers and knee-length socks, one of which had been dragged down around her ankle, were planted on the bed, her knees raised and together. When she let them fall to the sides, her hairless sex was seen to be gaping open, ready to claim her prize.

Rosper, who must have supervised this kind of operation before, stepped forward, stuffed a pile of pillows under her bottom and explained the routine. A guy would start off by sticking his cock in Poppy's mouth. Once it was hard he would move it to her pussy, while a second guy was getting sucked. He would then move away to be kept stiff by the girls in attendance, the second guy would move down to screw her and a third would go for her mouth. And so it would continue until they had all ejaculated.

'Now,' Rosper went on, 'we have a health and safety issue here. I'd love to invite any of you lads to flip her legs up, roll her back a bit and use her cute little arse instead of—or as well as—her cunt. OK, you can do that. But if you go down that path there's no going back. You're out of it. Sure, if young Timothy fancies it that way there's obviously no problem. He can stay in there as long as he likes.'

Even before Rosper had finished this lecture and while Poppy's sex was still open and waiting, Seb was fucking her mouth. He was followed by Mark and Roger in rapid succession, then Peter and Clinton, as the first three lovers withdrew to enjoy the attentions of the giggling wives around the bed. Jason was hanging about on the sidelines, seemingly disinclined to take part in the orgy. Tim stood at the foot of the bed, his arms folded, waiting patiently for his slice of the action. His prick stood up proud against his belly, leaking pre-come juices.

While the men were taking their pleasure in ever more frenzied turns, Poppy's hands were reaching out and playing rather roughly with the girls' cunts. It would have been hard for her young friend to be gentle, Sophie supposed, while those solid cylinders of flesh packed and pounded her. But it seemed the girls could take a bit of abuse.

Tracy had wandered over to join the miserable-looking, slightly tipsy Jason at the buffet. On impulse, Sophie left the little crowd round the bed and hurried over to them. 'Let's go back to your room,' she said. 'I want to help you to consummate your marriage.'

Jason looked puzzled. 'Consume what?' he said, chewing on a cocktail sausage.

'Consummate. It means having full sex. Putting your penis in your wife's vagina and ejacu—coming.'

'Oh, that. Sounds awesome. Yeah, let's do it.'

The three of them passed rather unsteadily through the hotel corridors, vestibules and courtyards. A little party of revellers smooching about by one of the groups of erotic statuary had been on the island long enough to be unfazed at the sight of a naked, semi-erect youth, a half-naked bride and a blonde young woman in nothing but the top of a purple bikini, one of her tits exposed.

In the couple's room they turned the lights to a dim, romantic setting. 'First we've got to get this lovely bride ready and gagging for it,' Sophie explained. She made Tracy lie comfortably on the bed, knelt between her parted thighs and started licking her while Jason watched, nursing a burgeoning hard-on. When the girljuices were flowing freely, she pulled back, helped Tracy to her feet and pushed the bridegroom down on the mattress. His cock stood upright, a bead of clear liquid gathering on the tip.

Sophie now straddled his hips, gave him a quick kiss and told Tracy to get behind her, lightly clasping his thighs between her legs in their white silk stockings. She lifted up. 'Put him in me, dear,' she cooed.

Tracy complied. The bare fingers of her gloved hand appeared below the golden fur of Sophie's cuntmound. The lace of the glove was secured by a loop of cord running between the middle and index fingers, and the wedding ring winked in the seductive light. Running her fingers lightly up over his ballsack, Tracy took hold of her husband's stiff member and forced it back until the bulb was lodged at the opening of her friend's vagina. The hand was withdrawn and Sophie plunged down, her wet flesh swallowing the offering greedily.

I must control myself, she thought. Control is crucial.

'I want you to come,' she crooned. 'Then, when you're nice and big again inside me, we'll let Tracy take over and see what happens.'

'Afraid I know what'll happen,' he replied. 'Like it always does, innit.'

Sophie stooped right down to murmur in his ear. 'Not this time. This time you're not—repeat, not—going to disappoint your lovely wife. She's right behind me now. Play with his balls, dear. You like that, Jason? I can feel her nipples digging into my back like little bullets. People think she's amazingly fuckable, even though she's never been fucked. Just relax, now, and get shot of all that troublesome spunk. Feel my muscles squeezing your prick? And when you've come, we're going to keep you nice and stiff to get into her. Just think of your bride's beautiful, fresh pink cunt with that little tuft of curls matching the ones on her head. Never had a man's cock up it—not even a boy's, she says.'

Before she had finished speaking, Sophie was aware of a powerful rush of hot semen flooding into her in pulse after pulse. She kissed the inflamed youth. His rod was still erect inside her.

Suddenly jumping up and flopping to the side, she indicated to Tracy that she should shift forward to take her place. The joining was effected without mishap. Jason clasped his wife tightly and rolled over on top of her so that he could shag her like a wild beast. Lifting up on his elbows, he gazed down into an enraptured, freckled face framed by the gauzy veil spread out on the pillow on either side and the copper-coloured tresses falling over her shoulders. Tracy's gloved hands grabbed hold of his buttocks to urge him on.

As Sophie rose to leave the room she stole a last glance at the happy couple. Her eye was caught by the glint of a gold ring on a finger working away between the cheeks of Jason's bottom.

The door to their own room had been left ajar for Sophie. She slipped in and closed it behind her. Mild applause greeted her—from Cathy, sitting on Peter's lap, and Mark, who had been nursing his own erection. The three of them were perched on the stools in front of the mirror, which had been switched to its see-through mode. In the room beyond, Jason and Tracy, more relaxed than they had been the whole week, were romping on their bed. Tracy moved to kneel sideways-on to the viewers, her gloved forearms supporting her. The veil and her auburn hair concealed most of her face. The bright pink tips of her grapefruit-sized breasts almost brushed the sheet. The welts of her white stockings showed off the shining smoothness of her thightops and bottom. Her husband knelt behind her and drove his stiff prick into the proffered cunt with new-found confidence.

Sophie looked at her companions. She felt a slight twinge of jealousy at the sight of her Peter's cockstem clasped by Cathy's pink cuntlips. The tight sac hanging below looked ready to spew its contents into the sheath of flesh. But soon it would be hers again. Hers.

This thought made it easier for her to lower herself on to Mark's hairy thighs and let his manhood find its own way into her opening. After all the excitement at the party and with the couple in the next room, she was desperate for relief. His hands reached round to the front to her to fondle her tits. She took hold of the one stroking her through the bikini, leaving the other one to pleasure the exposed nipple of the other breast. She pushed this hand down firmly over her stomach and into the yellow bush between her thighs. Mark found the bud of her clitoris and gave it a little pinch. Removing her hand from his, she reached down to grab his dangling balls.

She fixed her gaze on the young couple beyond the mirror, who were now writhing in newly discovered ecstasy. At this moment Cathy and Peter howled out their lust, both slumping forward on the shelf below the mirror, and Sophie stiffened as such a powerful orgasm racked her body that she had no idea whether Mark was discharging into her at the same time. And she didn't care.

Afterplay

A few weeks later, on a hot, sunny afternoon in Barnes, Sophie and Peter are hosting a reunion of the four couples who have had so much fun together on Pothos. Sophie and Cathy have been seeing each other on a regular basis, with the full approval of their husbands, and it was Peter who had suggested this get-together. Addresses had been exchanged before they left the island, so there was no problem about making contact. The four younger ones were quite surprised to learn about the wife-swapping that had been kept secret on the island but now had to be revealed as they were to be received at home by Sophie and Peter.

For the party Sophie has slipped on one of Peter's white shirts. It is open down the front except for the two bottom buttons. As she moves about, her breasts are sometimes exposed, sometimes half hidden and sometimes completely covered. For most of the time it is not possible to make out what, if anything, she is wearing down below. The light tan of her shapely legs contrasts with the crisp whiteness of the shirt. Because the party is going to be in their own house and small but secluded garden, Peter has decided that a black posing pouch is all he needs.

Cathy and Mark are the first guests to arrive. Mark's outfit is unexceptional enough: a white T-shirt and black jeans. But his wife Cathy is almost unrecognisable in a straw boater, an outgrown gymslip, white shirt and striped school tie, and to complete the picture white ankle socks. Her dark hair is plaited into two pigtails tied with blue bows.

'Wow!' exclaims Peter. 'You look simply demure.'

'Not bad yourself,' she replies. 'Not exactly *demure*, though. More sizzling hot and horny.'

At these words Peter's horn begins to strain against the cotton of his thong. It remains in that condition when the two younger couples arrive together in a taxi paid for, they say, by Jason's father.

Jason wears a scarlet singlet with the very loose, very brief white shorts he occasionally favoured on Pothos. His yellow hair has grown a little longer. His wife looks as girlish as ever in a candy-striped, green and white summer dress buttoning down the front and knee-high white socks. Instead of flopping all over her freckled face, her coppery curls have been swept back and tied with a broad pink ribbon.

Tim looks a bit ordinary (though appealingly young) in ragged blue jeans and a navy pullover. As soon as he has greeted his hosts he strips off the pullover, exposing his pale torso. Poppy, Sophie thinks, looks like her idea of a typical teenage girlfriend rather than a newlywed. This impression is created by a baggy black jumper, black tights or stockings and a denim microskirt, its hem frayed to match Tim's custom-torn jeans. The length of the skirt is hardly more than the width of the black belt that holds it up.

For the first half hour or so the guests and their hosts circulate in the living room and garden, making casual conversation and helping themselves to the drinks and other refreshments laid out on the kitchen table—the table on which Peter had fucked Sophie after that dinner party when she first met Mark and Cathy. Apart from some of the costumes, there is little to suggest that this is anything but an innocent social gathering. Sophie, however, senses a certain erotic tension in the atmosphere and her loins tingle in the knowledge that the guests know they will soon be having sex with each other.

Tracy leads a rather reluctant Jason over to Sophie. 'Got somefink to tell you,' she announces.

Sophie looks at her, musing. 'Everything's working properly now, is it? With you two, I mean.'

'Oh yeah, fanks to you. Once Jace gets it in he likes to keep it in me all night—tops me up wiv his stuff whenever he wakes up, see. But the fing is, like, his dad's ever so chuffed cos . . . '

'You're pregnant!'

'Yeah. And that means we don't have to be so careful now.'

'You mean the paternity won't be an issue.'

Jason coughs. 'You what?'

He puts an arm round his wife's still slender waist. He coughs again.

'There's free fit blokes here what she never slept wiv, know what I mean? Well, see, I want her to, like, do it wiv all free of em. OK?'

As he says this, he is staring into the open front of Sophie's shirt. Sunlight from the garden highlights a white breast and its stiff pink nipple.

Peter comes over with a tray of drinks and whistles at Tracy's radiant appearance. 'She's lovely,' he comments. 'Jason, you remember on the boat I told you what a lucky guy you were? Well, was I right? You've had a chance to find out now.'

'You was dead right, mate. Out on the island someone said she's, like, awesomely fuckable. Well, we want her to get awesomely fucked by everyone here, know what I'm saying?'

'So I'm in with a chance.'

'I ain't stopping you. She'll be gagging for it.'

Now that everyone is in a relaxed mood, Peter announces that they are going to watch some hot action Mark had filmed on Pothos, as well as a selection of CCTV material Rosper has sent as continuing payment for legal services that have preserved his freedom. His very considerable freedom . . . Everyone settles on sofas, chairs and cushions strewn on the floor. The plasma screen lights up.

Mark's opening sequence is innocuous but still saucy, and whets the appetite of the viewers, who are beginning to fondle each other as they watch. It had been filmed on the launch taking them to the island. How long ago it all seems, Sophie reflects, gently cupping Peter's sexpouch. After a close-up shot of Sophie herself, smiling coyly, the camera finds Tracy and Jason, *JUST MARRIED* written all over their shy faces. Tracy seems to be unable to stop playing with her wedding ring.

The next sequence, still on the boat, very briefly shows Sophie smiling innocently at the camera and sipping ouzo from a paper cup before Mark pans round to catch Tim and Poppy up at the front, getting to know Peter and Cathy. Poppy has her feet up on the bench she is sitting on. She has allowed her knees to drift apart and her denim skirt to ride up. The camera zooms in on her panty-covered crotch.

Memories come crowding back as the viewers are led through the corridors and courtyards of the hotel with its kissing, pissing, ejaculating and copulating statues. Next a snatched scene filmed through a half open bathroom door. A woman with her back to the camera is soaping herself. After rinsing off she turns and is briefly glimpsed stepping out on to the bath mat. It is Sophie, who even now feels indignant at the liberty Mark had taken. Peter, who has slipped a hand into her shirt, gives her tit a little squeeze to reassure her.

The film now cuts to the next morning. There is Sophie in the woods behind the hotel. In quite an artistic sequence, backlit, she is prancing about and showing off topless in a broad-brimmed straw hat and white wrap-around skirt through which not only her legs but a minute black bikini bottom are plainly visible. She flashes a lithe leg through the opening in the skirt and poses, offering her tits to the camera and grinning. She has gained confidence, it seems, after being taken by Mark on her wedding night. She is now much more comfortable being around other people in a sexual context.

A very brief sequence now shows a rear view of Jason and Tracy taken a few minutes later as they loiter in dappled shade in the same woods. Jason is wearing long shorts. His back is bare. With Tracy it is the other way round. Her little white suntop emphasises the transgressive impression created by her bare bottom—bare, that is, apart from the narrow white strip running down between her buttocks. White socks and trainers complete the erotic effect, or rather the finishing touch is the way her husband's hand hovers about on her hip, apparently resisting a powerful urge to slide down over the virginal white cheek just below it.

Then comes the action on that orange towel in the little cove. Sophie observes that over in a corner of the room Jason and Tracy have huddled together in embarrassment. Everyone claps and hoots as the scene unfolds. On the screen the girl is holding the petals of her cunt wide open in close-up. Yes—there is the wedding ring displayed as if on purpose. A purple cockhead is shoved into the sexmouth and immediately expelled, gushing its hot discharge over her belly and russet tuft.

This little episode ends with the shots Mark had taken as

the youthful pair made their way back through the woods. There is Tracy's beautiful reddish hair waving from side to side and her firm little breasts jiggling as she advances. Mark has zoomed in and focused on the diminutive white pouch at the base of her belly, to the skin of which, as Mark points out, lacy flakes of dried sperm adhere. Wisps of red pubic hair curling out from the edges of the thong show up charmingly against the creamy skin of her inner thightops. The bulge moves suggestively as she walks.

Beside her, and viewed from the same level, the front of Jason's green swimming trunks is seen to be moving even more decidedly. The camera zooms out to give a full length view of the couple, who are now facing each other as Jason's hand strokes his wife's bottom and begins to ease the back of the thong down. Although the sound is turned down fairly low, Tracy's voice can be heard telling him to play with her and get her 'mushy', ready for a 'real fuck' when they get back to their room. Then he whips her round to face the viewers, and stands behind her for his next move. One hand begins to play with a pert breast while the other one dips down to her sex. Zoom in: his fingers scrabble frantically at the little thong, pushing it into her slit and then tugging it aside so that he can work directly on the clit that stands proudly in its nest of coppery curls.

Tracy wriggles wildly and falls forward, out of the picture, which now displays a wet stain spreading over the front of her husband's swimsuit, darkening the green and clearly issuing from the tip of the stiff member trying to burst through the fabric.

Over in the corner of the room Sophie sees an embarrassed Jason being comforted by Tracy. He is sitting on the floor with his back against the wall, his white legs stretched out in front of him. The comfort she is offering consists of petting the penis which has emerged from the loose leg opening of his shorts and extended itself some way down his thigh. She seems to be trying to coax the foreskin down to cover a mauve knob that simply swells even huger the more she pulls. Sitting next to him with her knees pressed up against her chest, Tracy may not be aware that the skirt of her dress has fallen back. Yes—there are the backs of her soft thighs, and just a glimpse of her bottom, with a hint of her red-fringed pussy peeping through. Catching Sophie's eye, she blushes and straightens her legs. The white socks and black shoes accentuate her girlish appearance. At the top of her thighs her flame-furred mound is fully displayed for a moment before she tugs the knee-length dress down. She places her hand over Jason's prick, either to provide some decency or to continue comforting him—probably both.

Sophie looks up to see Tim standing over her. Ever the exhibitionist, he has taken his jeans off and his lean, hairless body is adorned with a fine erection. He strokes her face. 'I think you're so pretty, Sophie,' he says, and she is tempted to return the compliment. Instead, she drops to her knees in front of him and takes the rampant prick between her lips. Her hands wander over the backs of his thighs and buttocks. Her shirt is open and the points of her breasts rub against the boy's thighs. She sucks. As the tip of a finger prods his arsehole, her tongue and palate receive the streams of salty juice that jet from the succulent plum.

The next episode to animate the screen is the 'reconstruction' of Cathy's sixth-form dalliance with Peter and Mark. As Peter snogs his schoolgirl date under the envious eyes of Mark, the 'real' Cathy steps forward to stand beside the plasma screen.

In her straw boater, gymslip and socks she looks a bit different from her on-screen embodiment in blazer and short skirt, but the difference is a piquant one. The attention of the audience is divided when she lifts the hem of her gymslip with one hand and uses the other one to part the dark hair of her pussy. The puffy lips are revealed and she soon has herself whipped up into a frenzy as her filmed double's face and neck are painted with a coating of lubricant from the head of her lover's prick. Most of this gets licked off as Peter prepares to plant a hot kiss on her lips.

Sophie notices her own reflection in the mirror behind this action. She stands there nude apart from her little black G-string, holding the camera. Tim notices this detail as well, and shoots another thick wad down her throat.

The exciting action on the screen is soon over as Peter, kneeling between his girl's thighs and flipping her skirt up to her waist, fucks her and ejaculates into her cunt. Mark has tugged her shirt open and stuck his cock in her mouth. As his friend comes, Mark pulls out and sprays her face and breasts with spunk.

In the real life world of the party, Jason stands up, his erection still protruding from the leg of his white shorts. He swaggers across to Cathy as she flaunts and frigs herself. Bending his knees a little, he grasps his tool and forces it into the passage she stretches open for him. Now that these two are locked together the spectators are deprived of the sight of their genitals. Jason realises this and, to compensate, swivels round so that Cathy has her back to them. He lifts the skirt of her gymslip up over her bottom. The buttocks are clenching and unclenching to the rhythm of Jason's fucking.

Although the volume is turned low, a resounding THWACK

draws everyone's attention back to the filmed action. There is Sophie, who has taken over the role of schoolgirl, bent forward in front of the mirror, her pleated skirt tossed up over her back. And there is the reflection of a nude Cathy using one hand to film her while masturbating with the other one. The 'headmaster', Mark, has just left the imprint of his hand on a behind bare except for the narrow black tape running down between the cheeks. Mark tugs the thong halfway down her thighs, where the crumpled-up black fabric contrasts with the whiteness of her socks.

As a naked and rampant Peter steps up beside her, Mark grabs the thong and smooths it out to show the whitish deposit contained in it. He rubs it vigorously against Sophie's cunt and then spreads the fresh juices all over her bottom, working them well into the cleft before pulling it down again. The 'real' Sophie feels a sympathetic, stabbing pain in her bowels as her filmed husband drives his cock up her filmed arse. In the mirror her cute face topped with the maroon beret is contorted and her tongue sticks out.

Hold on—as she kneels on all fours where Jason has left her after spending in her mouth, she realises that the stabbing is more than a sympathetic twinge. The 'real' Peter has come up behind her to tug aside the tape of her thong and emulate the action of his filmed counterpart. Ouch!

When he has finished sodomising her, Sophie, lying on her stomach, looks up blearily to take in the episode now unfolding on the screen. She and Cathy are shown in the hotel room posing as brides. Cathy has a wreath of peach-coloured flowers on her head. A white suspender belt supports a pair of sheer white stockings, and white lace gloves adorn the lower part of her forearms. Otherwise she is nude. Sophie has on the familiar wedding outfit modelled on stage by Poppy when she was 'married' to Tim. Minus the bra. And there are those odd wisps of blonde hair peeping out round the edges of the lacy thong.

The shot of these two lovelies, arm in arm, is not held for long. Cathy is seized by Peter, who throws her on the bed and starts to tongue-fuck her. In no time she has released the stiff prick from his jeans and is thrashing about on the bed as he churns the tool in her vitals.

Sophie wishes Mark had been able to set up the camera to work automatically, but that is the end of the sequence and she has to make do with memories of how he stripped and hurled himself on her. He had torn her thong in his eagerness, hadn't he? And nearly torn her cunt.

Mark's home movie has come to an end, but he says he has some more stuff to show them later. The party is really getting under way, fuelled partly by a generous supply of liquor and a certain amount of the white powder Rosper had absolutely prohibited on the island but mainly by the sheer exuberance of youthful lust. All except the naked Tim, and Mark, who now wears nothing but his white T-shirt, retain the clothing they had come in, making the most of its erotic suggestiveness.

Sophie is watching her husband flirting with Poppy. The teenager has lifted her arms to let him pull off her baggy black sweater. Under it she is wearing the top of that famous shocking pink bikini. But at this moment Sophie feels a hand on her arm. It is Mark, who leads her gently out on to the shady patio. He holds her at arm's length and looks her up and down—she, for her part, can't help noticing the almost upright dick projecting from the dense black thicket below the hem of his T-shirt. He reaches for the buttons fastening the bottom of the white shirt she is wearing.

'My lovely hostess has no business covering herself up like this from her guests,' he says. 'That's it. Let's slide it off your beautiful white shoulders and down off your arms. Oh yes. Look, before I take you in there to show you off as if you were my own wife again, I'm going to give you my full appreciation out here. Yes, what a cute smile, and just a hint of a blush, is it? Just under the corner of your mouth here, this must be a little flake of dried spunk from that Tim—I saw you suck him off, you naughty girl. These shoulders are so smooth. Put your arms round my neck—that's it—so that I can enjoy your most unusual feature.'

'What's that, you beast?'

'These gorgeous silky tufts in your armpits. They're so sexy. So womanly.'

She feels him tickling her. Wasn't part of her appeal supposed to be her girlishness?

'And now those perfect tits. So soft, so firm. Hey, me just talking about them makes the nips stand up like little pricks.'

'And seems to make your prick stand up like Nelson's column.'

Mark is mouthing the nipples as she makes this observation, which is inspired by the pressure of his knob against her belly. His encomium continues as he draws back from her to take in more of her radiant appearance.

'Oh, look. I've already left a trail on your tummy like a snail. But you're used to that kind of leaking, aren't you, sweetheart? That thong you're wearing's covered in stains. What colour was it originally? Light green, I'd say. Yes, Cathy's told me all about this one. Got it on your honeymoon, didn't you, off some American lezzie. Those are girl stains.'

Sophie giggles. 'Well, I've had it on once or twice for Peter. It's caught quite a bit of his spunk, too. I've got another one with girljuice only.'

'Turn round, dear. God, that bottom! Let me stroke it. Yes! Let me kiss it. Sophie, it's a crime to deprive all the other guests of these delights, but believe me, I've simply got to screw you right here and now. You can have them when I've finished with you.'

'Will you ever be finished with me, though?'

'Good question. I was hoping we might still get to see each other like this now and then, for old times' sake.'

He doesn't wait for an answer, but lowers her on to a cushion, draws the stained, pale green thong to one side and lets her part the moist lips of her sex to facilitate a smooth entry. Sophie feels him thrusting right up her. His lunges are powerful and rapid. And then she feels the hot, pulsing gushes he shoots into her womb.

They both rise to their feet and Sophie pulls the thong back to receive the trickle or flood that will surely soak it. She has not come herself, but certainly feels appreciated and knows the omission will be rectified before very long. Mark escorts her back into the sitting room, topless and flushed. She is greeted by clapping and whistling, although the flirting couples in there are giving most of their attention to the DVD now playing.

It is Rosper's edited record of their stay on Pothos, culled from the hundreds of concealed CCTV cameras around the hotel.

Sophie sees herself (from behind the mirror in that hotel

vestibule) standing in her blue one-piece swimsuit. Behind her is the grinning Mark. He could be naked, except that the waistband of his red thong is just visible crossing his hip. His hairy arms go around her. One hand moulds a breast, while the other one slides down to cup the prominent pubic mound. How differently she had felt about him on that first evening, while still in a manner of speaking his unravished bride.

Suddenly the picture cuts to the bed in Sophie and Mark's first room. The light is dim, but strong enough to show the white-clad figure of Sophie throwing herself face down on the covers. She is wearing that baby-doll nightie. Her golden hair is spread wildly over the pillow and her athletic legs are bare.

Buck naked, Mark jumps on to the bed beside her. His hand strokes the backs of her knees. She is trembling. He sweeps the hem of the nightdress right up to the small of her back and stoops to kiss her bottom. Sophie eases herself on to her side with her back to him and facing the camera. The front of her nightdress can now be seen—low cut and secured with two little pink bows just below and above the breasts, one of which Mark begins to massage through the flimsy material. He brushes the hair from her face and plants a kiss on her cheek before moving down to lick her naked hip while petting her bottom. His tongue traces a wet path down into the crease of her groin and over into her golden pubic fuzz.

And now the lovely young woman is ready to give herself to her lover for the first time. She stretches out on her back and opens her thighs. The tip of his tongue flicks over her clitoris and rasps up over her belly. His fingers fumble with the pink bows and he pulls the top of the nightie wide open, easing the small, firm globes out to meet his wet mouth. Her arms are extended limply above her head on either side, the yellow tufts on show, and with the nearer one she reaches out to switch on the bedside lamp. The picture is now sharply illuminated.

As Mark mouths her teats, one of his hands cups her sex and gently squeezes it. Then both hands move up to toy quite roughly with her breasts as his tongue lashes her pussy and slices the succulent lips apart. His nose plays against her clit and her voice is audible to everyone in the room.

'Fuck me, you gorgeous man. Fuck me now. Shoot your spunk up me. This is our wedding night, remember?'

Mark replies. 'You are beautiful, Sophie. I guess this is the moment I've been dying for. What a honeymoon this is going to be! Just feel how heavy my balls have gone with all the spunk in them.'

The 'real' Sophie holds her breath and can hardly bear to watch, so poignant are the memories this scene evokes. On the screen she reaches for Mark's balls to give them a feel and a little squeeze. In a bound he is straddling her chest. She leans forward to take the oozing cockhead between her lips.

But not for long. He pinches her nipples as a warning for her to release the bursting plum before leaping back between her thighs and drilling it into her cunt.

'Okay for me to come inside you—wife?'

'Go ahead. Give it all to me. Fill me up. Do it—now!'

Cut to Peter and Cathy's room. To their 'marital' bed. Friends reunited—at last that charming relationship that had blossomed in their school days has been resumed with the mature man now 'wedded' to his erstwhile girlfriend. This is the scene Sophie has been waiting for. It is short, simple and powerful.

The couple are sporting in beautiful nudity. Sophie's husband drags his tongue up through her new friend's sexual gash before plunging the massive tool which the younger woman has come to regard as her own straight up into it. Cathy's legs embrace his heaving buttocks. A deep, gurgling sound comes from her throat as he draws a purple teat into his mouth. And then it is all over. Peter's muscles go rigid, twitching, and the frantic pumping stops. He lifts his head. His eyes are wide as he jets everything he has into his temporary wife's cunt.

The show continues with Jason's repeated and always frustrated attempts to penetrate and impregnate his bride on this first night they have been saving themselves up for. His movements become more and more frantic, and then more and more lethargic. Both Tracy and the bedsheets are soon awash with his spewed fluids.

Sophie feels a light touch on her arm. It is Poppy, who draws her aside to an unoccupied sofa from which they can still see the screen. The two young women sit side by side, admiring each other. Those narrow pink triangles of lycra do nothing to hide the stiffness of Poppy's nipples, any more than the stained and still damp green thong can conceal the yawning cleft between the twin segments of Sophie's puffed-up pussy. Poppy grins and unfastens her broad black belt, followed by the clasp of her denim microskirt. She lifts her bottom and slips that garment down to the floor.

Sophie expects to see revealed the indecently minuscule pink thong. But no—above the darker welts of her black hold-up stockings her hairless and naked sex is as lewdly distended as Sophie's own. Poppy leans over and kisses her, kneading her firm breasts as her tongue forces its way into her mouth. The teenager's hands begin to pull Sophie's thong down. But Sophie stops her. 'No,' she insists. 'We're keeping that on. You can do me through it or inside it, right?'

On screen Jason is licking his slippery spendings from Tracy's belly. But Sophie is intent on getting some relief from young Poppy. She takes hold of Poppy's legs in their black stockings and lifts them across her own—the feel of the woollen material against her naked thighs is perversely delicious. The girl lies back, her head supported by the arm-rest of the sofa. Her chest looks completely flat, the lycra strips and the gold ring in the middle of the black tape that connects them merely decorative. Her stomach too, of course, is flat, but quivering with sensual excitement, the navel winking prettily.

Sophie slips a hand between Poppy's thighs and separates them. A delicate scent is released as the petals of girlish sexflesh pout in readiness, a beautiful flower framed by the smooth whiteness of belly and thightops. Sophie's fingers seek out the little stamen nestling among the petals, while with her other hand she plunders the girl's fuck hole and stirs the juices welling up in that buttery, soft receptacle.

'You're just so sexy,' she purrs. 'Ah, those stockings . . .'

She dips her mouth. It takes no more than a moment of licking to bring on a fierce climax. The fit young cunt clenches so tightly that Sophie's fingers are expelled. She sucks them and lifts Poppy's legs so that they can change places.

Now the pale green thong is displayed bulging obscenely as Sophie lies back on Poppy's lap. A connoisseur would be able to distinguish several layers of evidence from the stains on it, most of which have originated inside the little pouch and soaked through. Faintest are the original traces of the American girl's lust. Then, numerous tokens of the conjugal pleasure Peter has enjoyed when aroused by the sight of his wife in this garment with its sentimental associations. It is from some of these encounters that the spots of white crust on the outer surface derive. And now, almost dry but still pungent, those darker patches at the bottom of the triangle testify to Mark's recent debauch on the patio. But even as the patches dry in the warmth of the room, Sophie's cunt contracts in anticipation and fresh sperm pours out to soak the dainty scrap of fabric.

Poppy is not concerned with the archaeology of these deposits and the great floods of which they speak. Easing a perky little tit out of the pink triangle stretched over its centre, she thrusts the nipple into Sophie's mouth. At the same time she uses a slim finger to work the sodden thong up into her friend's pussy. Her thumb rubs the material over the distended nub of the clit. Sophie can tell that this action must make Poppy as aware as she is herself of the tangled blonde bush being pulled this way and that inside the thong.

The girl slowly draws the cotton out of the vagina, bringing with it a fresh load of spunk. She then reaches down into the thong from above, letting her fingers and fingernails work directly through the pubic hair. The thumb vibrates over the lovebud while two fingers curl up into the mush of the sex canal.

Sophie stiffens and shouts out as the orgasm hits her and continues to roll through her body for what seems an eternity.

The screen shows what must still be Jason and Tracy's room, but now bright sunlight pours in from the pool area outside. The occupants enter through the glass sliding door. Tracy is wearing that blue one-piece swimsuit identical with the one Sophie owns. She is followed by the golden-skinned Jason, his erection sticking out of the leg of his flimsy white shorts as it is right now, as stiff as ever after shagging Cathy.

He throws his young wife face down on the bed, drags the straps from her shoulders and tugs the costume down below her buttocks. Grabbing her hips he pulls her bottom up and presents the head of his cock to her red-fringed cunt. While it is probing about in the moist folds, Jason reaches round her thighs with both hands and diddles her to a shattering climax. What happens next is a foregone conclusion, and over in a flash. As she flops forward, the shining bulb skids up between the girl's buttocks and spews a stream of white cream up her back.

The Bridewell. By the light of flaming torches poor Tracy is seen spreadeagled, chained to the iron grid above the water. She is blindfolded and gagged. All in black, her torturer, now known to be Jason, tugs her little red pubic tuft before opening her cunt with rough, gauntleted hands. He rams a black dildo into her—this is the moment when, technically speaking, she loses that long-preserved virginity, and a muffled scream echoes in the torture chamber. The insides of her white thighs are splattered with streaks of blood that have squirted out round the implement.

Jason stands back and contemplates his victim, who writhes and struggles in her chains. When he steps forward he is holding a feather. With the tip of this he tickles her armpits, her nipples and her belly down to just above her straining cuntmound. The studded fingers of a black leather gauntlet draw back the clitoral hood and the feather teases the exposed nub. As she is forced to climax, Tracy's vaginal muscles clench and expel the dildo.

Her ankles are now unchained, but fastened again to the iron bars when her tormentor has bent her double so that he can apply his swishy cane to a bottom that is soon criss-crossed with pink stripes. He flings the instrument of correction down and strips off, standing over his chastised bride, black-booted and menacingly erect. Then he is in her. In her rectum.

In stark contrast, the next scene shows the stage of Rosper's theatre. Tim stands beside Poppy—the couple are all nervous smiles, about to be married. Tim is naked apart from his crown of ivy, the white sandals with their thongs criss-crossing up to his knees, and the little scrap of gold-fringed white silk attached to the band of gold braid round his waist and just covering his genitals. The hanging silk is stirring as the excitement of the situation kicks in.

Next to him stands his bride. His lovely, eager young bride. The outfit is familiar to everyone by now (they were gazing at it just a little while back in the part of the film showing Sophie herself wearing it), but Sophie still feels a thrill every time she sees it. The gauzy veil floating down from the flowery headdress to halfway down the back. The white gloves. The semi-transparent bra and matching thong. The sheer white stockings.

The real-life Tim looks up from the floor, where he is shagging Cathy, her gymslip bunched up round her waist. Sophie can see that her friend is all flushed and well on the way to satisfaction. Yet Cathy too takes time out to gaze up at the screen, knowing that the boy's erection will stay hugely stiff in her belly until they resume their fuck.

By this time the near-naked temple maidens and youths, the 'sacred prostitutes' Rosper had called them, have stripped off the bride's bra and thong and Tim's little white covering and withdrawn to give the audience a clear view of the hairless bodies. Sophie wonders if the prick now gripped by Cathy's vagina is as engorged as the one displayed on the screen, upright and trembling in anticipation. She realises that she has a powerful need for cock herself right now.

Sitting beside her on the sofa, Poppy is getting it from Peter. She is obviously fully occupied in all senses. Sophie catches Mark's eye and beckons him over. He is more than happy to oblige his 'wife' of a few weeks back and is soon snugly sheathed. Poppy's hand reaches over to take hers. How good it feels to enjoy this shared loving!

Meanwhile, Rosper has taken the couple on stage through his lewd litany and the business with the rings. He declares: 'I pronounce you man and wife. You, Timothy, may kiss your blushing bride, Poppy, on her mouth, nipples, bottom and cunt. And you, Poppy, may return your husband's kisses.'

On the purple bed the bridal couple lie down and perform this fourfold ritual. They end in a sixty-nine with Tim on top.

On the sofa, Mark moves from long, slow strokes to short, jabbing ones. He is almost there. Sophie draws Poppy's hand over, kisses it and inserts it between her own abdomen and her lover's. The youngster, who seems to be close to her own climax, nevertheless stretches her fingers through Sophie's bush and begins to dab at her clitoris.

By this time the youths and maidens in the film have covered the bodies of the bridal couple with their slippery spendings. It is now time for the consummation. Poppy opens her legs and pulls her labia apart. Tim mounts her, missionary-style, and plunges his stiffness into her depths. She groans.

Because the youths and maidens have made such a good job of lubricating their whole bodies, Tim is able to slide and slither all over his bride as he pumps and pumps. The picture is greatly enhanced by the way the skimpy garments Poppy still wears—her veil, gloves, stockings and the narrow chain around her loins—contrast with Tim's almost total nudity: he is bare except for the wreath of ivy leaves still perched on his head, his strappy sandals and the belt of golden braid round his hips. On each upstroke the viewers can make out his swinging balls.

After a few minutes of this fucking the couple freeze. Tim's buttocks clench, hollows forming in his flanks. Then Poppy's white-stockinged legs flash up in the air and her arms wave about on either side as she beats the mattress. She howls out her delight. Tim's balls bunch up in readiness to shoot their load; he makes a final thrust and collapses, gurgling, on her breast.

Now almost about to come on Mark's prick as Poppy's fingers play with her clit, Sophie reaches her own hand over and thrusts it between the bellies of her husband and his teenage fuckbuddy. She feels Peter's hairs on the back of her hand and Poppy's moist smoothness on her palm. She works two fingers down to grip the thick cock as it slides in and out. As Peter rams it in for the last time, she can actually feel the surge of spunk rushing through it to fill the clasping cunt. And overfill it—Sophie's fingers are swamped with the overflow. She scarcely notices this, because her own orgasm is bursting through her and her own vagina is already expelling the surplus of Mark's outpouring. There's going to be some tricky cleaning after the party!

By this time the filmed ritual is drawing to a close. Poppy and Tim join hands and step forward to take their bow to thunderous applause. The husband's ivy wreath now sits on his dark locks at a jaunty angle. His golden girdle intersects white skin gleaming with dried girljuice. Although his dick droops from its efforts, it already seems to be thickening up in

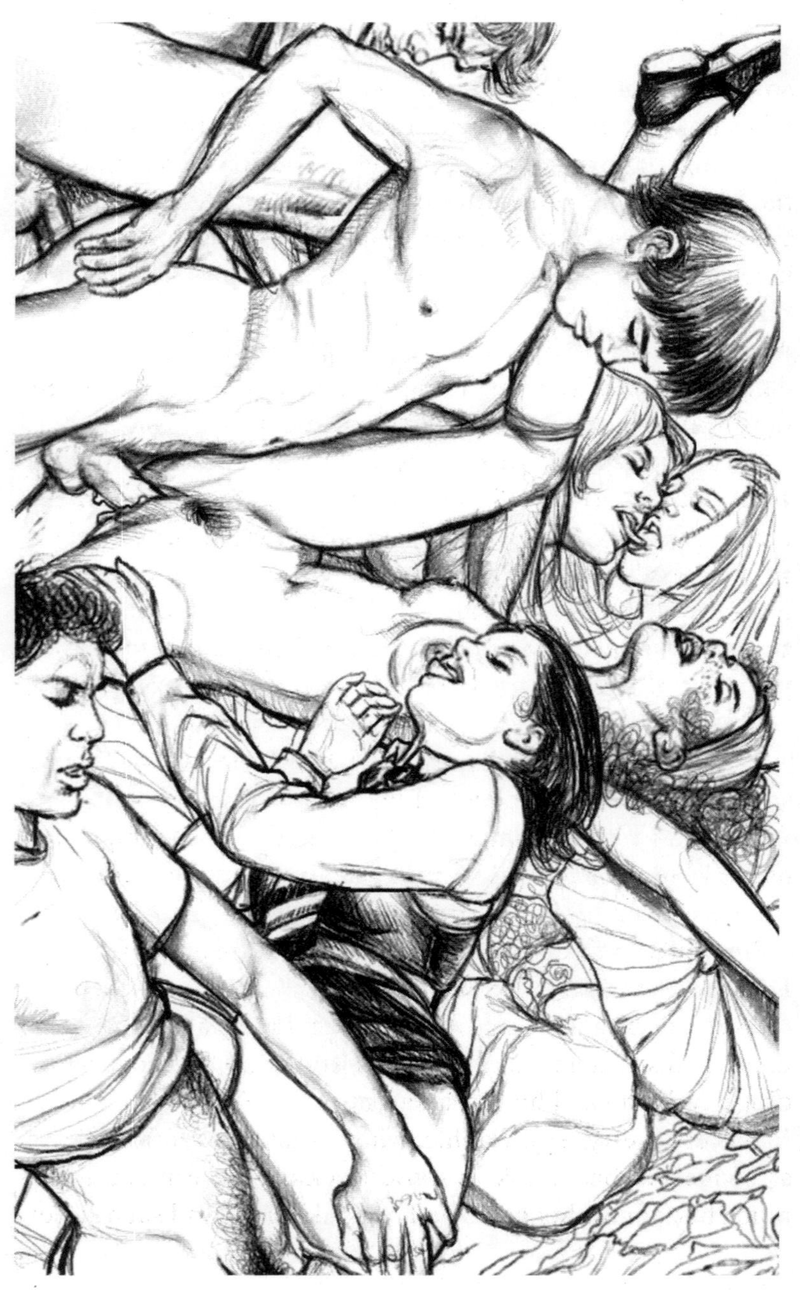

anticipation of further conjugal treats behind closed doors.

In contrast, his wife's body is wet and streaming with the spendings of her servitors in the ceremony. She still maintains the image of the radiant bride with her stockings, gloves and veil. A travesty of the conventional image, to be sure, but still lovely and still blushing.

After this display the plasma screen is switched off and everyone takes some much-needed refreshment into the garden. When they return, Peter makes an announcement.

'Time for what we've all been waiting for, friends. But first an invitation. Jason tells me his dad's off on a cruise next month, so we're all invited over to his place in Barking for a great poolside party. So our fun won't be over after tonight. As for what happens now, though, Jason's had a word with Sophie and made it very clear what he wants. You want it too, don't you, Tracy darling?'

'Oh yeah—I want it. I *need* it.'

'Right, then. First of all, just pull down Jason's shorts, Tracy, so we can all get a good look at him.'

Blushingly, Tracy complies. Her tanned husband steps out of the little garment and stands naked and half erect. He, too, is embarrassed.

'Now you must do the same for Tracy. Display her for us— I'm sure you can be proud of her.'

Jason fumbles with the buttons down the front of his wife's dress, and she helps him. She slips it off her shoulders and it drops to the floor. The onlookers gasp.

'So very pretty,' says Sophie, who has taken over from Peter as spokesperson. 'Look at those freckles. We can see them much better now her hair's tied back like that. And such sweet titties. Sweet, yes—the nipples are like sweets waiting to be sucked and chewed. Turn round for a moment, darling. What about that for a bottom, guys? And I don't know why but I can't resist the backs of those legs. Now give us the full frontal again, my poppet. Well, I'm sure we all adore that touch of colour down there. Don't you dare shave it. Oh, and the little socks and trainers complete the picture, don't they just.

'Right, people. What Jason has explained to me is that he wants to see her fucked by everyone here. And Tracy agrees.'

Tracy chips in. 'You know—like when Poppy got done for winning that musical chairs game.'

'Except we've got to be gentle with her. Remember, she's only ever had Jason's cock inside her. Anyway, we've got three guys to do her one after the other. Let's say Peter, Mark and Tim in that order, then her husband to finish off so he can stay in her as long as he likes.'

'Yeah,' says Jason. 'Sometimes I stay up her all night, know what I mean.'

After a whispered consultation with Peter, Sophie suggests that during this serial fucking she, Cathy and Poppy should kneel beside the willing victim to assist with her pleasuring. And they should kneel in such a way that their pussies are available for their partners as soon as they have spunked in Tracy—if they have anything left to offer.

Cushions are arranged on the floor and the unbelievably fuckable girl sinks down on them. She raises her knees and lets them fall apart, her knee-length socks contributing to the seductive effect. Her sex gapes pink and wet. Cathy, still in her gymslip, gets down on her left and Poppy, now nude, on her right. They begin to stroke the insides of her thighs and to lick her stiff-standing orange nipples. For her part, Sophie, also kneeling on the girl's right, bends forward to kiss her mouth. A seemingly unending, tonsil-tickling, salivating kiss.

Peter is fully aroused and ready to go. He gets down on his knees and kisses Tracy's quivering tummy before having a quick munch of her reddish fur when Cathy and Poppy raise her pelvis from the cushions. Then he is up her. Sophie is almost suffocated by Tracy's manic kissing. Peter ruts furiously and comes. Still stiff, he pulls out, his rod all gleaming with sexjuice.

Next it is Mark's turn. Sophie takes in very little of this performance, since her own pussy lips are being separated by her husband's fingers and the head of his wet cock is nosing into her channel. Mark drills the young Tracy enthusiastically until she orgasms. Without coming himself, he withdraws and hurries round to flip up the gymslip and finish his fuck in Cathy's belly.

If the two older men have acquitted themselves well, their agility and sheer lustiness is outshone by Tim when he splays Tracy's labia and plunges his long, slim prick into the mass of semen that now bubbles out of her to make room for the intruder. Sophie interrupts her wet snogging for a moment to turn her head and enjoy the sight of Tim's steady plundering of the much-coveted cunt. The hairless white flesh around the base of his tool makes a thrilling contrast with Tracy's little coppery tuft.

Someone else is getting a thrill from the sight, too. Jason stands over the group, slowly jacking his own hard prick. He looks as if he can't wait. Suddenly he takes hold of Tim's shoulders and forces him back. Ropes of Tim's cream spew from his purple cockhead and shower the girl's tummy, mound and thighs. He has lost hardly any of his youthful rigidity and immediately slips round to grab Poppy's buttocks and thrust deep into the gaping young cunt that pouts back at him in invitation.

Jason takes his place. He fucks his wife with abandon, and the other three women can tell from the way she responds that Tracy is being carried over the top. The young lovers soon lie luxuriating in the enjoyment of each other's post-orgasmic bliss, with the boy's penis soaking in his darling's sperm-filled vagina. The other three couples draw away to separate corners of the room and the husbands fuck their wives silly.

Sophie congratulates herself on the way the party has gone. Quite a lark, she reckons.